"Suzanne Woods Fisher's *The Haven* is a heartwarming story of faith, family, and renewal filled with characters that come alive on the page like old friends. The story will captivate fans of Amish fiction and readers who love an endearing romance."

—**Amy Clipston**, bestselling author
of the Kauffman Amish Bakery Series

"Shy Sadie Lapp returns to Stoney Ridge to find her quiet Amish farm life has turned upside down: two suitors, a nesting peregrine falcon pair, and one whopper of a secret. *The Haven* is a warm, touching novel about the power of familial bonds. Once you dip into this novel set in the charming town created by Suzanne Woods Fisher, you'll be hooked."

—**Beth Wiseman**, bestselling author
of the Daughters of the Promise series

"Suzanne Woods Fisher's novels are always such a joy to read! I found *The Haven* charming, humorous, and compelling—so much so that I had to remind myself to put the book down and get back to work! I'll be joining her many fans by the calendar, anxiously awaiting her next book to be released."

—**Shelley Shepard Gray**, *New York Times*
and *USA Today* bestselling author

The
HAVEN

Books by Suzanne Woods Fisher

Amish Peace: Simple Wisdom for a Complicated World
Amish Proverbs: Words of Wisdom from the Simple Life
Amish Values for Your Family: What We Can Learn
from the Simple Life

LANCASTER COUNTY SECRETS
The Choice
The Waiting
The Search

A Lancaster County Christmas

STONEY RIDGE SEASONS
The Keeper
The Haven

The HAVEN

A Novel

Suzanne Woods Fisher

Revell

a division of Baker Publishing Group
Grand Rapids, Michigan

© 2012 by Suzanne Woods Fisher

Published by Revell
a division of Baker Publishing Group
P.O. Box 6287, Grand Rapids, MI 49516-6287
www.revellbooks.com

Printed in the United States of America

Library of Congress Cataloging-in-Publication Data
Fisher, Suzanne Woods.
    The haven : a novel / Suzanne Woods Fisher.
        p.   cm. — (Stoney Ridge seasons ; 2)
    ISBN 978-0-8007-1988-3 (pbk.)
    1. Amish—Fiction. I. Title.
PS3606.I78H38 2012
813'.6—dc23   2012010638

Most Scripture used in this book, whether quoted or paraphrased by the characters, is taken from the Holy Bible, New International Version®, NIV®. Copyright © 1973, 1978, 1984 by Biblica, Inc.™ Used by permission of Zondervan. All rights reserved worldwide. www.zondervan.com

Published in association with Joyce Hart of the Hartline Literary Agency, LLC.

Any internet addresses (websites, blogs, etc.) and telephone numbers used in this book are provided as a resource. Baker Publishing Group does not vouch for their content for the life of this book, nor do they imply an endorsement by Baker Publishing Group.

12   13   14   15   16   17   18   7   6   5   4   3   2   1

To Lindsey, my darling daughter.
My first cookie turned out! She turned out *great*.

1

It never failed to amaze Sadie Lapp how the most ordinary day could be catapulted into the extraordinary in the blink of an eye. She was still a little dazed. She couldn't shake the feeling that it seemed her whole life had been leading to this particular moment. She had a strange sense that this day had come into her life to change her, to change everything.

But that didn't mean she felt calm and relaxed. Just the opposite. She felt like a homemade sweater unraveling inch by inch. As she caught her first glimpse of Windmill Farm, she hoped that, maybe, things could get straightened out, once she reached home.

Sadie had spent the winter in Berlin, Ohio, helping Julia and Roman, her sister and brother-in-law, settle into Rome's childhood home. A part of every day was spent shadowing Deborah Yoder, an elderly Old Order Amish woman who was known as a healer. Knowing of Sadie's interest in healing herbs, Rome arranged a meeting with Deborah that resulted in a part-time job. A part of Sadie wished she could have spent years studying and watching the wise old woman.

But last week, Sadie woke and knew she needed to return home. When Sadie told Julia, her sister's face fell with disappointment. She had expected Sadie to stay through the summer and tried to talk her out of leaving. But Old Deborah understood. "The wisest people I know," she had told Sadie, "learn to listen to those hunches."

The taxi swerved suddenly, jerking Sadie out of her muse. A few more curves in the road and she would be at Windmill Farm. She hoped the family was there for her homecoming. Wouldn't it be sad to try to surprise everyone, only to arrive to an empty house?

Maybe she should have called first, to let her father know she was coming. But he would have asked her why she was changing her plans and she didn't want to say. Maybe she should have at least tipped off Fern, their housekeeper. The one person she knew she couldn't confide in was Mary Kate, her twelve-going-on-thirty-year-old sister. It was well known that M.K. liked to babble and tell. She was the self-appointed bearer of all news—truth or otherwise.

Sadie gazed out the window. Coming home felt harder than she thought it would be. The family was much smaller now. It would be quieter without Rome and Julia. Without her brother, Menno. Even Lulu, Menno's dog, was living with Rome and Julia now. Sadie leaned her head on the back of the seat and closed her eyes for a moment, remembering. They used to be a family with a mom and a dad, three sisters and a brother, and crazy Uncle Hank. Pretty normal.

Until her mom passed and her dad, Amos, developed heart trouble. Then Uncle Hank found a housekeeper in *The Budget*. The sisters secretly called her Stern Fern. She took some time to warm up to, but she was just what the Lapp family needed. Sadie would have to add the Bee Man to the "just what we needed" list too. When Roman Troyer came to live at Windmill Farm last summer, life took a happy upturn. For Julia, especially.

But then Menno died in a terrible accident and his heart was given to his father. Everything changed again.

They weren't a normal family anymore. Julia had married Rome and moved to Ohio. And wasn't that also the way life went? Sadie thought, moving the basket beside her out of the direct sun. One minute you felt like laughing, and the next thing you knew, you were crying. She glanced at the basket. Would she ever feel normal again?

As the taxi passed along the road that paralleled Windmill Farm, Sadie scanned the fields, horrified. Dozens of cars were parked along the road. Near the barn, horses and buggies were stacked side by side. The amount of people up there looked like ants at a picnic. There was even a television van with a large satellite dish on top, like a giant sunflower turning to the sky. She unrolled the car window to get a better look. What on earth was going on?

She told the taxi driver to pull over at the base of the hill rather than go up the drive. After paying the driver, she stood by Julia's roadside stand, a small suitcase flanking her on one side, an oval-shaped basket on the other, a small box in her hand. She wasn't quite sure what to do next. The thought of walking up that hill into a crowd of strangers mortified her. Strangers were on Sadie's avoid-at-all-costs list. She was shy to the point of sickness among strangers. When she was out in town, she almost swooned with fear.

Why had she let the taxi drive off? Why hadn't she called her father first, to let him know she was on her way from Ohio and to find out what was going on at home?

What *was* going on at home?

Suddenly, a familiar voice came floating down the hill, followed by pounding footsteps. "Saaaa—dddieeeee!" Mary Kate was running toward Sadie, full blast, arms raised to the sky, a look of pure joy on her face.

Sadie threw open her arms and hugged her little sister. "Mary Kate, you've gotten so tall!" Fresh and tall and sleek, though starting to fill out her dress. Her little sister was on her way to becoming a woman.

"You didn't let anyone know you were coming!"

"I wouldn't even recognize you if I passed you on the street!" She handed M.K. the small container. "Rome sent along a new queen bee for your hives. I worried through the whole trip that the queen would escape out of that box and sting me."

M.K. peered through the screen top of the box. The brown bee queen was gripping the screen with its tiny fuzzy black legs. "Oh, she's beautiful!" M.K. was enamored with bees. Sadie liked to stay clear of them. "You won't believe what's been going on around here!"

"Take a breath, M.K., and tell me what all these cars are doing here. Is everyone all right? Is Dad doing all right?"

M.K. put the bee box on top of Sadie's suitcase and glanced at the house. "Dad's having a good day today. I've never seen him look so proud and pleased. When the president of the Audubon Society gave him the letter for Menno, I thought Dad was going to bust his britches."

"What letter? What are you talking about?"

"For all those rare birds Menno found! Turns out he spotted more rare birds than anyone else in the state of Pennsylvania. The Audubon lady brought a newspaper reporter with her." She stretched her arms over her head and released a happy giggle. "And right when they were presenting the letter to Dad, the game warden drove up. He sent an intern to stock the creek with trout and he spotted another couple of rare birds. This pair is an endangered species, and it looks like they're settling down to raise a family right on Windmill Farm! So that meant the game warden had to put No Trespassing signs up all over the farm. Of course, that was like sending out a skywriter with the news that Windmill Farm has another rare bird. Suddenly the whole town arrived. Even a telly-vision crew." She pointed to the news truck. "They're trying to film the birds. That's got the Audubon lady all upset. She's worried so much interest will disturb the birds. But the game warden says that the public has a right to observe the birds, as long as they're not trespassing on private property. I don't think there's anyone left in town—they're all up there listening to the game warden and the Bird Lady and the news reporter. It's better than a volleyball game." She spun herself in a little circle and clapped her hands, her grin wide. "And now you're home too! This is the best day, ever!"

"The entire town is up there?" Sadie said. *Oh no.* "Even folks from our church?"

"Everybody! Even on a perfect spring day—folks just dropped their plows in the fields and hurried over. Fern is trying to figure out how many think they're staying for sup-per." M.K. turned to look up the hill. "There's Dad!" She cupped her hands around her mouth and called out, "Hurry, hurry, hurry! Sadie's home!" She turned back to her sister. "Uncle Hank is trying to get himself on the local news. It's making Edith Fisher mad as a wet hen." She drew herself as tall as she could, hooked her hands on her hips, made a terrible prim face and, in a husky voice that sounded eerily like Edith Fisher, said, "Pride goeth before a fall, Hank Lapp!"

As kerfuffled as Sadie was, she couldn't help but laugh. M.K. was a regular little mimic, as good as a tent show, Uncle Hank said, and he would know. Under normal circumstances, Sadie would have enjoyed M.K.'s imitation of Edith Fisher, but these weren't normal circumstances. She was preoccupied with the mighty flood of news M.K. had dropped on her. The timing for her homecoming could not be any worse. How had this happened? Why, oh why, did she feel she should come home on this day, of all days? Why did she happen to be in the bus station—at that exact moment—earlier today? She had to believe it was meant to be. What other explanation could there be? The circumstances of the day couldn't be accidental.

Nearly down the driveway, Amos Lapp held his arms out wide for Sadie and she ran into them. She breathed in the sweet familiar smells of her father, of rich coffee and pine soap. Maybe . . . everything was going to be all right.

"What a wonderful surprise, Sadie! Today of all days! Why didn't you let us know you were coming?" Amos leaned back to look at her, hands on her shoulders. "I shouldn't be surprised. Not a bit. You always had a way of knowing the right place to be at just the right time." He sounded so pleased. "Did M.K. tell you the news about our Menno?

Did you hear that the president of the Audubon Society brought a letter congratulating us on Menno's keen eyes for birding?" He shook his head. "Our Menno. He would've been pleased."

"I think Menno would have wondered what all the fuss was about," Sadie said. "He would have told all these folks that they should be out looking for rare birds themselves."

Amos smiled, a little sad. "You're probably right. You always knew him best."

Sadie looked at her father, really looked. He had gained a little weight and it suited him. But his warm brown eyes had dark circles underneath, as if he wasn't sleeping well. He looked positively careworn.

"Let's get you up to the house, through that clump of people, so you can wash up and get something to eat." He reached down for her suitcase, noticed the bee box, picked it up, and peered into it. Then he handed the bee box to M.K.

"Dad, there's something—"

"Say, does Gideon know you're coming?" Amos lifted his head as he picked up the suitcase. "He'll be anxious to see you. I wish I had a silver dollar for every time he asked me when I thought you'd be coming back."

"Gid's my teacher this spring, Sadie," M.K. said, eyes fixed on the queen bee. "Did you know that? He's the best, the very best! So much more interesting than his crotchety old maid sister—"

"Ahem," Amos interrupted, giving M.K. the look.

"Yes," Sadie said. "Of course I know Gid is your teacher. You've told me hundreds of times. And no, Gid doesn't know I'm coming. I was trying to surprise all of you." She turned to her father. "Dad, before we go up to the house, I need to tell you something—"

A strange little squeaking sound came out of the basket behind Sadie's feet. M.K. peered into it and looked up, shocked. "Sadie, it's . . . you . . . you have a baby!"

Amos crouched down to look. He pulled back a little quilt blanket to reveal a tiny baby. The baby started waving his arms and crying like a weak lamb. Amos looked up at his middle daughter, stunned. "Sadie, what's this?"

Sadie took a deep breath. "Dad, that's what I've been trying to tell you. I need . . . some . . . help."

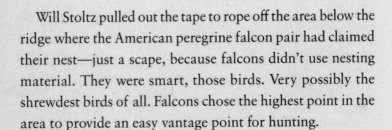

Will Stoltz pulled out the tape to rope off the area below the ridge where the American peregrine falcon pair had claimed their nest—just a scape, because falcons didn't use nesting material. They were smart, those birds. Very possibly the shrewdest birds of all. Falcons chose the highest point in the area to provide an easy vantage point for hunting.

A week ago, in late March, Will had been stocking streams with trout for the game warden, and lo and behold, he spotted a pair of American peregrine falcons. The male—actually called a tiercel—was about one-third smaller than the female, and the pair seemed to be soaring in the sky in specific flying patterns. When Will saw the male bring food to the female, he knew they were courting. He smiled. Falcons mated for life. The male would select a few sites for a scape and let the female pick the place she wanted to raise her clutch. Very civilized, he thought. He would do the same, if he ever married.

He nailed one end of the yellow Keep Out tape to a tree. There was a line of people standing behind the tape, with telescopes and cameras fitted with enormous zoom lenses. This was a big event to hit Lancaster County. Even for the state of Pennsylvania—an endangered species on its list had chosen a little Amish farm to nest in. Will knew the game warden was determined to squeeze every ounce of publicity he could out of this American peregrine falcon pair—partly for the sake of the falcon pair but mostly to breathe life into his sagging career.

Last year, Game Warden Mahlon Miller had been criticized for not giving enough protection to a bald-headed eagle pair that had built a nest in a tree in an unfortunate location—a popular civic park. One of the eaglets had been killed by a kid messing around with a BB gun and Mahlon Miller had been publicly chastised. Eagles were increasingly common to parts of Pennsylvania, unlike falcons, and Mahlon wasn't going to let anything happen to jeopardize these rare birds.

Will thought Mahlon was taking the right precautions as game warden, but he felt a little sorry for the Amish family who hosted these falcons. He didn't know how the family would be able to stand having a protected nesting site on their farm. Talk about a loss of privacy for utterly private people! Strangers would be crawling all over the farm, eager to see the falcons. And these falcons weren't going to be leaving soon. They looked like they had taken their time finding just the right piece of real estate and were settling in for a long stay. If these raptors liked the location, they would return year after year.

A crow flew into a nearby tree and let out a loud caw. Another answered back, and soon it sounded like a full-fledged heated family discussion was going on.

Will started to walk back to the farmhouse to tell the game warden that he had finished marking off the area for the falcons. At the top of a ridge, next to a red windmill with spinning arms, he paused to look around. It was a beautiful farm. It was talked about in the birding community. There were more species of birds identified on this farm than any other farm in the county, including eight rarities. It made Will curious. Why here? Why this farm? What made this place more bird friendly than another? So many farms around here were Amish—most were very eco-friendly, used minimal pesticides, and welcomed birds. So why were more birds sighted on this farm than the one next to it?

Will had been to Windmill Farm once before, though no one would have recognized him. Last year, he had come to see for himself when he heard about the American pipit on the Rare Bird Alert. He couldn't believe it when he saw it, but there it was. A small, brown, nondescript bird, half the size of a robin, sitting on a woodpile. It ate crickets out of an Amish teenage boy's hand.

Will's interest was piqued. He wanted to know more about this farm and this family. Especially now. Windmill Farm might prove very useful to him, if he went through with this opportunity that had fallen, out of the blue, into his lap and promised him a way to get out of the mess he was in, without having to involve his father . . .

———— ❖ ————

Late in the afternoon, Twin Creeks Schoolhouse was bathed in warm, sleepy sunlight that fell in speckled patterns across the polished wood floor. The old walls and ceiling beams creaked and moaned, sounding every bit like an old man stretching as he rose from his favorite chair. Gideon Smucker had been hearing the sounds for a few months now, and found them oddly comforting.

Gid closed the math book, took off his glasses, and rubbed his eyes. He was barely able to keep one day ahead of his brightest scholar, Mary Kate Lapp. He thought the complicated problems in this book would keep M.K.'s nimble mind busy, but he didn't realize how many mental cobwebs he would need to brush off just to correct her work. He leaned back in his chair and clasped his hands behind his neck. He was glad the other scholars weren't as precocious as Mary Kate. He'd be sunk.

He still couldn't believe he was here, teaching the twenty-one scholars of Twin Creeks School. He loved book learning but never imagined himself a schoolteacher. His sister, Alice, had been teaching at Twin Creeks for seven years. A week before school started up again after Christmas, Alice was injured in an unfortunate sledding accident. She broke both of her legs, requiring a long, slow rehabilitation. Desperate, the school board asked if he would fill in for Alice. How could he refuse the three members of the school board, or Alice? But even more startling was the discovery that Gid loved teaching. He felt he had been born to teach, in a way that he never felt behind a plow. His mind felt so challenged by teaching, so active and alive.

Gid glanced at the clock on the wall: five o'clock. He needed to get home soon and help his dad with evening chores. He wanted to finish the letter to Sadie before he went home. He'd been writing steadily to her over the last few months and was hoping she'd be coming back from Ohio soon. If he mailed it tomorrow, she would receive it on Saturday. Too soon? Did he seem too eager? He didn't want to come across like he was pining for her. He wasn't. He most definitely wasn't. Not much, anyway. Maybe he should hold off mailing it for another day or two.

He went through this every week. He would send her a favorite book or two of his, scribbled with marginalia, along with a brief note at least once a week. He worried constantly that he was going to push Sadie away by being too obviously smitten by her.

To him, Sadie was like a delicate hummingbird, easily frightened off. And why should a girl like her ever be sincerely interested in a fellow like him? He was clumsy, tongue-tied, awkward socially. He hoped that through the books they shared, she might see what was in him that he couldn't seem to express in person. Why was it so much easier to write something to her than to say the same thing to her? If he could describe things with written words, couldn't he do the same aloud? Maybe when Sadie came back, he would be able to say these things to her.

He overheard someone describe him once as a young man without deep feelings. He did feel deeply, he knew he did. But what he felt was so confusing and required so much work to figure out, and then even more to get it to the surface and express it, that it was easier to keep quiet and concentrate on writing, something he could see. He imagined all kinds of sweet things he wanted to tell her: how there were times in church when a beam from the sun caught her hair and glinted and he thought she looked like an angel. How much he loved those pronounced dimples in her cheeks. And those freckles that covered her nose and cheeks. He knew she hated them and tried to get rid of them with lemon juice, but he wished she wouldn't because he liked them. And her laugh . . . it was like the sound of wind chimes. He sorely missed Sadie, as much today as when she left for Ohio four months ago.

Gid was in eighth grade when he first realized he was in love with Sadie Lapp. Not that he let anybody know he was besotted. Especially not Sadie.

He had learned the hard way that just because you felt something didn't mean you had to tell other people. His friends had a way of twisting things around, finding something in the most commonplace remarks to jab at a person and make fun.

He had plenty of reasons to keep his mouth shut on any romantic topics. First off, nobody would believe he knew what love was at his age. Second, Sadie was even younger than he was. Third, Sadie had never given him the slightest indication that he was anything more than just another boy to ignore at school.

But then, last December, Gid gathered enough courage to ask Sadie if he could take her home from a singing, and she nodded shyly. The night was clear and cold and their breath was frosty on the air as the horse pulled the buggy across the frozen ground. In the soft moonlight it was easier to talk, and both of them seemed reluctant to reach her farm and have the evening end. That one time led to another ride home from a singing, then an ice skating party, and a few other times when they didn't need a gathering as an excuse to see each other. Then came the last time together, just after Christmas, the night before Sadie left for Ohio with her sister and brother-in-law. Gid didn't know when he would see Sadie again.

Gid had stopped the horse near the side of the barn, where M.K. couldn't peek out the farmhouse window and spy on them like she did on a regular basis. He helped Sadie out of the buggy.

Sadie glanced toward the house. "Perhaps we should say goodnight here," she said.

Gid moved in front of her to block the cold wind. He had never kissed a girl, but he'd given it a great deal of thought. Quite a great deal. He lifted her chin so she would look at him. For a moment they stood absolutely still. Then he dropped his head down to softly cover her lips with his. Her hand came up to touch his cheek, and when he lifted his lips from hers, they stood there with their warm breath intermingling for a moment. None of the books or poetry he had read had done kissing justice.

It was the single finest moment in Gid's nineteen years of life.

2

As the sun started to dip into the horizon, the excitement over the falcons slowly petered out. Cars and buggies left the farm. Will had just finished taping off the area near the falcons' scape and was walking back to the farmhouse to let the game warden know he had finished. When he reached Mahlon, he quietly mentioned the concern he had about so many onlookers. The scape was situated in a place on the farm where there weren't any fences. Folks could easily trample through the fields, he explained to the game warden, and climb up that ridge to get a closer look at the scape. It worried him, he said. The female might not lay eggs if she became stressed by the presence of onlookers.

"I know all that," Mahlon said, sounding annoyed that an intern for the game commission would try to tell him basic bird facts. Then his face relaxed. "Imagine if the clutch ended up with four or five viable eyases. Even two or three."

Will whistled. "It would be big."

"Might be the first successful breeding pair in this county."

Will scratched his neck. "We could do a drive-by each day on our way to work and back." Since his internship had started last week, he had been boarding at Mahlon Miller's house.

"Oh, I've got a better plan to protect those falcons than Keep Out tape and a daily drive-by."

"What's that?" Will asked.

Mahlon gave him a smug smile. "You."

Will's eyes went wide. "Uh, but . . ." This wasn't exactly what he had in mind for his internship—not that this internship was his idea in the first place. It wasn't. It was his father's idea. A way to make Will pay for getting suspended from the university for the semester. That was why he was living with the game warden—it was part of the deal his father struck with Mahlon. A few years ago, Will's father, a doctor, had performed a risky operation on Mahlon's mother and saved her life. There wasn't anything Mahlon Miller wouldn't do for Will's father.

Will took off his cowboy hat and spun it in his hands. "Just seems like it's asking too much to stay with an Amish family."

Mahlon dismissed that with a wave of his pudgy hand. "I've already thought that out. I'm going to see if you can stay in that empty cottage over there." He pointed to a small, tidy-looking cottage underneath a stand of pines, not far from the falcons' scape. "That way, you won't interfere with the family at all. You're going to babysit those falcons until the chicks are banded and ready to leave the scape." Mahlon folded his arms across his chest. "I'm friends with Amos Lapp, the Amish farmer. I don't think he would mind having you stay, especially after I offer your help around the farm. He could use the help and you could use the work. Kind of a barter arrangement."

Will felt a little stunned. He had always made it a point to dodge physical labor—academics were more to his liking. Plus . . . he was lazy. He knew that about himself and accepted it happily. And here he was, about to be offered up as a farmhand. He didn't even know what farmers did all day. Watch their crops grow? Muck out horse stalls? Oh, this wasn't good. Not good at all. He opened his mouth to object as Mahlon tossed his truck keys to him.

"I'm going to go clear it with Amos," Mahlon said. "You go pack up your belongings from the house and get back here. Pronto." He spun on his heels to go find the farmer, a wide grin on his face which, Will thought, had something to do with the thought of having his intern move out of his house. Just last night, Mahlon's wife seemed particularly touchy about the three-day-old forgotten meatloaf sandwich left in Will's backpack that had attracted a mouse in his room. Maybe two. Maybe a family.

Will walked down the driveway to the truck, reviewing this turn of events. As he backed the truck to turn it around, he pedaled down a new lane of thinking. Maybe this was a gift in disguise. A beacon in the gray fog that covered his future. He woke up this morning wrestling with his conscience about a recent opportunity that had been presented to him. With this last swift decision, made by Mahlon, Will was going to take it as a sign to stop overthinking the situation. The matter was decided.

At the kitchen table, Mary Kate waited patiently for Sadie to pass the potatoes, but her sister seemed to be deep in thought. Sadie's eyes kept misting over like she was trying to not bust out crying. Something was bothering her.

M.K. wasn't sure why Sadie was suddenly in such a mood, but for now, she was hungry, especially after spending the last hour carefully introducing the new brown bee queen to the hive. Bees were very fussy about newcomers, especially one that would now reign over them. She reached over Sadie and tried to help herself to a large cloud of mashed potatoes, but her sister moved the bowl out of her reach.

Amos lifted his eyebrows. "Sadie, would you mind passing food around the table?"

Sadie made a point to pass the bowl of mashed potatoes to Fern, bypassing M.K. She lifted her chin. "Mary Kate is oblivious to the kind of trouble she created today."

M.K.'s eyes went round as saucers. "What did I do that was so bad?"

Sadie looked at her, astounded. "You told people that I brought a baby home from Ohio."

M.K. raised her palms in wonder. "But you did! That's the truth!"

"That's NOT the way it happened!" Sadie glared at her. "I did not *bring* the baby from Ohio. The baby found me, in the bus station in Lancaster, while I was waiting for a bus to Stoney Ridge." She passed the platter of roast beef to Uncle Hank, seated across from her. Then she picked up her fork and poked at the mashed potatoes on her plate. "Who all did you tell?"

M.K. had her eye on Uncle Hank, who was spearing large slices of roast beef onto his plate. She hoped there would be some left. "Just a few people."

Sadie narrowed her eyes. "Who, exactly?"

M.K. put up her hand and counted off her fingers. "Ruthie. Ethan. Solomon Riehl and his little boy, Danny." Uncle Hank passed her the platter and she grabbed it eagerly.

Relief covered Sadie's face.

M.K. lowered her head and quietly added, "And maybe Edith Fisher."

"Noooooooooo!" Sadie looked like she'd swallowed a firecracker. "Edith Fisher will spread the news through this entire town by morning."

M.K. took a large mouthful of roast beef and mumbled, "I still don't understand why it's so bad."

Sadie glowered at M.K. "Lower your voice or you'll wake the baby up. I just got him to sleep."

M.K. looked at her father and raised her palms in exasperation. She mouthed the words, "But I'm not talking loud! Sadie is!"

Fern, sitting to the right of M.K., placed her hand on her forearm. "Denk zehe mol, schwetz eemol." *Think ten times, talk once.* "How many times have I told you that?"

Too many to count, M.K. thought. Along with zillions of other bromides about talking too much, moving too fast, acting without thinking, accepting correction, being humble, on and on and on. Fern was famous for her sayings. M.K. thought she must study them so that she could whip one out at just the right moment.

Sadie got up and checked on the baby, sleeping in the little basket in a corner. "M.K., you had no right to tell people anything about the baby. I was barely home for five minutes and you couldn't keep quiet. You just don't *think*. And now you've started all kinds of rumors about me."

Uncle Hank's fist hit the table. "NO SIR! No one would dare say a mean word about our Sadie. I WON'T HAVE IT!" He clamped his jaw, but his emotions passed quickly, like a racing thundercloud. He picked up a few biscuits and generously lathered them with butter.

"Don't be so sure," Fern said. "Folks think that a rumor is truth on the trail."

Uncle Hank took a bite and chewed it thoughtfully. "I did hear someone say something about Sadie's absence being mighty suspicious. But, DAGNABIT!"—that was the only cuss word Fern would allow out of Uncle Hank, so he made plenty of use of it—"I set them straight. I said she was exiled to be with relatives for the winter."

"Exiled?" Sadie said, horrified. "You used the word 'exiled'?"

Uncle Hank stroked his chin. "Exiled? I said excited."

Sadie was mortified. "You *said* exiled!"

Uncle Hank frowned. "I said excited and I meant excited! Your ears must be full of cotton. I said 'Sadie was excited to be with relatives for the winter.'" But he didn't look quite convinced.

Sadie crumpled. "See? I told you! Folks are going to think I *had* this baby! And it's all M.K.'s fault!" Looping her arms to rest on the table, she slid lower and let her forehead rest on her fists.

M.K. was disgusted. It was a scandal how often the finger of blame pointed to her. She thought she was sharing happy news. What could be so bad about having a baby come to stay with them? Her friend Ruthie was thrilled!

"Would you go over everything one more time, Sadie?" Amos said.

Sadie lifted her head and sighed. "I arrived at the Lancaster bus depot and had to wait for the Stoney Ridge connection, so I started to read my book and must have nodded off. When I woke up, there was a basket by my feet." She pointed to the basket. "And in the basket was *that* little baby."

"No note?" Fern said.

Sadie shook her head. "Just a bottle and a can of powdered formula. And some diapers."

M.K. pinched her nose with her fingers. "Not enough of them."

"You didn't remember seeing anyone?" Amos said.

Sadie shook her head. "It was pretty busy when the bus arrived, but then, when I woke up, it had cleared out. I walked all around the station looking for someone, and then I went to ask the stationmaster if he had seen anyone who was holding a basket."

"What did he say?" Fern asked.

"I tried to explain myself a couple of times, but I don't think I did a very good job of it. He finally pointed to the basket and asked if I was feeling okay, and maybe he should call the police or paramedics because they can help with confused people." Sadie frowned. "I didn't want the police or paramedics to take the baby away. Or me, either. And just then the Stoney Ridge bus arrived and I got on it. With the baby." She set her elbows on the table and rested her chin in her palms. "Dad, what are we going to do?"

Amos sat quietly for a long while. Too quiet for M.K.

Finally, she couldn't hold back any longer or she would pop. "We should keep him! Don't you see? He was brought to Sadie by an angel! Ruthie said there are angels all around us. Ruthie knows about these things, now that her dad's a minister." As soon as the words flew out of her mouth, she regretted them. The entire family looked at her as if she had spoken Chinese.

Then Sadie spoke. "Mary Kate might have finally said something today that was worth saying." She looked at her father. "I think she's right. That baby was meant for me. For all of us. I think that's why I felt such a strong pull to get back here today, Dad. I was meant to be in that bus station, at just that moment. On this day, of all days. I'm just sure of it, and I think I felt sure of it in the bus station too. Today was no accident. That baby is meant for us."

Amos fingered a seam on the tabletop. "Sadie, I'm not sure that's for you to decide."

Sadie's eyes went wide. "Well, why ever not? The baby was given to me."

Fern picked up the basket of biscuits and passed it to Amos. "Bringing home a baby isn't the same thing as bringing home a stray kitten or puppy."

As Amos broke a biscuit in half, a puff of white steam was released. His eyes were fixed on the biscuit as he quietly said, "We need to do what's best for the baby. And what's best for the baby is to find his family."

Something awful began to break in M.K.'s mind, and Sadie's too, judging by the stunned look on her face. *This isn't fair! The baby was given to Sadie! To all of us.*

Sadie's eyes started to well with tears. "Dad, we have to keep this baby. We just have to."

Amos looked a little puzzled. "We'll get it all sorted out, Sadie. But we want what's best for that baby."

"We're what's best for that baby," Sadie said, more forcefully. "I know that's what the mother wanted. I'm sure of it."

"What makes you so sure of that, Sadie?" Amos said. "Anyone who would abandon a baby in a bus station must not be thinking too clearly."

"But she left the baby with me." Sadie had stopped crying now. "Not with anyone else but me."

Uncle Hank slammed his palms on the table. "SHE'S ABSOLUTELY RIGHT!" He was getting excited now, and that meant his raspy voice would get louder and louder. "THAT ANGEL KNEW OUR SADIE WOULD BE A STELLAR CHOICE!"

This was starting to get interesting, M.K. thought, observing the exasperated look on her father's face. She had never seen Sadie so adamant about anything before. She always thought Sadie could sit on a fence and watch herself walk by. She was *that* prone to changing her mind, to seeing a situation from all directions. But as she looked over at her sister, she realized a change had come over Sadie since her visit to Berlin. More than one change. Usually, Sadie was the one to mollify others, a peacekeeper, determined that no one should remain unhappy for long. Tonight, she held her chin up high, a look of determination set in her eyes. She looked trimmer, taller, and even held herself differently. Shoulders back. Why, she was practically perpendicular! A 90 degree angle.

And wouldn't Gideon Smucker be proud of M.K. for finding geometry in something as mundane as a person's posture? Watching Sadie, M.K. straightened her back, hardly aware she was doing it.

Just as Uncle Hank opened his mouth to jump in on the

what-to-do-with-the-baby discussion, Fern lifted her hand to ward him off. "It's been a long day. And if I know newborn babies—and that baby can't be much older than a month or so—it's going to be an even longer night."

Sadie looked confused. "Why is it going to be such a long night?"

Uncle Hank burst out with a snorting laugh. "By tomorrow morning, Sadie girl, you might just be changing your tune about keeping that baby!"

In that way Fern had of bringing the whole world up short, she pointed to Uncle Hank and said, "Whether that baby is here for a day or a month, he's going to need some things we don't have. You need to go to the Bent N' Dent tonight to buy more supplies." She pulled a list from her apron pocket and handed it to him. "Lickety-split. Store closes at seven."

Hank shoveled one last biscuit into his mouth. "Better hurry up and pray, Amos, since I seem to be Fern's factotum." He winked at M.K. "See? I'm using them big words you keep trying to jam into my head."

M.K. beamed. She adored her father's uncle. "I'll go with you, Uncle Hank."

Amos bowed his head and the family followed suit. As soon as he lifted his head, M.K. jumped up, grabbed her black bonnet off the wall peg, and slipped out the door before Fern could call her back to help wash dishes.

As Uncle Hank went to get the horse to hitch to the buggy, M.K. stayed on the porch, tying the bonnet ribbons under her chin, listening to the conversation continue at the table through an open window. She heard Sadie ask her father, "What exactly did Fern mean about babies and long nights?"

"Babies need to eat every few hours," Amos said.

"What?" Sadie said. "You can't be serious!"

M.K. saw Sadie turn to Fern for confirmation. Fern was at the kitchen sink, adding dish soap into the basin.

"He's right," Fern said loudly, over the sound of running water. "Around the clock."

Sadie groaned and dropped her forehead on the table with a clunk. Then her head popped up. "Maybe we could all take a shift!"

M.K. saw Sadie look at her father, who was not uttering a peep behind his nest of beard. He was studying the ceiling with great interest. Then she saw Sadie whip her head over at Fern.

"Oh no, don't look to me," Fern said in her crisp way. "This is *your* miracle. Besides, I don't do babies. They're a heap of trouble."

M.K. popped her head in the window and whispered to Sadie, "I know all about babies. It can't be that hard. I'll help." Then she jumped off the porch and ran down to Uncle Hank, waiting for her in the buggy.

3

The next morning Sadie woke up with a start, a jittery mess. The morning sun beamed bright through her front window. How could it be morning already? She had been up with the baby four times, maybe five, no signs or stirrings of M.K. or her father or Uncle Hank, until Fern finally came into the kitchen around 4:00 a.m. and told her to go to bed, that she would take a turn.

That was the way it was with Fern. She complained about having to take care of everybody, but then she took care of everybody.

Sadie was exhausted. How could such a tiny baby eat so much and cry so much? Downstairs, she heard the sounds of morning going on. Familiar, contented noises. The hinge of the kitchen door squeaked as her father went out to the barn. Bacon hissed and sizzled in a frying pan on the stove. She heard M.K. gallop down the stairs, talk to Fern for a moment, then gallop back up. Sadie's bedroom door burst open. "Fern says to get up. She said that baby is starting to make noises about breakfast. She said to tell you she can't be expected to be babysitting while you're sleeping 'til noon."

Sadie yawned. "Can't you take a turn and feed the baby?"

"Me?" M.K.'s eyes went wide. "Oh no. I've never actually fed a newborn baby before. I might break him. Besides, Dad needs me out in the barn."

"What happened to your big promise to help me with the baby last night?"

M.K. shrugged. "Never heard him." She spun around, and then turned back. "Are we just going to call him That Baby or are we going to give him a name?"

Sadie looked at her blankly. The thought hadn't even occurred to her. "I don't know. I guess we should."

M.K. whipped a list out of her apron pocket. "Here are my suggestions: Kayak, Level, Radar, Murdrum—"

"What kind of names are those?"

"They're palindromes. Words that can read backwards or forwards. Gideon Smucker taught us all about them. I've been naming all of the new chickens these names."

Sadie put up a hand like a stop sign. "I'm not naming that baby after one of your chickens."

"Solos. Tenet. Racecar. Rotor. Madam. Dewed—"

Sadie threw a pillow at M.K., but she had seen it coming and was halfway down the stairs by the time the pillow reached the floor.

Sadie stretched and yawned, then rolled her feet onto the cold floor. She dressed quickly, pinned her hair in a tight knot, and covered it with a bandana, pondering baby names. M.K. was probably right—they did need to call that baby something other than That Baby. But naming him seemed so . . . real. So permanent. If only she could have somehow hidden the baby from the eyes of other people in Stoney Ridge, just to have time to think this all through. But nothing stayed hidden in Stoney Ridge for long, and by the end of the first day, everyone in the community would know this baby had been dropped on the Lapps like an unwanted puppy.

When she reached the kitchen, Fern was already giving the baby a bottle of formula. Silently, she handed the baby to Sadie and went outside to hang a load of wash on the clothesline. After Sadie finished feeding the baby, she changed his diaper, placed him in the basket, and carried the basket outside to help Fern. She rubbed her eyes with her right hand, then rested her palm over them against the brilliance of the day. From an oak in the yard, a plump red robin whistled and chattered, and another answered from across the yard.

As soon as Fern saw her, she handed the bag of clothespins to Sadie. "I need to get out to the garden before it gets too warm. You finish up here."

Fern went around the back of the house to reach the garden and Sadie picked up where she had left off, hanging wet towels. The baby had fallen asleep, and the morning sun was warming Sadie's back. As she clipped a towel onto the line, worries swooped down on her like pigeons on bread crumbs. What was she to do about this baby? What if no one ever claimed him? She wasn't ready for this. She looked forward to getting married one day, dreamed about it, planned every detail of her wedding. Someday, she wanted children. But someday wasn't supposed to have arrived yet.

Maybe it would be the best thing for everybody to let the church find a family who could raise him. She was glad that her father didn't know what she knew about the baby—what she *thought* might be true. She considered telling him last night, but there didn't seem to be a quiet moment for such a conversation. And her concerns about her father's health spiked last night. He looked so tired after dinner. She had assumed that the heart transplant would have cured him. Fixed and done, like replacing a new engine in the lawn mower.

Maybe a heart transplant is never really over. She saw the amount of pill vials in the kitchen. The pills, she knew, were to suppress his immune system so that it wouldn't reject the heart. But it also made him susceptible to all kinds of illnesses. He couldn't even plow the fields this year like he used to because of the fungus that was in soil. Too risky. Maybe a heart transplant was a way to prolong a person's life, but the life might never be quite the same.

The baby let out a sound and she bent down to check on him. One eye squinted open, followed by a big yawn, then he drifted back to sleep. He was a cute little thing, with downy dark hair and a rosebud mouth.

It wouldn't be hard for someone to love him. She thought of Mattie and Sol Riehl. Mattie was always taking in foster babies. Maybe Mattie and Sol would want this baby. But then she frowned. If Mattie and Sol took in this baby, the state of Pennsylvania would get involved. The Riehl home was frequented by social workers who checked up on the foster children. She had heard Mattie complain about what a headache it was to work with government agencies. And there had been that time when Mattie and Sol were hoping to adopt a little girl who had lived with them for over a year, only to have the Child Protective Services return the little girl to her mother. It had broken Mattie's heart. No, Sadie did not want the government to catch wind of this parentless baby and make decisions for his welfare.

Last night at dinner, her father had said that they would all need to decide what was best for the baby. What would he say if he knew what she knew? But then, she reminded herself, she didn't know anything for sure. It was just a hunch. That was all. Nothing more than a hunch. She should probably do a little investigating before she said anything to anyone.

She reached a hand into the clothespin bag and came up empty. Since the baby was sleeping peacefully in the basket, she decided to leave him as she scooted back to the house to get another package.

After Sadie found the spare bag of clothespins that Fern kept in a kitchen drawer, she opened the kitchen door and froze. A stranger—a man—was crouching down by the baby's basket. She'd never seen him before. He was wearing a straw cowboy hat and cowboy boots. Her heart started to race when she saw him reach down to pick the baby up. Without thinking, she grabbed her father's rifle off of the wall rack next to the kitchen door and shouted from the porch.

"You there!" She aimed the rifle at the young man.

The man spun around to face Sadie. His eyes went wide when he saw the rifle aimed at him.

"Don't make any quick moves, you . . . you . . . baby thief!" Sadie spoke distinctly and authoritatively. She surprised herself.

The man carefully put the baby back in the basket and stepped away from it, hands held high like he was surrendering.

Sadie felt like a mother tiger protecting her kit. "Who are you and why are you trying to steal that baby?"

"Ma'am, I'm . . . I'm not trying to steal your baby." His eyes were wide and innocent looking, but Sadie wasn't going to be fobbed off that easily. "I was walking by and heard him crying and I was just going to hold him. That's all."

The baby was making noises, little mewing complaints at first, and now was starting to wind up like a siren. How could a tiny baby have such a loud, ear-piercing cry?

The cowboy pointed to the baby. "I've always been pretty good at getting babies to stop crying." He took a step closer to Sadie and she lifted the rifle, so he backed up. "I'd feel a little better if you would stop aiming that rifle between my eyes."

A thick strand of hair whipped loose from her simple bun, effectively shielding her eyes. "I'd feel a whole lot better if you'd identify yourself and try to explain what you're doing on my farm at this time of day."

"Sadie Lapp!" Amos was marching from the barn over to Sadie. "Put down that gun. What on earth are you thinking?"

Sadie lowered the gun. Her father reached her and snatched the rifle out of her hands. "He was trying to kidnap the baby!"

The man visibly relaxed as soon as the rifle left Sadie's hands.

M.K. came skipping out of the barn. "What's going on?"

Silence. Finally, Amos said, "With all of the hoopla yesterday, I forgot to tell you girls about this game warden intern . . ." His face scrunched up as he tried to remember the young man's name.

"Will Stoltz."

"That's right. Will Stoltz is staying in the cottage and babysitting the falcons."

"Not exactly babysitting," Will Stoltz said, holding a finger up in the air. "More like protecting an endangered species from an overly zealous public."

Sadie stared at the man. Now that she wasn't shaking from holding a gun at him, she noticed that he wasn't very old. Twenty, twenty-two, tops.

"I'm not a kidnapper," Will Stoltz said earnestly. "I'm with the game warden."

"You thought he was a kidnapper?" M.K.'s eyes grew as wide as saucers. "Sadie, were you going to *kill* him?"

Amos rolled his eyes. "Not with an empty rifle, she wasn't. And Sadie, what were you thinking? Since when does a Plain person point a gun at another human being?" He shook his head. "Will, the daughter that gave you a scare is Sadie, my middle daughter. And this one here is Mary Kate, my youngest." He raised an eyebrow at M.K. "She needs to be heading off to school." He flipped the rifle up on his shoulder. "Sorry for the cold reception." He turned and walked back to the house with the rifle.

"No problem!" Will called out to him cheerfully. "Easy mistake to make."

Sadie scowled at Will and brushed past him to pick up the baby. The baby was really crying now, howling mad. Louder and louder. Sadie was starting to panic. Maybe something was seriously wrong with the baby. Maybe that's why the baby was abandoned in the bus station. This baby was defective. "M.K., go get Fern."

"Why?" M.K. said.

"Because I can't get the baby to stop crying and I don't know what's wrong with him."

40

"Let me try," Will said. As Sadie hesitated, he added, "Like I was trying to tell you, I'm pretty good with babies."

Still, she was reluctant to pass the baby to him, so he added, "I won't hurt your baby."

"Oh, that's not her baby," M.K. offered, giving Sadie a look that said "See? I am *not* spreading rumors" look. "Sadie found that baby at the bus station. Just yesterday. We don't even have a name picked out yet. But I'm working on it. My latest suggestion is Otto."

"Hush, M.K.," Sadie whispered.

The baby's face was bright red and a tiny little tear leaked down his cheek.

"No kidding, you're not the baby's mother?" Will said. "The way you were coming at me with that gun, you reminded me of a mama bear, thinking I was a threat to her cub."

Sadie hardly heard him. She was at her wit's end trying to calm the baby. Nothing seemed to work. She gave Will one more head-to-toe look and decided he didn't look terribly threatening, so she handed the baby to him. He swept the baby against his chest and gently patted his back, bouncing gently as he walked around in a circle. M.K. was peering around Sadie, watching the young man. Sadie could tell that M.K. was fascinated. They both were.

The baby's crying slowed, then stopped entirely. Sadie and M.K. exchanged a look.

Sadie looked Will up and down. "How did you do that?"

"It's all in the jiggle," he said in a loud whisper. "And babies like to be pressed up against your shoulder, not held low in your arms like you were doing. Must help with gas pains."

It wasn't long before the baby drifted off to sleep again.

Ever so gently, Will bent down and tucked the baby into the basket. He rose and brushed his palms against each other. "Easy, once you get the hang of it."

Standing this close to the intern, Sadie saw that he had blue eyes. Really blue eyes, framed by thick brown lashes and strong straight brows darker than his hair, blond hair that swept into his eyes. He was sunburnt and needed a shave, but he was quite nice looking, sort of rugged. He was wearing jeans, dirty at the knees, and a plain white T-shirt under his short-sleeved khaki shirt. He tipped his cowboy hat to them, smiled, and went on his way. He had the kind of a smile that could have melted a glacier.

Sadie and M.K. watched him stroll over to the barn, thumbs hooked in his jeans' pockets, whistling a tune.

"Good thing you didn't kill him, Sadie," M.K. said. "We might be needing him." She sniffed the air and scrunched up her face, zeroing in on the odor wafting up from the baby in the basket. "Think the cowboy changes diapers?"

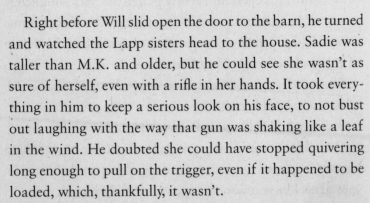

Right before Will slid open the door to the barn, he turned and watched the Lapp sisters head to the house. Sadie was taller than M.K. and older, but he could see she wasn't as sure of herself, even with a rifle in her hands. It took everything in him to keep a serious look on his face, to not bust out laughing with the way that gun was shaking like a leaf in the wind. He doubted she could have stopped quivering long enough to pull on the trigger, even if it happened to be loaded, which, thankfully, it wasn't.

Most of the guys he knew probably wouldn't notice Sadie

so much at first. She wasn't the blonde bombshell that his fraternity brothers panted after, but she was pretty in a simple, soft way. Sandy blonde hair, a small nose, a stubborn chin. Freckles. She had the prettiest eyes—big and blue, kind of skittish, the way a doe looks when she's deciding whether to bolt for the woods or stand her ground. She wasn't thin but she wasn't fat. Average-sized, maybe a little round and curvy, but it seemed to suit her. Her voice was low, like music. And she walked back to the house, holding that baby's basket, with a gracefulness that seemed surprising for a farm girl. As she opened the kitchen door, she turned and gave a shy look back at him. Cute, like a soft summer day. That's how he would describe her looks. Very, very cute. It was quite possible being here was going to be more tolerable than he had feared only yesterday.

He slid open the barn door and waited until his eyes adjusted to the dark. He heard Amos Lapp rummaging around in a back room. He followed the noises but stopped just before he reached the feed room. High on a shelf was an assortment of empty birds' nests. He pulled out an empty butter tub and found tiny eggs no bigger than the tip of a finger, pecked with a hole. The thieving work of a blue jay, he surmised. Another tub held random feathers. Somebody on this farm loved birds like he did.

Will found Amos in the feed room, pouring out scoopfuls of oats into a bucket. Amos looked surprised at the sight of him.

"Well, hello there," Amos said. "I thought you might be my girls, coming to help."

"I think I might have scared them off," Will said.

Amos stopped scooping. "Sorry about that. Completely

43

slipped my mind to tell them you were staying at the cottage for a few weeks. So much excitement going on last night."

"That was sure a lot of people yesterday. Do you mind all of those visitors?"

"Used to it, I guess." Amos dug the scooper into the barrel of oats. "We've always had a lot of rare bird sightings on this farm."

Will saw that Amos had filled one bucket and grabbed another for him, replacing it so he didn't miss a beat. His nails were clipped short, Will noticed. Large hands, working hands.

Amos nodded. "How are the falcons this fine morning?"

"I saw the male head out to hunt. The female is sticking close to the scape, which might mean she's getting ready to lay a clutch."

Amos finished filling the second bucket. "Well, that's what we want." He stood up carefully, tentatively, as if he wasn't completely confident that his body would obey him. It surprised Will. Amos Lapp seemed healthy and strong, fit and slim. A craggy, chiseled, suntanned face. If he were trying to describe Amos Lapp to his mother, he would compare him to John Wayne—his mother's favorite spaghetti Western actor. She loved old movies. Will bent down and grabbed the buckets. He might as well start making himself useful.

Amos started walking toward the center aisle of the barn, stopping by each horse to scoop oats into their feed buckets.

"I was hoping for a chance to talk to you about the rare bird sightings on your farm," Will said. "I'm an avid birder, myself. It's interesting to me that Windmill Farm has had an unusually large amount of sightings. What makes your farm different from others?"

Amos walked to the next stall and lifted the feed tray. "It's not much of a mystery. A lot of Amish farms attract birds. One of the many benefits of plowing with a horse instead of a tractor. Using aged manure instead of chemical fertilizers. I'm not sure we have more birds on Windmill Farm than any other Amish farm."

"Still, there have been more sightings on this farm than any other in the state of Pennsylvania. Even the staff at the game warden's office talk about this farm."

"Well, we might not have any more birds visiting the farm, but we might have spotted birds more than others." Amos stopped and turned to Will. "My son loved birds. He spent 90 percent of his time outdoors and had a gift of noticing God's creatures. He could identify each and every variety of fowl that migrated through our area."

Will noticed that Amos's cheeks were flushed and he was slightly out of breath. He also noticed that he spoke of his son in the past tense. He wondered if that might be how his own father referred to him lately, as if Will were dead to him.

When Amos finished scooping the last of the oats, he turned to Will. "Menno was his name. He'd be about your age. He kept a list of all the birds he sighted. I'll get it for you, if you want to see it. I think he'd be pleased to share that information with a fellow bird lover."

Will lit up. "I'd like that very much. Does he live far away?"

Amos paused and cast his eyes up. "Menno passed on, six months ago."

"Oh, I'm sorry. I thought maybe . . . he had just left your church." Will didn't know a great deal about the Amish, but he had taken a course in sociology in college. He knew about shunning.

Amos lifted his dark eyebrows in surprise. "No, not Menno. I don't think he would ever have left the church. He died in a shooting accident."

"Oh no," Will said. "He was in the wrong place at the wrong time. I'm so sorry."

"No. Menno was in the right place at the right time. His life was complete. The timing of his passing was in God's hands. But his heart lives on."

"Of course," Will murmured, feeling he should say something. "Of course it does. You'll never forget him."

Amos gave him an odd look, with a sad smile. Then he opened the top of his shirt to reveal a large scar that ran down the center of his chest, starting just below his throat.

"Oh," Will said. "You meant that literally."

※※※

Amos heard the wail of a baby as he walked up to the house from the barn. He wasn't sure just what to do about this baby. Should he contact the deacon? But would that mean the baby would be given to a childless couple? Maybe that was for the best. And maybe the sooner, the better. It troubled him to see Sadie's protective, unreasonable attachment to that baby. Imagine—a daughter of his, holding a rifle against another child of God! The sight was almost comical if it weren't such a serious breach of judgment. So unlike his Sadie! He walked into the kitchen and heard footsteps overhead. "Fern?"

"Upstairs."

Just the sound of her voice made him feel better. She'd know what to do about the baby. She'd distract him from worrying about his heart, from his tension over keeping up the farm when he couldn't even plow the fields himself. She had a way of making him forget things—she could make him smile, make him mad. Fern was like a buffer. No, she was more than his buffer. She was his—

He took a deep breath and leaned against the counter. He didn't know what Fern was to him. Not exactly a friend, although she understood him better than other people he'd known for years.

Fern came downstairs and held out her hand to him, palm side up, with pills in it. "I found these on your bedside table, when I was changing your sheets." She placed a hand on her hip. "You forgot to take them last night."

"I meant to. I fell asleep. I'll take them now," he said.

A slight frown creased her brow, but she replied patiently. "No. You're not supposed to double up."

Amos frowned right back at her. "I can manage my own pill taking, Fern."

"Apparently you can't. I called your cardiologist and made an appointment. He wants to see you Monday afternoon." She held up two fingers. "Two o'clock."

Amos glared at her. "You had no right to do that."

"Something's not right lately and you know it. You look as worn out as an old man's slippers. You're not getting enough exercise. You're as limp as a boiled noodle. And I know you aren't sleeping well. I hear you prowling around in the kitchen in the middle of the night. You're—"

He held up his hand like a stop sign. "Fine. I'll go."

Fern's voice softened. "Don't look so woebegone. It might be that your medications need adjusting. Might be as simple as that."

Amos watched her head into the kitchen to put his pills back in the little amber vials. *Or it might be that my body is rejecting this heart, this beautiful, precious heart that once belonged to my son.*

— 4 —

M.K. held a glass up to the wall between Fern's downstairs bedroom—where she had been sent to put freshly ironed pillowcases on the bed—and the kitchen. It was a trick she had read in *Case-Solving Tools for the Everyday Detective*, a book she had checked out from the library. She listened for less than a minute before she was overcome with shame at what she was doing. The thought was tantalizing, but oh, how awful if she got caught!

But then she heard voices in the kitchen. She put the glass back up against the wall, listened carefully for a few minutes, then bolted upstairs to find Sadie. She burst into Sadie's bedroom without knocking and found her lying on her bed reading a book about baby care. "Sadie! You won't believe what I just heard."

"Wunnernaase!" *Nosy.* Sadie frowned at her.

M.K. offered her a smug smile. "Wunnernaase un Schneckeschwenz." *Nosy and curious.*

"M.K., how many times have we told you to stop eavesdropping?"

She lifted her chin. "Fine. I'll just keep the news to myself."

"Fine."

M.K. hung around for a few minutes, peeked at the baby sleeping in his basket, and waited until Sadie couldn't stand it any longer.

Sadie sighed and put down her book. "What exactly did you hear?"

M.K. sidled up to the bed and sat down. "Dad's heart is acting up."

Sadie sat straight up, stunned. "What do you mean? Tell me exactly what you heard. No embellishment. No exaggeration. No editing. And who was doing the talking?"

"Fern and Dad. She's making him see the heart doctor on Monday."

Sadie leaned back on the bed, her face ashen.

"The doctor can fix him. I heard Fern say that very thing. She said that maybe he was just tired because his pills needed adjusting." M.K. patted Sadie on the shoulder. "He'll be fine. Fern said so."

"How has Dad been the last few months? Think, M.K."

"I'm *always* thinking." She rose from the bed and tucked one hand under an elbow, then tucked her chin into the palm of her hand, pacing the room as she thought about Sadie's question. Now that Sadie mentioned it, something did seem a little off with their dad lately. "He seemed fine up until a few weeks ago. Then he started acting tired again, like he did when he first got sick." She brightened. "But yesterday, he sure seemed happy after the Bird Lady brought him the fancy letter for Menno. And then, you came home." She peeked into the basket as the baby let out one tiny squeak. "Last night, though, he seemed sort of sad. Maybe the baby's got him worried."

Sadie was quiet for a long time, watching M.K. fuss over the baby. "I think we need to try and reduce Dad's stress."

M.K.'s eyes went wide. "What stress do I possibly cause? You're the one who nearly killed a harmless game warden intern this morning."

Sadie ignored that reminder. "Mind that you don't get into any trouble at school."

M.K. knotted her forehead. "That is a perfectly ridiculous comment. Especially now that I have a teacher who actually makes the day interesting."

Sadie snorted. "Probably helps that you haven't broken his legs in a sledding accident like you did the last teacher."

"That was not entirely my fault!" M.K. was outraged. People were always blaming her. "Why would anyone in their right mind stand at the bottom of a hill when folks are sledding?"

"Especially when one of those folks happened to be Mary Kate Lapp—a girl known for speeding out of control on hills," Sadie said smugly. Then she clapped her hands to her cheeks. "Gid! I haven't even thought about him since I got back. He's probably heard by now that I'm back."

"Not to worry," M.K. said, bouncing back on the bed. "He knows you're busy with the baby."

Sadie jerked her head toward M.K. "You told him too?"

"No! You told me not to." She studied her feet. "But Ethan Yoder might have," she mumbled under her breath.

"What did you say?"

M.K. cleared her throat. "I said . . . Ethan Yoder might have."

Sadie shot to her feet. "And how would Ethan have heard?"

"Maybe . . . Susie Glick."

"How would Susie Glick know?" Sadie was really mad now, steaming like a teakettle.

M.K. was very focused on a shadow of a tree branch, dancing on the wall. "Ruthie might have said something."

Sadie propped her fists on her hips. "And Ruthie only knows because of you! It always circles back to you and the words that tumble out of your mouth."

M.K. scratched her head. "I think that's a bit of an over-reaction, Sadie."

Sadie glared at her. "What did Gid say?"

M.K. looked up at the ceiling. "Nothing, actually. He didn't say a word. Not a thing. Just got real quiet. He had every-body read for the rest of the afternoon, which suited me just fine because I'm in the middle of *Taming of the Shrew* and I want to find out what happens between Kate and Petruchio."

The baby started making noises and Fern bustled into their room. "There, there," she cooed, as if he had been hollering for hours.

"I'll get the baby's bathwater ready," Sadie said.

"I'll help," M.K. said.

"The both of you are making that baby spoiled as can be," Fern said, snuggling the baby on her shoulder and patting him gently on the back. She tucked her chin over his head, nuzzling him.

M.K. stood behind Fern and tapped the baby's tiny nose. "Dad tried to change his diaper this morning. You've never seen such a complicated process. We'll have to ask him to do that chore more often, just for fun." Because changing a diaper was one task she was never, ever going to perform. You had to draw the line somewhere.

Late Friday afternoon, Gideon Smucker drove the buggy down the road toward Windmill Farm, following another buggy.

A little girl was watching Gid through the open back window. She'd turned in her seat, climbed onto her knees, her head tilted slightly to the side, as if she were curious about him, or confused by him. Her dark hair floated in wispy, tangled curls around her face, her pale blue eyes regarded him with a concern that seemed out of place in the round orb of a child's face. She couldn't have been more than five, maybe six. He didn't recognize her, but in another way, she reminded him of his own boyhood. He loved sitting in the back of the buggy when he was that girl's age, watching the world unroll around him. Life seemed so simple, so unencumbered.

Unlike now.

When Ethan Yoder told him that Sadie had returned with a baby, he felt as if she had delivered a blow to his gut. He was completely, thoroughly shocked. He couldn't stop thinking about it, wondering about it, hoping Ethan had his facts wrong. But then he returned home after school let out and his sister, Alice, had heard the same story from two friends who had stopped by to visit with her.

He knew he had to see Sadie, to talk to her, face-to-face. Maybe this was all a terrible mistake. He couldn't believe it. Sadie, his Sadie, had a baby. This sting of betrayal was the sharpest emotion he'd ever felt. It was like someone was carving his heart out with a dull kitchen knife.

As he drove up the road that led to Windmill Farm, he

saw Sadie up by the farmhouse. "Whoa." Gid pulled back on the reins, drawing the horse to a stop by the side of the road. He reached a hand under the buggy seat and pulled out a pair of binoculars. It felt wrong, like he was a Peeping Tom. He'd never done anything like this before, but he justified his spying on Sadie by telling himself he was just gathering facts.

He saw Sadie walking on the porch, back and forth, with something in her arms. Then he heard a wailing sound carry down on the wind. That was the sound of a crying baby. He focused the lens. Yes, there was definitely a baby in Sadie's arms.

Gid let the binoculars drop. Should he go up to talk to Sadie? To find out more about this baby? He should. He definitely should. He needed to be man enough to get up there and ask her directly. Whose baby is this? What's happened to us since you left? He picked up the reins to get the horse moving, but then his attention was distracted by someone coming out of the open barn, pushing a wheelbarrow filled with hay. A stranger. Or at least a stranger to Gid. A young man with shingled hair, cut differently than Plain men wore theirs, and a confident way of holding his head. When the stranger saw Sadie, he set the wheelbarrow down and crossed over to her. Gid picked up the binoculars again and focused them on Sadie. He saw the man lift the baby out of her arms and press the child against his shoulder. The wailing sound stopped.

Tears prickled Gid's eyes. He couldn't do it. He couldn't see Sadie. What if she told him the very words he didn't want to hear—that there was someone else? He slapped the horse's rump with the reins, startling it to lunge forward. As Gid came to the driveway to Windmill Farm, he drove right past.

———◈———

Will handed the baby, now quiet, to Sadie and went back to pushing the wheelbarrow filled with hay out to the horses in the pasture. He had to keep his chin to his chest to keep from smiling. He could hardly resist releasing a snort of amusement when he observed the deep shade of red Sadie Lapp's face blazed whenever he spoke to her. She was so painfully shy! It was charming. Refreshing, in a way; so different from the kind of girls he was accustomed to at the university.

When the youngest daughter, Mary Kate, had rushed to find him in the barn, begging him to help Sadie get that baby settled down, Will found himself powerless to turn her down. He was getting a kick out of being the only person who could quiet that baby. Twice in one day! It felt good to solve someone's problem. True—it was pretty much a given that it's easier to sort out other people's issues than your own. If only his problems could be solved so easily. Still, his mother would be proud of him. She always said he had a special knack with children. She wanted him to be a pediatrician.

Then his smile faded. Like an echo in his mind, he could hear his father's voice, riddled with disgust, stamping out his mother's compliment. "Snotty noses and ear infections. That's the main job of pediatrics." If he was really in a snarly mood, he would add, "Women's work."

It was ironic that Will's father didn't have any daughters. He had often wondered what his father would have been like with a daughter, but then, Will would never have wished such a fate on any girl. It was hard enough being Charles William Stoltzes' only son.

A tiny slice of movement snagged Will's attention. Someone was watching him from the kitchen window. Mary Kate. He didn't doubt for a minute that girl knew everybody's comings and goings. He could tell her mind spun faster than the arms of the red windmill on a blustery day.

A woman came out on the porch to fill a bird feeder. She was an older woman, in her forties or fifties, as thin as a broom handle. When he saw her face, he could have sworn he was looking at Katharine Hepburn. A handsome woman, unsmiling, yet with unfathomable depths in those steel flint blue eyes—that's how his mother described Katharine Hepburn's appearance. His mother was a nut for Katharine Hepburn movies. His father indulged her on her birthday and watched a few movies with her. This woman on the porch could have been Katharine Hepburn's double. Wouldn't his mother have enjoyed this coincidence? He would have loved to take a picture of her on his cell phone, but he didn't dare. He had a hunch the Katharine Hepburn look-alike would have boxed his ears.

Two horses trotted over to the fence and leaned their heads over the railing to pick at the hay. Will split up a flake of hay and tossed it over the fence. A mother and colt walked up to the hay on the ground. The mother horse pushed her head against one of the horses that had beat her to it. The gelding gave up and looked at Will to solve the problem, so he tossed another flake at the gelding. Even in nature, Will thought, mothers protected their young.

A buzzing sound startled him. His cell phone! It seemed

so out of place on an Amish farm. He reached for the phone and held it against his ear. "Will Stoltz."

"You were supposed to call in yesterday."

Will's heart plummeted. He gulped back panic. "Mr. Petosky, I thought we had an agreement. We left it that I would call you. You don't call me."

"I don't like having to track you down," Mr. Petosky said. "That's not our deal. What's going on?"

"It's too soon to tell. Look, I just got here yesterday."

The voice turned dark. "Please tell me you have some good news for me."

"Mr. Petosky, I've barely unpacked. And the Amish farmer has a long to-do list for me."

"Hey, all I'm asking for are updates. And as soon as the time is right, you complete your task. It's as simple as that."

Simple. Right. That's why Will's stomach was rolling like a tiller in the fields.

The voice softened, as if reading Will's mind. "Remember, Will, this is a win-win. The bird wins and you win."

"And you win," Will said. "Don't forget that, Mr. Petosky."

A husky laugh filled the air. "Right. A three-way win. Everybody wins." Mr. Petosky cleared his throat. "Check in tomorrow."

Will snapped his cell phone off.

Sadie tucked a strand of hair behind an ear, her gaze following the tall cowboy as he strode to the pasture. Earlier today, she hadn't looked directly into his face, too embarrassed by her mistake of assuming he was a baby thief. Now, though, as

Will Stoltz helped her quiet the baby again, she had an opportunity to peruse his features without his knowledge. And she liked what she'd seen. His thick, wavy hair, combed straight back, reminded her of her father's hair. Where Amos's was dark brown with streaks of gray, the cowboy's hair was brown with sun-bleached streaks.

When she came into the kitchen and tucked the sleeping baby into his basket, Fern had just put a casserole into the oven. She asked Sadie to finish cleaning up some pots and pans for her while she went to the basement to get a jar of canned peaches. That's all they'd been eating lately—peaches for breakfast, lunch, and dinner. Fern wanted to use them up before the new crop set on the trees.

Sadie picked up a mitt to put a hot skillet in the sink, then ran some water into it and braced herself. She had always felt frightened by the reaction of a hot skillet to cold water, both the quick angry hiss and the clouds of rising steam. Fern said she had to get over all of these silly fears. Skillets and steam didn't scare Fern one bit. But then again, nothing scared Fern.

Sadie looked out the window at the cowboy who, she just learned, wasn't a cowboy at all. He just liked the hat and boots. He was a student at a university in Philadelphia. Taking a semester off to find himself, he had said. Had he been lost? she wanted to ask, but thought twice before saying it aloud.

She saw Will glance up at the farmhouse as he fed hay to the sheep in the pasture. He waved to her and she waved back. He picked up a baby lamb in his arms and pretended it was his dance partner, sweeping it around as if he was waltzing in the pasture. Then he gently set the lamb on the ground, turned to Sadie, and made a grand bow. Alone in the kitchen,

Sadie laughed out loud. When Will popped back up, his lips spread into a grin beneath the brim of his felt cowboy hat. For a minute, Sadie caught herself just . . . watching him smile. He had a really nice smile, actually. A little impish. The expression seemed kind of mischievous, as if the two of them shared a private joke and Will was enjoying it.

She would think a fellow like Will Stoltz would have a lot of girls fluttering around him at that fancy college. It wouldn't be hard to fall for a boy like that. She tilted her head, wondering if she could hear his heart beat if she laid her cheek against his chest. She had such foolish thoughts as these. *Sadie Lapp, just where will that line of thinking get you? Into trouble!* she upbraided herself. Another part of her brain answered back: *What's so bad about a little bit of trouble?*

Such questions seemed to constantly buzz in her head like mosquitoes, but she felt far short of answers.

As Gideon Smucker pulled the buggy up to the barn at Goat Roper Hill, his family farm, his father came out to meet him. Gid leaped from the buggy and walked around to release the horse from its tracings. Wordlessly, his father pulled the buggy and leaned it up against the barn. Gid led the horse into the stall and filled a bucket with fresh water. He tossed a forkful of hay into the horse's stall. His father followed him in, standing in the center aisle of the barn.

"Something on your mind?" Gid asked. It wasn't like Ira Smucker to not have his hands busy.

Ira sat down on a hay bale set against a wall, leaning forward, steepling his fingers in front of him.

Gid paused in lifting another pitchfork of hay to look at his father. It was strange. His father couldn't seem to look Gid in the eye, as if it was taking everything in him to try to act calm.

Finally, Ira spoke. "Being a minister, well, it's not easy."

Gid knew that to be true. His father was chosen by lot to be a minister nearly three years ago, just before Gid's mother had passed. Gid often thought that the timing of becoming a minister had been a gift to his father. His father was a quiet man, well respected by others. He would have become even quieter if it weren't for the demands of being a minister. And Gid knew that folks counted on Ira's sound judgment. He didn't say much, but when he did, folks listened. Gid tossed a forkful of hay over the stall's door and moved onto the next stall. He faced his father, hooking his elbow on the rounded end of the pitchfork's handle. "What's happened?"

Ira cleared his throat. "There's some talk brewing about . . . about Sadie Lapp."

He leaned the pitchfork against the wall. "About the baby." Gid closed his eyes. "I just drove past Windmill Farm and saw her walking that baby. I didn't talk to her, though. I just couldn't."

Ira nodded sympathetically. "I know my own son well enough to realize Sadie hadn't told you anything about having a baby." He sighed. "I remember what it's like to be a young man. There are certain temptations. Sometimes, a couple in love gets ahead of their wedding day."

Gid's eyes popped open. It hadn't occurred to him that Sadie had been in love with this other fellow. What had gone so wrong? When had she met him? Was she seeing him while she was going out with Gid last December? He counted back the months and slammed his palm against his forehead. Stupid, stupid, stupid! She must have been seeing this other fellow at the same time she was spending time with him! Who could it have been?

Ira's cheeks turned scarlet. "In a . . . situation . . . like this . . . I think it's best to face things head-on." His father kept his eyes on a piece of hay that he was twisting in his hands, back and forth, back and forth.

A horse shuffled straw with his hoof in his stall. A starling flew from one side of the barn to the other, disappearing into a nest in the rafters. In the silence that followed, it slowly dawned on Gid what his father was getting after, why he was acting so strangely.

Gid wondered what Sadie had told people. Had she led others to believe that Gid was the father of that baby? He wasn't! He most definitely wasn't! Gid bit down on his tongue to hold back words of protest.

If he told the truth, he thought about what that could mean for Sadie. She would be under the bann for six weeks, then confess her wrongdoing before the church. And even though she would be restored in full fellowship, there would always be questions, talk, murmurings. She would be raising this baby alone. The quiet pressure might be so intense that she would want to leave the church. To start fresh somewhere else.

With someone else.

And what would happen to them? There wouldn't be a "them."

It would play out the way it had with his second oldest sister, Martha, called Marty. She had met someone while visiting relatives and came home carrying that someone's child. What made it worse was that someone was a married man. Gid was only thirteen at the time, but he remembered the shame that fell over Goat Roper Hill, as real as a covering of deep snow. Marty sat on the front bench and confessed as their mother sat in the back row and cried. It seemed his mother didn't stop crying that entire summer. His mother claimed that everywhere she went, she heard a hiss of whispers: "*They're* the ones with the adulterous daughter."

His father said she was imagining things and to stop making Marty feel as if her life was over at nineteen. "It isn't," Gid vividly remembered his father telling his mother. "God is in the business of second chances." But his mother said that while God might give second chances, people weren't as generous. Then she told him he just didn't understand the way of the world and she started crying all over again.

Whether the pressure came from outside the home or inside it, Marty had enough. She left home before the baby was even born. She worked as a waitress over in Harrisburg and was living with another someone. Every so often, she called home and asked for money to fend off the bill collectors. Her father would always send a check off to her, no questions asked.

But no requests for her to come home, either.

Gid snatched up the pitchfork and jabbed it into the mound of hay with enough force to bend the tines. If he lied and said he was the father of Sadie's baby, it would mean that he, too, would be put under the bann for six weeks. He might even lose his teaching job. And then he and Sadie would be expected to marry. Immediately.

In a way, it wouldn't entirely be a lie. He could, essentially, become the baby's father. That baby was part of Sadie, and Gid would raise him and love him as his own. He loved Sadie. He didn't doubt that for a moment. And Gid couldn't imagine his life without her. He wanted to spend the rest of his days with her, filling a house with children and serving God.

He would do this for her. He loved her that much.

He gave a little jerk, setting his feet in motion. "Dad," he said, in a voice so steady that it could not be his own. "I want to marry Sadie Lapp. As soon as possible."

A broad smile lit Ira's face. He turned to his son and nodded, satisfied, then ambled toward the barn's wide opening, leaving Gid alone with his thoughts.

5

At first Sadie thought she was woken by the moonlight streaming into her window. Full, orange, the moon seemed to teeter on the windowsill. The light spilled into the bedroom and across the wood floor. Then a broad beam of light swept over her bedroom wall and along the ceiling. She popped up on her elbows. Heart pounding, she climbed out of bed and knelt at the window. At first she could see nothing; then she saw someone below her window. A tall, dark figure silhouetted against the moonlight. He held the flashlight up to his face so she could see him. It was Gideon Smucker, looking up at her, motioning with his free hand for her to come down. She pulled up the window sash.

"Hang on a minute, I'm coming down." Her heart zinged into her throat, and before she could talk herself out of it, she dressed, slipped downstairs, slid her feet into flip-flops, and went silently through the back door.

He was waiting for her. "You've come home," he said, holding out a hand to her as she approached him.

She smiled at him. His eyes were beautiful—a deep, clear blue, as blue as a robin's eggs, with impossibly thick lashes fanning outward. Looking into his eyes ignited something in her and she never quite knew how to describe it. Unsettled was the closest feeling she could claim. He was so sure about her, so certain that she was meant for him. It made her nervous, but pleased too. More pleased than nervous. "No one knew, not even Dad. I wanted to surprise everybody."

"You did just that. You certainly did."

They headed toward the maple tree in the side yard—on the opposite side of the house from M.K.'s bedroom. Sadie plunked down on the swing that hung from the tree's large branch. Gid leaned his back against the tree trunk and stared at the clouds rushing through the night sky. Gid wasn't much of a talker, but those eyes of his—they told her everything he felt. Tonight, there was something in his reserved expression that spilled out sorrow. Something was wrong.

Gid's gaze shifted to a spray of lightning bugs dancing past them. "I remember coming here once and watching M.K. chase lightning bugs."

He stopped and swallowed, then looked up into the trees. It hit her then that he was just as nervous as Sadie was.

"Gid, you might have heard things," Sadie whispered.

He kept his gaze angled toward the night sky. "It's okay, Sadie. I want to make this better for you."

She caught his sleeve and gave it a tug, forcing him to look at her. "Make what better?"

He looked at her for a long moment, dropped his head, then squeezed her hand that was still on his arm. "Your . . . circumstances."

She was confused. "I don't know what you mean. What needs to be made better?"

"You know. The baby."

She blew air out of her cheeks. "M.K. told me that you were told."

His head snapped up. "I didn't know it was a secret."

"It's not. Not exactly." She watched the moon pass behind a cloud. "I mean . . . I would have preferred the news to not have gotten out like it did. So that I could figure out what I needed to do without everybody's opinion."

Gid didn't say anything for a long time. "Folks are quite surprised at this . . . situation."

Okay. Now she was mad. This wasn't a situation! This was an orphaned baby. "Why is it anybody's business?"

Gid looked flustered.

"I'm sorry if I sound testy," she said, still sounding testy, "but I have a hard time understanding people who talk about you behind your back."

"It's just natural, I suppose. I remember a lot of talk when the same thing happened to Marty—"

"Marty? Marty!" She flinched, as if suffering a physical blow, and yanked her hand out of his. "But it's not the same thing. Not the same thing at all!" She searched his eyes. "You believe that, don't you, Gid?"

There was a beat of silence. "I want to," he said quietly. Gid scuffed the dirt with the toe of his boot, eyes down.

"How many others are thinking what you're thinking?"

He rubbed his neck. "Quite a few. Most."

A chill swept through her soul. How far was this rumor traveling? She envisioned the faces of her neighbors—Sol and Mattie to the east, her Zook relatives at Beacon Hollow to the south, Jonah and Lainey of Rose Hill Farm to the north,

Carrie and Abel to the west. She couldn't imagine any of them believing such a lie. She lifted her chin. "So our friends and neighbors would just prefer to believe the worst about me."

"You have to admit, it doesn't look good." Gid ducked his head, bright color staining his cheeks. The singing wind shifted the clouds again, flickering shadows and light over Sadie's face. He took a deep breath. "Love covers all wrongs. I forgive you."

Such beautiful words, and yet, from somewhere deep inside, Sadie felt a well rising, filled with fury. She was livid. "If you're going to pull one verse out of the Bible and toss it at me like a preacher"—she stood and faced him—"then how about this one: 'Love believes all things, hopes all things.'"

His eyes sent her a silent plea. "That's exactly what I'm trying to do, Sadie."

"Then why don't you ask me for the truth?"

Gid tipped his forehead against Sadie's. "I'm sorry," he murmured.

She leaned against him, breathing in his familiar scent: sandalwood. She could feel his breath, his words, falling onto her.

"All right then, Sadie. I'll ask you for the truth. Who is the baby's father?"

Gid's question set off a cavalcade of emotions in her. She was on the cusp of bursting into tears right in front of him. "Gideon, do you trust me or not?"

"I trust you," he finally said.

"No. You don't. Not really." She stepped away from him. "If you did, you would never have needed to ask me that question."

She ran to the farmhouse and went inside, bolted up the

stairs, and flopped herself on the bed, making the springs squeak.

How could so much have changed, in such little time? Why didn't she just stay in Berlin with Julia and Rome? And Old Deborah? She wouldn't have to deal with a boyfriend who believed lies about her, with a newborn baby who cried like he was getting stuck with a pin, with a father whose second heart was giving him trouble. A week ago, life was so much simpler. How could she stay here? How could she face going to church, knowing what people were thinking about her? What Gid was thinking about her!

Sadie turned toward the window and curled into a ball. She wished her mother were here to ask advice. It seemed the older she got, the more she missed her mother. A shred of a memory, long forgotten, flashed through her mind—a day when Sadie came home from school with hurt feelings because someone had told her she was as dumb as a box of rocks. Book learning came slowly for Sadie. She just couldn't remember details the way M.K. and Julia could. She was forever slowing her class down, causing them to lose spelling bees and math quizzes. On that day, she had missed the word "utter," spelling it "udder." An innocent mistake! But one that brought whoops and howls of belly laughter from the boys. Even the girls. They teased her about it all day long.

Her mother had met her at the door with freshly made gingersnaps. When Sadie told her about the spelling bee, her mother said, "There are two kinds of smarts in this world: book smarts and people smarts. Frankly, I think people smarts is worth much more than book smarts. And you've got more people smarts in your little finger than most folks have in their whole bodies." Then she covered Sadie's small hand with her own and gazed steadily into her eyes. "Someday, Sadie, folks are going to be coming to you for advice to solve their problems. You just mark my words."

Fat chance.

Sadie slipped out of bed and sat by the window, resting her fingertips against the smooth glass. She propped her arm on the windowsill and rested her chin on the back of her wrist. Stars glittered overhead, beautiful against the velvety backdrop of black sky. The round moon hung low in the sky. How often had she sat here and made wishes on the stars? She scrunched her eyes tight and started to cry again, softly at first, until tears were flowing down her cheeks and she could barely hold back a sob.

She felt someone rubbing her back. Sadie's eyes opened wide, blinking out at the soft night scene. Fern had come to comfort her. Sadie turned her head slightly. She took a few deep breaths.

"Was that Gideon's voice I heard out there?"

Fern. She heard everything.

Sadie gave a quick nod of her head. "My little sister did me the great favor of telling a few people that I returned with a baby, and a few people told a few more. I just found out that everyone in the church thinks this baby is mine."

Fern let out a sigh padded with exasperation. "Mary Kate never meant to hurt you."

"I know. But what about everyone else? I can't believe people are spreading lies about me."

"So Gideon believes such nonsense too?"

On a strangled sob, Sadie barked out, "He told me . . .

he forgave me!" New tears threatened, but she sniffed hard and brought herself under control. "For what?! I didn't do anything!"

Fern bit on her lip, as if to hold back a smile. "Gid's a man of deep convictions. Responsible. Those are good traits, Sadie. Schtill Wasser laaft gern dief." *Still waters run deep.*

"But his convictions are wrong!" She frowned, fighting back a wave of worry. "Why do people only believe what they want to believe?"

"Easier, I guess. They don't have to think."

"How am I going to be able to face everyone in church, knowing what they are thinking about me?"

"Don't pay any attention to such idle gossip."

"You're the one who always said, 'A lie can travel across the country and back again while the truth is lacing up its boots.'"

Fern sighed.

"And you've also said that gossip is like mud thrown on a clean wall. It may not stick but it leaves a dirty mark. And how many times have you said a rumor is about as easy to unspread as butter."

"I've also said, 'Was yeders duh sott, dutt niemand.'" *Everybody's business is nobody's business.*

Sadie wiped a tear off her cheek. "Maybe I should go back to Berlin. It was easier there. People didn't gossip there."

"Sadie, look at me," Fern said in a gentle but authoritative voice. When Sadie twisted around to face her, she continued. "It's time you got your wits together. After all, you're nearly full grown, aren't you?"

Sensibly, Sadie left that unanswered.

"You want to rein in that line of thinking—lumping everyone in the same pile. So, maybe a few are spreading tales. But more than a few want to help. Mattie Riehl and Carrie Miller stopped by today to see the baby. They brought over a bag of baby clothes and blankets. Mattie said she'd love to babysit, anytime we need help. Bess and Lainey offered to have a baby shower. Never forget—these neighbors are your friends, through thick and thin. Nobody ever said they were perfect. They make mistakes, just like you do. And they make mistakes in Berlin, Ohio, too. You just weren't there long enough to notice."

Over in his basket in the corner, the baby started making noises. Sadie groaned. She was growing familiar with his noises. Those little peeps and squeaks would start getting bigger, and bigger, until that ten-pound bundle was screaming bloody murder.

"I'll take this shift," Fern said. "You get some sleep."

Sadie lifted her head to look at her. "How do you do it, Fern? How do you handle coping with all of the problems my family seems to have?"

Fern brushed Sadie's cheek with her rough fingertips. "I do what I have to do," she said matter-of-factly. "You of all people should understand."

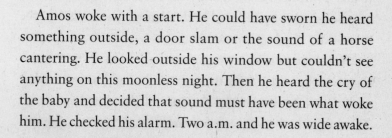

Amos woke with a start. He could have sworn he heard something outside, a door slam or the sound of a horse cantering. He looked outside his window but couldn't see anything on this moonless night. Then he heard the cry of the baby and decided that sound must have been what woke him. He checked his alarm. Two a.m. and he was wide awake.

He hoped it wouldn't be another sleepless night. It could be worse, he thought. It could be a night with dreams.

Amos ran a finger along his scar. It still amazed him—his sternum had been buzzed open by a saw and held apart with a metal spreader. His weak, damaged heart was replaced with a vibrant, healthy heart. His beloved son's. He held his hand against his heart, taking comfort in the steady beat: *thump, thump, thump.*

Even though Amos knew there was no scientific evidence to support this theory, he couldn't deny it: he felt as if Menno's heart was altering his psyche. It wasn't like some of the strange stories of cellular memory that people liked to tell him about. The latest story he heard was about a man who gained a miraculous ability to paint after receiving a heart from an artist. When Amos heard that, he wanted to ask: what if the fellow just had extra time on his hands after his surgery? What if he just had a desire to try something new? No—Amos thought the whole notion of cellular memory was a bunch of mumbo jumbo.

But ever since the transplant last fall, he kept having strange dreams that involved Menno. He woke in a cold sweat, unable to remember the dream but left with the same feeling each time—that there was some unfinished business he had to take care of. When he mentioned the dreams to the doctor, he was asked if he believed in the theory that souls on "the other side" tried to contact us.

"Now," Amos said, trying to hold back from obvious scorning of such a ridiculous theory, "why would a soul bother with that if he were in the presence of the almighty Lord?" The doctor had no answer for him.

Amos had no doubt that Menno, enjoying heaven, was untroubled by the worries of this world. His son was wholly restored, from imperfect to perfect, and he was in the company of his mother and others who went before him. Menno knew the end of the story, and it was good. "In your presence is fullness of joy," wrote the psalmist.

But Amos couldn't shake these dreams. It felt as if maybe God was trying to remind him of something he had forgotten, or misplaced, or more likely, to nudge him to pay attention. He prayed about them, asking God to reveal the meaning of the dreams to him, the way he had to Joseph in Egypt. Once, he had even gone through Menno's belongings to see if there might be a clue. Nothing, other than an overdue library book. And it was a book of Charlie Brown and Snoopy cartoons! What unfinished business could there have been of a nineteen-year-old whose mind was that of an eight-year-old boy? He just couldn't figure it out.

It was Friday. It had rained all night, a hard, driving, drenching downpour. As M.K. toyed with her scrambled eggs, she could feel the edge of danger mounting within her. She knew that today would be the day.

"Will you listen to me while I'm talking to you?" Fern said to her.

"Ah . . . what?"

"When I'm talking to you, I want you to listen. You sit there like you've got cotton stuffed in your ears."

Fern always had a thing about M.K. not listening. She

scrunched around in her seat, pretending to listen to her, but her mind was a million miles away, working out a plan.

"You'd better be home right after school today," Fern said. "No dillydallying."

M.K. lifted her chin. "I don't dilly and I don't dally."

After breakfast, M.K. and Sadie worked in silence as they cleaned up dishes. Finally, she tapped Sadie's shoulder. "Are you going to stay mad at me forever?"

With a sigh, Sadie turned from the sink. M.K. tried to make her face look as contrite as possible. "I'm not angry, M.K., I just don't think you realize the kind of trouble you stirred up when you told people I brought back a baby from Ohio. It's just . . ." But once again, she fell silent.

When Sadie wouldn't talk, M.K. knew it was best to just try to change the subject. "If you're not angry, then let's go find out who might be missing a baby."

Sadie turned to face her.

"I've been doing some thinking by using my crackerjack detective skills. I know the baby was wearing a Onesie—something that any baby might wear. No clue in that. No clue with the brand of diapers. Just regular old Pampers. But the basket the baby was left in . . . I think that basket might hold a clue."

"How's that?"

"I was examining it earlier. It's handmade. And it's pretty new. There's a tag on the bottom. I'm thinking we should take it to a basket shop and see if they might know who made it, or who it was sold to."

Now Sadie looked at her with interest. "You might be on to something, M.K."

M.K. nodded, her eyes sparkling with mischief. "It's called connecting the dots. I'm particularly good at it."

Then Sadie's face clouded over. "Maybe . . . we don't want to know."

"What do you mean? Dad said that the baby should be with his mother."

"What kind of mother would abandon a baby? Maybe the baby is better off with us."

M.K. wrinkled her forehead. "Sadie, maybe you shouldn't be getting too attached to that baby."

"I can't help it. There's something about him. I just feel he is meant for me. For us. I can't explain it. It's like a deep-down knowing. This baby is for us."

M.K. shrugged her small shoulders. "Maybe you're right. Maybe Dad's right. But I'm going to take a trip to that bas-ketmaker as soon as I can slip out this afternoon without Fern catching me. Are you coming with me?"

Sadie hesitated. She looked at the sleeping baby. "We'll go. But I'm driving." She gave M.K. a look as if she was bracing herself for a challenge.

Would M.K. dare to miss a ride with Sadie as pilot? It could be more exciting than sledding down Flying Saucer Hill on an icy day.

— 6 —

At five foot three inches, Sadie had to sit on a telephone book to see over the dashboard of the buggy. Her buggy driving skills were not exactly her strongest suit. She had always avoided driving the buggy. One sibling or another usually wanted to be in the driver's seat and she happily acquiesced. But last night Fern had reminded her that she was nearly a grown woman and Sadie hadn't stopped thinking about that comment. If she was going to start her life as an adult, she was going to have to be brave.

Then she couldn't find M.K. Nothing unusual there; M.K. never came when she was called. M.K. said it was because her mind was always on other things. Sadie finally found her up in the hayloft, reading.

"Let's go," Sadie called up to her. "The baby is asleep on Fern's bed and she has a long list of things she wants me to get at the store." She held up the baby's basket. "A golden opportunity!"

M.K. flew down the hayloft ladder and beat Sadie to the buggy, hopping in on the passenger side.

Sadie banged her door shut, and the horse startled and

reared a few feet. Sadie screamed and dropped the reins. Her high-pitched scream made the horse startle even more, and then, the mare bolted. The buggy shot forward on the curving front drive, then veered straight off the drive. M.K. was holding on to the door handle with both hands. They were gunning over the grass, shade trees were looming by, fences flickered past, the entire world was a blur. Chickens scattered, feathers flying, as they saw what was headed in their direction. Sadie was pinned against the seat and M.K. seemed to somersault on the front seat.

Think, Sadie, think. You're a grown woman now. Think!

Sadie grabbed the loose reins and yanked as hard as she could. They blasted between two trees, and right over Fern's newly planted flower bed. They sailed over neat rows of impatiens—red, pink, then white—but the front wheels of the buggy dug into the soft flower bed and caused the horse to slow from a canter to a trot, a trot to a walk, and finally, to a stop. Sadie collected her wits, at least those that hadn't been shaken out of her, and turned to check on M.K. Her little sister had both feet braced against the dashboard of the buggy, and her eyes were really big. She never saw M.K. scared, except maybe when Sadie was driving.

M.K. took a few deep, gulpy breaths. "Cayenne? Why in the world did you harness up Cayenne? She's barely buggy broke. She's as skittish a filly as they come."

Sadie wiped perspiration from her forehead. "She was the only horse in the barn."

M.K. peeled out the door on her side, ending up in a pile on the grass. "I hate to say it, Sadie, but being in a buggy with you at the helm could be hazardous to a person's health."

She spit a feather out of her mouth. "You kill more chickens driving the buggy than the Fishers on butchering day." She brushed herself off and checked for damages. "Either I drive or I'm staying home."

Ten minutes later, Mary Kate steered Cayenne into the Bent N' Dent, a small Amish corner store without any signage out front. Sadie went into the store to get the items on Fern's list and told M.K. to wait in the buggy. Waiting was never a strength for Mary Kate, and she soon grew bored with watching the horse's tail swat flies.

Another buggy pulled into the Bent N' Dent and she poked her head out of the window to see who it was. She scowled when she saw Jimmy Fisher, her arch nemesis, jump from his buggy. They'd had a running feud since the first day she started school. It was set aside briefly after Menno died, but soon resumed again. It was unfortunate, M.K. always thought, that Jimmy happened to be blessed with good looks and a charming personality, because the spoiled youngest son of Edith Fisher was usually up to mischief. He was the sort of boy who couldn't settle until he'd jerked a girl's bandanna off her head or tripped someone walking down the aisle at church. And he was the only boy Mary Kate knew who smoked on a regular basis: cigars, cigarettes, pipes, or corn silk. He was a scoundrel of the worst kind.

Under ordinary circumstances she wouldn't pay any mind to Jimmy Fisher. But as she watched him stride toward the store, she realized he had grown tall as a stork, seemingly overnight. It must have been coming on him in stages, but she hadn't noticed until today, and she couldn't believe it. Mostly, she saw him from afar, and he was always striding in the other direction.

Jimmy Fisher had begun to leave the skinny boy behind and was cutting the fine figure of a lanky man. His knees were working through his britches, and his wrists had grown out of his sleeves. She noticed how fuzzy sideburns were beginning to grow down the sides of his face. He would turn fifteen this summer.

With a smug look on his handsome and horrible face, Jimmy saw her and sauntered over to her buggy.

"Well, if it isn't Mary Kate Lapp," he said, placing his hands on the open window. "I see you're taking your old nag out for an afternoon stroll. Hope she can get you home by supper."

Blond though he was, you could see a whisper of whisker under his nose. His neck was filling out, and she thought he had a cold he couldn't shake off before she realized his voice was changing. She looked down, and his boots were like boats.

It was amazing. She couldn't get her mind around it. One day Jimmy Fisher was a bratty little boy, and the next he was a bratty young man.

"My filly could beat your bag-of-bones gelding any day of the week," she said, lifting her nose in the air.

He leaned closer to the buggy. "So I hear there's a little scandal happening out at Windmill Farm."

She ignored him.

"A little ten-pound, bald-headed, diaper-bottomed scandal."

She continued to ignore him.

"Funny how life goes, isn't it? Who would have ever thought

sweet little Sadie would have a race with the stork." He tsked-tsked, shaking his head, as if he were scolding a small child for dripping an ice-cream cone.

Now that really got M.K.'s goat. A person could only take so much, especially from the likes of Jimmy Fisher.

Mary Kate pointed a finger at his chest. "You. Me. Your worthless gelding. My sleek filly. From here to Blue Lake Pond and back again." She glanced at the store. She needed to get back in time before Sadie came out.

Jimmy perked up. "Now?"

"Now." She gave him a sweet smile. "Unless, of course, you need some practice."

"Me and my gelding, we don't need any practice," he shot back. "What's at stake?"

"When I win, you will keep your mouth shut about anything that has to do with the Lapp family."

"And when I win?"

M.K. narrowed her eyes. She hadn't thought this through. Then a brilliant thought bubbled to the front and the corners of her mouth curled up in a devilish grin. "I won't tell anyone that you were the one who let Jake Hostetler's bull out."

Jimmy's mouth opened wide in outrage. Clapped shut. "I never did!"

"That's a big lie, Jimmy Fisher, and it'll only get bigger."

The bull breakout had been the talk of the town for a week. Jake Hostetler's bull had broken through two neighbors' fences to get to the Masts' dairy farm. It had taken eight men over two hours to get all of the Masts' cows gathered and contained and Jake's bull back home. The Masts were not entirely unhappy about the outcome as they had a prize sire visit their farm without the usual stud fees, but Jake Hostetler was furious. "The Masts sure would like to know who got their cows all stirred up and crazy with desire." She lifted her voice and carefully enunciated the word *desire*, just to rub it in.

Jimmy's eyes shifted to shifty. She was getting nearer the truth, never a short trip.

"On. The. *Sabbath*."

Jimmy's ears burned like fire, and his broad shoulders slumped. So she was right! She wasn't entirely sure it was Jimmy who had started the mischief, but she had a strong suspicion. She wondered if the pressures of life had unhinged his mind. Even at the best of times, his mind hung by a single, rusty hinge.

He glared at her. "Down to Blue Lake Pond and back again." She gave a short jerk of her head.

Jimmy ran back to his buggy and hopped in. They lined up the horses, side by side, at the edge of the Bent N' Dent parking lot. "Ready?" he said, watching M.K. from the corner of his eye. She was doing the same.

The horses quickly surmised that something was up. Their ears, cocked forward, were sharpened to a point. They were retired racehorses and knew the drill. Cayenne pawed at the ground with her right front hoof.

M.K. made sure she had the reins tightly held. She looked for traffic and saw no car in sight, either direction. "Go!" she shouted, and her mare hurtled into action. Jimmy slapped his reins on his gelding's rump and his buggy lunged forward.

The race was on and they were off.

Sadie walked out of the store just in time to see the backs of two buggies kick up dust as they thundered down the road. It didn't take a genius to figure out what was going on. Through the window, as she had paid for her groceries, she had seen Jimmy Fisher buzzing around M.K. She sighed and reviewed her options. This might be a blessing in disguise. She wanted to go do a little sleuthing that didn't involve her little sister's nose for news. She put her groceries on a bench, told the clerk that she'd be back soon, and hurried down the road. She cut through one field and came out on a seldom-traveled lane that led to a run-down old farm. At least, it looked run-down to someone from the Old Order Amish, who took pride in the upkeep of their farms even though they weren't supposed to be prideful. This farm belonged to an elderly Swartzentruber man. He lived there with his granddaughter, Annie.

As Sadie approached the house, she saw it looked even worse than a year ago, the last time she had been here to visit Annie. An old house without a speck of paint stood set back from the dirt lane. A few outbuildings had caved in, and the privy stood at an angle. A handful of scrawny chickens pecked dirt. The big shade tree in front of the house had just leafed out and made shadowy patterns. The yard wasn't mowed. Even in full daylight, the place had an eerie feel to it, a little like a graveyard when you're all alone, and you could almost feel ghosts lurking about, even though Sadie didn't believe in ghosts.

A skinny, pathetic-looking yellow dog let out a halfhearted "woof!" as Sadie walked along. The dog cocked its head, then came forward cautiously to sniff her. Sadie went down on one knee.

"Where did you come from, big guy?" Sadie held out her hand, palm up. "It's a wonder you haven't been eaten up by a bear." She ran her hand along the dog's side. "Your ribs are poking through. How long since you've eaten?" The dog sauntered off to lie in the shade.

Sadie hadn't noticed an old man sitting in a chair on the porch, slumped, with his jaw dropped. He could be dead. He could be a dead body somebody left here. But then something made him stir, maybe the dog's gentle woof. His eyes opened, and he looked up under his worn black hat, then yanked it off to have a better look at her. He was as bald as an egg and needed a shave. His neck shrank back from the collar on his shirt. He was looking at Sadie like he thought he knew her. Sadie's mind whirled. She wanted to run away, but she had to see this through.

"THERE YOU ARE. I WANT MY DINNER." The old man's jaw wobbled as he spoke, and Sadie could see there was not a tooth in his head. He had an unusually loud voice for such a withered old man. The old man squinted at her over his glasses. "I WANT MY SUPPER IS WHAT I WANT." He looked around the front yard. "ANNIE, I'M HUNGRY. IT'S PAST SUPPERTIME."

Now Sadie was up on the porch, gripping the post. She was Annie, and he wanted his supper, and she didn't know what to do. "I'm not Annie. I'm Sadie. SADIE LAPP. NOT ANNIE."

The old man's eyes were just watery slits now, and he was getting really excited. A big cane was tucked behind his chair. The old man thrashed around in his chair, looking for his cane, and she wanted to keep out of its range.

The yellow dog gave out another feeble woof. Sadie looked at it again. Something dawned on her—this was the puppy her brother Menno had given to Annie a year or so ago, now full grown. The realization made her sad. Menno took pride in his pups' well-being.

"WHEN IS ANNIE COMING HOME?"

"I'M HUNGRY. I WANT MY DINNER."

"WHEN WILL ANNIE COME HOME TO MAKE YOUR DINNER?"

"YOU'RE ANNIE AND I'M HALF-STARVED."

"I'M NOT ANNIE. I'M SADIE LAPP. HOW LONG HAS SHE BEEN GONE?"

"WHAT?"

"HOW LONG HAS ANNIE BEEN GONE?"

He blinked at her a number of times, like a fog was lifting. "DON'T YOU HAVE SOMEPLACE YOU NEED TO BE?"

He had a point. It was definitely time to get going. Sadie was in new territory here, but she knew where she wanted to go next. She had to try one more time. "I'LL GET YOUR DINNER FOR YOU."

The old man brightened.

Sadie walked up to the porch, expecting the old man to tell her to leave, but he seemed to be delighted to have someone solve his immediate problem. She slipped into the house and found the kitchen. The furnishings were sparse. Bare necessities only. It worried her to see what little food was in the house.

She didn't know much about this tiny Swartzentruber colony. They seldom interacted with Sadie's church, but she would have thought they'd be looking out for this old man. She found some bread, peanut butter, and jam, made a sandwich for him, filled a glass of milk—sniffed it first to make sure it hadn't gone sour—and found a small tray to take it out to him. She peeked out the window and saw he had his eyes closed. She put the tray down and looked around the room. Emboldened, she went down the hallway, opened a door, and poked her head in. It must be the old man's room, because it was dark and smelled musty. Then she looked into another room, tiptoeing in as her eyes adjusted to the dark. Something familiar caught her eye and she bent down to examine it.

So this was it.

The breath she hadn't realized she was holding whooshed out of her.

"WHERE'S MY DINNER?" sailed through the open window from the front porch.

Sadie closed the door to the bedroom and picked up the tray with the sandwich and glass of milk in the kitchen. She hurried outside and handed the plate to the old man before he could rise from the chair. "Perhaps it's time to be running along," she said in a loud and strange voice. "GOING." She waved goodbye to make her point.

The old man was gumming the sandwich and didn't even look up. The yellow dog followed Sadie down the path to the road, despite her efforts to shoo him home. Finally, she turned and tried to drag the dog back to the old man, but the dog sat back on its heels and wouldn't budge.

"TAKE IT!" the old man yelled. "THAT DOG IS A DOOZY. I DON'T WANT IT."

Sadie walked back through the fields to the Bent N' Dent, deep in thought, with the yellow dog trailing behind her.

When she arrived at the store, Mary Kate was waiting for her with an odd look on her face and a very lathered-up buggy horse. She waved to Sadie to hurry. "Maybe we'd better skip the basketmaker today and get on home."

Sadie opened the buggy door and let the yellow dog jump in. M.K. seemed so distracted, she didn't even look twice at the dog. Sadie barely shut the door as M.K. slapped the horse's rump with the reins and headed home. Sadie watched her for a while, amused by the tense look on M.K.'s face.

"What happened to Jimmy?" Sadie finally asked.

Eyes straight forward, M.K. said, "Jimmy who?"

"M.K., he's not bleeding to death in a ditch somewhere, is he?"

M.K. flashed her a look of disgust. "No!" But she wouldn't offer another word.

M.K. was always up to something and Sadie wondered what. She had this urge—just a slight one—to grab her little sister by the ankles and dangle her over the side of the buggy until she started talking.

As they pulled up to the barn at Windmill Farm—in record time, Sadie noted—Fern walked out of the house to meet them with a crying baby in her arms. M.K. rushed to get the horse out of its shafts. She waved Fern's questioning glance off. "Got to take care of the horse, Fern," she tossed over her shoulder as she walked the horse down the hill to cool it off before returning it to the barn. Fern turned to Sadie with a question in her eyes.

Sadie shrugged. "I'm not entirely sure what happened, but it had something to do with Jimmy Fisher."

Fern, who had heard all this before, released an effluvial

sigh. "It always has something to do with that boy. Those two are like oil and vinegar." She lifted an eyebrow. "What happened to my impatiens?"

Sadie's attention was suddenly riveted to the sky, where the male falcon, the one Will called Adam, soared above them. The baby let out another big wail and Fern passed him off to Sadie. "He's fed, he's dry, and he keeps on crying." She cocked her head. "And where are the groceries?"

Sadie smacked her own forehead. "Oh. Oh no! I left them at the store."

Fern looked at her as if she might have a screw loose.

The yellow dog leaped out of the backseat of the buggy and jumped up on Fern, drenching her face with wet licks. Fern pushed it off and walked back to the house, muttering away about how it was easier just to do things herself.

7

Sunrise would stir Will in just moments, and he could hardly lift his head off the pillow. Every single muscle in his body ached from the farmwork he had been doing. It was backbreaking work, day after day. It was the best time of his life.

On a Saturday morning, he knew there would be plenty of bird-watchers lined up with their scopes to watch his birds. His birds. He was already thinking they belonged to him. He felt oddly protective toward them. It started when he named them Adam and Eve. He stuck his stocking feet in his boots and looked around for his binoculars. He had just moved in a day or so ago, and the cottage was already a mess. Clothes were strewn all over. Some groceries he had bought were still on the kitchen table, next to a banana peel and a half-eaten piece of wheat toast, and a dirty napkin. He frowned, looking around the room. He really was a slob. He drank milk and orange juice from the carton. He dipped his toast in the peanut butter jar. He left the cap off the toothpaste and squeezed it in the middle. He didn't pick up his socks or make his bed. Why bother? He was just getting back into it tonight.

He finally found his binoculars under a newspaper, and grabbed a granola bar out of a box to stave off hunger. He wasn't quite sure how he was going to manage cooking for himself. Not that he had much experience with cooking in the first place, but he sure couldn't figure out the appliances in the kitchen. Where were the wall switches? And he still had to learn how to light the kerosene lamp. He tried again and again last night, went through a box of matches, and finally gave up and went to sleep. But he liked this little cottage. It was simple living at its best. As he lay in the snug bed last night, covered in homemade quilts, he could have sworn he smelled a faint scent of beeswax, infused in the walls. The scent was very homey and appealing.

He jammed his hat on his head and hurried outside to scan the sky. Adam and Eve were already up, soaring over the creek bed that wove through Windmill Farm. He watched Eve—the larger of the two—soar high and key in on something down below. He watched her virtually stop in the air, then dive straight down as if she was heading right into the water, only to make a last-minute turn and soar back up to the sky with a small bird in her talons. Effortless! Will kept his eyes trained on her. Just as he expected, she flew to a nearby place on the ground and tore the bird to pieces, quickly swallowing them. The falcons were vulnerable on the ground and preferred to spend as little time there as possible. They have a special pouch in their throats to hold food. It would be digested later, when Eve was safely in her scape.

Adam flew over a field and caught a small bird in the air. He disappeared into a treetop. Will noticed a group of bird-watchers had just arrived and were setting up their telescopes.

He walked over to politely remind them to stay off the property. He wasn't too worried about this crowd—anyone who set an alarm for predawn to watch a bird catch his breakfast was a pretty tame type. It was the feeding at dusk that seemed to bring out a rowdier crowd.

Eve flew back to the scape, which Will thought was indicative of impending motherhood. He followed Adam's flight path and ended up passing the farmhouse. Sadie was out on the porch, filling a bird feeder with sunflower seeds. He'd never seen so many bird feeders or birdhouses at one home. It was a regular feeding station. Tall purple martin houses, stacked like condominiums, lined the far end of the driveway. Hollowed-out gourds hung from the limbs of a large maple tree in the front yard. Small wooden birdhouses sat on tall poles. If a bird were smart enough to get to Windmill Farm, it would find plenty of food and shelter.

"Mornin'," Will called out. "Your birds sure are regular customers. I thought I saw someone filling up that feeder just yesterday."

"Well, it's springtime," she said.

"You must spend a fortune on birdseed."

"Not at all. We grow dozens and dozens of sunflowers along the back side of the vegetable garden." She put the container of seeds on the ground. "Have you ever noticed how much birdsong there is, so early in the morning?"

"The race to reproduction," Will said professorially, as he watched her replace the top on the feeder.

Sadie's face went a shade of crimson.

Will tried hard, without success, not to smile at her modesty.

"I didn't think you'd be awake yet on a Saturday," she

said. "You're welcome to join us for breakfast. That is, if you haven't eaten yet." She stammered her request in embarrassed politeness, then finally looked up at him with an almost mortified expression on her face.

How could he refuse?

But he hadn't expected this. He hadn't thought about being invited over so soon. Or so early in the morning. The effects of the granola bar had worn off long ago and his stomach was growling. "Well, sure . . . I guess so. I don't usually eat much breakfast, though, but I wouldn't mind a cup of strong coffee."

A shy smile curled Sadie's lips. "Oh, wait until you try a cup of Fern's coffee. She's known for her good cooking." She took the broom that was resting on the porch rail and swung it at a few curled brown leaves along the stairs. *Swish, swish.* "We figured you might be having some trouble figuring out how to live without electricity. You'll have to be sure to let us know if you need anything."

The broom was still swishing. Will found himself watching her. She reached up to her forehead and tucked a wisp of hair back under her prayer cap, then positioned herself again like a golfer at the driving range. She was a careful sweeper, going all the way to the edges. What a serious, methodical little person she was. He wondered what she did for fun.

She stopped abruptly and straightened up when she noticed he was observing her. "The problem with sunflower seeds is that the hulls make a mess." Then she went down the steps and out in the yard to fill a bluebird feeder. A dinner plate with a hole drilled into it was positioned on the pole under the feeder to deter squirrels. Pretty clever, Will thought, but the feeder itself was a sorry excuse; the roof was rotting and the pole was leaning over precariously as if it would topple right over if a crow or blue jay landed on it. She needed a new one. Maybe he should get her one after his time at Windmill Farm came to an end, a parting gift. But by then she might know what he had been up to, and she might not want a bird feeder or anything else from him.

But he had nothing to worry about, he told himself again. He kept reminding himself of that. What he was doing wasn't wrong. Not wrong at all. In fact, you could say it was very right. A good thing to do. A win-win.

Wonderful aromas greeted his nose as he stepped up on the porch. He was even hungrier than he had thought. The kitchen door began to swing open slowly, with a squeak as if its hinges needed oil. Then he saw a face peering around the edge at him—the woman who looked like a middle-aged version of Katharine Hepburn. His first impression was that she was scowling at him, but when he looked more closely, he saw that she was merely looking him over and sizing him up. She seemed as lovable as a mountain thistle. They stood there looking at each other for a moment, and then he heard Amos's voice from behind her.

"Well, for pity's sake, Fern, let him in." Amos looked at Will over the woman's shoulder and smiled. He pushed the door wide open and motioned for Will to come in.

Amos pointed to a straight-backed chair across from him on the other side of the large kitchen table. The seat sounded like a creaky hinge when Will sat down. The girl who had watched him from the window, Mary Kate, galloped down the stairs like a newborn filly but stopped abruptly when she saw he was sitting at the table. She sidled into a chair, across from Will, eyes glued to him. Fern brought Will a cup of coffee and, nervously, he gulped it down. No one spoke for a few moments and he wondered if he had done something wrong. He had seen *Witness*. He knew they drank coffee. Should he have waited to drink it? Was there a certain tradition to drinking Amish coffee that he should have known?

What was he doing here? he asked himself. Not just the breakfast invitation but the whole business.

It was so hot in here. Was he getting sick? He wondered what made it so hot in the room, but then he realized it was the woodstove. He'd forgotten how much heat radiated from a woodstove. Will glanced quickly around the large family room. Everything was in its place. And plenty of seating—two large sofas, a rocker, a bench with a colorful knitted afghan folded on it. Bookshelves lined the far wall, filled with titles. Large picture windows brought in plenty of natural lighting. What would his mother say about this room and its decor? What would she call it? At times, she could be a snob. He could hear her brittle voice: "This isn't shabby chic—this is just plain shabby."

Sadie finished sweeping the porch and came inside. She peeked at the sleeping baby, tucked into a corner in the room, and sat next to her sister. Fern finished bringing in platters of food and sat down. Will had never seen so much food in all of his life: stacked blueberry pancakes, pitchers of maple syrup, smoked sausages, a bowl of steaming scrambled eggs, grapefruit. It looked like a smorgasbord! Will picked up his fork but stopped when he realized that Amos Lapp had bowed his head and everyone had followed. Except for him. Will wondered what went on during those seconds of silence.

Then Amos lifted his head and everyone dug in like it was their last meal.

The kitchen door opened and in blasted an older man with wild and wiry white hair sticking out from under his black felt hat. "WHO HAVE WE HERE?" he hollered as he caught sight of Will. His face practically beamed with happiness.

"Uncle Hank, this is Will Stoltz," Sadie said. "The game warden wants him to babysit the falcons." She passed the stack of pancakes to her father.

Will lifted a finger in the air. "Not really babysitting," he hurried to explain. "More like protecting an endangered species from an overzealous public."

Uncle Hank emitted a noise that was part laugh and part snort. "So you're set on trying to give the love birds a little privacy!"

"Oh, fuss and feathers, Hank. Sit down and eat." Fern clucked at him until he settled down to eat, but he talked and joked and told stories throughout breakfast. Uncle Hank got Mary Kate giggling so hard that milk came out of her nose.

The food was better than any Will had eaten for a long time. The baked oatmeal was wonderful—crisp on the outside and soft and warm and mealy on the inside. Will wasn't fond of scrapple but took some to be polite. It was surprisingly good, heavily doctored with sage to mask the contents of offal. Sadie refilled his coffee. And when it was over, Amos bowed his head again, then everyone hopped up and got to work. Amos and Hank went to the barn, Mary Kate went off to feed her chickens, Sadie tended to the baby, so he helped Fern gather dishes from the table and take them to the kitchen.

"You can go on out and help Amos," Fern said. "Now that spring is in full gear, he'll need a lot of help."

"Is he healthy?" Will handed a big platter to her. "I mean, I saw this . . . long scar." He pointed to his neck.

Fern started filling up the sink with hot water and added liquid soap to it. "Don't ask Amos about the scar on his neck," she said. "He doesn't like to speak of it."

Will brought in the last two platters from the table. "You mean about the heart transplant?"

Her hands splattered the water. In her surprise, she looked right at him. "You mean he told you?"

Will nodded like it was natural. "Seemed like he wanted to tell me." She looked a little disappointed, so he thought it would be best to change the subject. "Have you known Amos for a long time?"

She let out a deep sigh. "Some days, it seems like forever. Other days, it's like I hardly know him." She swished her hand in the sink to get the water sudsy. Then she pointed to a towel for him to dry the dishes. He guessed he wasn't going to make as quick an exit as he thought.

"It plagues me," she said. "I have been taking care of his household for over a year now—"

Will gathered that she meant Amos.

"—through thick and thin. And there's been plenty of both. For days on end that man can hardly string two words together." She scrubbed the spoon she was holding until it shone before she went on. "I always knew he seemed to be drawn to a barn like a magnet, always finding something to tinker with out there. But I never thought there was much talking going on." She handed him the spoon to dry. Dishes

95

and utensils were coming faster and faster now, as she was starting to get herself worked up. Will was having trouble keeping up. Drying a dish wasn't something he had done much of. He thought letting dishes air-dry was more than good enough. Better still, paper plates.

"But the minute my back is turned, Amos starts talking, and freely, to you of all people. A bird sitter!"

Will lifted a finger. "Just to clarify . . . I'm not exactly a bird sitter. I'm trying to keep an endangered species away from an overzealous public." He had the spiel memorized now.

She wasn't listening to him. "To a boy who isn't much more than a stranger! I have half a mind to walk out to that barn and ask him why men are the way they are." She handed him a platter. "I suppose there just isn't an answer."

Will saw the conversation drifting in a no-win direction. For such a tight-lipped woman, she could talk a blue streak once she got started. When Sadie came to the kitchen to ask Fern a question, Will took the opportunity to leave. It was high time he should head out and chase off any bold bird-watchers.

Afterward, walking up the hill to the falcon scape, Will felt slightly stunned from the whole experience. It wasn't exactly the enormous quantity of food he had consumed or the Lapp family or the conversation. It was just everything together. He had never felt quite such a sensory overload.

The aroma of Fern's strong coffee triggered memories for Will of morning at the table with his father and his mother, at their grand home in Wynwood, a small upscale suburb outside of Philadelphia. But the smell of coffee was where the similarity ended. Breakfast was the one time of the day when his father was calm—before the busyness of his work claimed his energies and consumed his thoughts. Silence reigned. In fact, his parents rarely spoke during breakfast beyond an occasional polite inquiry after the other's health, or how they slept. But after the workday claimed his father, he treated everyone differently. Indifferently.

Yes, breakfast in the Stoltzes' home was a quiet affair, interrupted only by the rustle of newspaper pages as his parents exchanged sections. Cold cereal and coffee were the only items on the menu. Sensory underload.

No wonder Will felt stunned.

M.K. hadn't made up her mind yet about the yellow dog that followed Sadie home. He was a crazy dog, with an unpredictable streak running through him. They ended up calling him Doozy. He would bark at the silliest things without warning, like a leaf skittering across the driveway or a shadow moving across a windowpane, or a towel flapping on the clothesline. On the other hand, he was very predictable about other things. Every single time a buggy came to call, for example, Doozy could be found hiding under the porch. The poor thing was half starved and flea-bitten, and though Fern usually didn't have a sympathetic bone in her body, for some reason she took to this pathetic creature. When M.K. pointed out this contradiction to her, Fern raised one eyebrow and replied, "What I like best about dogs is that they wag their tails instead of their tongues."

Fern! So prickly.

M.K. left Fern baking in the kitchen to go see what Sadie

was doing with the baby. She curled up on Sadie's bed and watched her sister feed the baby a bottle. He would drink a little, then fall asleep, then jerk awake and start drinking as if he were starved. The baby held one hand up in the air, fingers splayed like a starfish. M.K. loved looking at his little hands. They were so small, so perfect.

Her mind drifted to the unsolved dilemma: to whom did this baby belong?

"Later today, maybe I can take the basket and go ask around town."

"No," Sadie said with an uncharacteristic firmness. "You've already created enough problems. The last thing I want is to have you poking your nose into this."

M.K. looked up at her, serious, and blinked once. How were they going to figure out who the baby's mother was with *that* attitude? This business with Sadie reminded her of doing math problems. Sometimes they worked out. Sometimes you were back where you started.

Sadie put the baby into his basket and covered him with a little blanket. "M.K., I think maybe we have a special job ahead of us. Something important."

Mary Kate was just about to ask what she was talking about as she heard the yellow dog wander up and down the hallway, completely stumped by this new environment. He wasn't the brightest of dogs. He came into Sadie's room and curled up on the small rug by the side of her bed. "Fern is going to have a conniption when she finds you indoors." The dog looked up at her with sad, brown eyes. Then he cocked his head, ran to the window, and let out a low growl.

M.K. jumped off the bed to see what he had noticed. "Oh

no," she said. Her mouth was suddenly very dry. Edith Fisher had rolled up the driveway in her buggy. Worse still, Jimmy Fisher was beside her, looking angry and sullen. She looked down at the dog, who was still growling a little. She patted his head. "Maybe you're smarter than you look."

She saw her father walk out of the barn to greet Edith, who was out of the buggy and walking toward the house. Jimmy followed behind, hands in his pockets, scuffing the gravel with his feet.

She knew what this was all about. She had hoped to avoid this, but it figured that Jimmy would try to pin this on her. She saw her father look up at the house and catch sight of her in the window. He motioned to her to come downstairs. She sighed, deeply annoyed with Jimmy, and went out to meet them. Sadie followed behind, far too happily, M.K. noticed.

When they reached Amos, he said, "M.K., I understand you challenged Jimmy to a buggy race, from Bent N' Dent to Blue Lake Pond."

She glared at Jimmy. "Nolo contendere."

Her father paid no mind to her Latin. "And I understand that a police officer pulled Jimmy over after clocking him at thirty-five miles per hour—" He stopped abruptly and turned to look at Jimmy. "Really? You got that old gelding up to thirty-five miles per hour?"

Jimmy brightened. "Sure did."

Amos whistled, one note up, one down, impressed.

"Amos Lapp!" Edith Fisher snapped, trying to remind Amos of the gravity of this matter. She could snap with very little provocation.

Amos turned to M.K. "And when you heard the police

siren, you made a fast break into someone's driveway, leaving Jimmy to get caught by the police officer."

M.K. started to smirk, but Jimmy saw it and glowered at her. Her smile faded.

Edith drew herself up tall. "The police officer brought Jimmy home and said he would forget about a ticket if Jimmy would complete thirty-five hours of community service. One for every mile per hour, he said." She touched the back of her bun. "Fortunate for us that policeman happens to be a regular egg customer at our hatchery." Her glance shifted to M.K. "It only seems fair to have Mary Kate do the community service. She's the one who tempted my Jimmy. After all, what boy can turn down a challenge?"

What?! M.K. was outraged. She wondered what would happen if she gave Edith Fisher the shock of her lifetime. *For your information, Edith Fisher, your son Jimmy has a ten-speed bicycle hidden behind your stinky henhouse! He sneaks out late on Saturday nights and goes roaring around Stoney Ridge.* It was a piece of valuable information M.K. had stumbled upon and tucked away, with many other Jimmy Fisher crimes and indignities and grievances, for future use.

"It's high time Jimmy took responsibility for his actions," Fern said. "You coddle that boy, Edith."

Everyone whipped their heads around to face Fern, who had appeared out of nowhere like she usually did. Just as Edith was about to get up on her high horse, Amos held up a hand to stop her.

"Now, Fern," Amos started. "We have no right to tell Edith how to raise her boy."

Let Fern talk, Dad! M.K. started to say but thought better of it. Jimmy Fisher *was* coddled. She tried to hold back from shouting by conjuring up a picture of Jimmy staked out in the desert with vultures plucking at his flesh and flies swarming all over his gorgeous head. Unfortunately, she couldn't make the image gruesome enough. Still, it was a satisfying thought.

"They should both do the community service," Fern said. "It would do them good."

Fern! So intrusive!

Amos nodded. "Now, that does seem only fair, Edith."

"I know of someone who needs help," Sadie said.

M.K. looked aghast into Sadie's steady blue eyes. *Et tu, Brutus?* She would have loved to say it aloud but what was the point? Gid was the only one who understood and enjoyed her references to Shakespeare. Everyone else always looked at her as if she were speaking Polish.

Sadie ignored her silent pleas. "An older man. Someone from the Swartzentruber colony."

"But they all left the area," Amos said. "A few months ago, the colony up and moved to Ohio to join a larger settlement."

"This old man must not have gone with them. He's all alone," Sadie said. "Maybe on Saturdays, Jimmy could do yard work and M.K. could help with the cooking and cleaning."

M.K. envisioned months and months of Saturdays down the drain. Worse still, she would have to spend them with the likes of Jimmy Fisher. She raised a finger in the air. "Before this is a fait accompli, I'd just like to point out that—"

Cutting her off at the quick, Fern said, "Sounds like an ideal solution."

And that was it. M.K.'s fate was sealed. Her Saturdays, for the foreseeable future, were ruined.

Even Edith Fisher looked placated. "I suppose that would suffice. I'll go along with them on Saturday, just to make sure everything is on the up-and-up." She arched an eyebrow in M.K.'s direction. "You've got no more direction than a new-born calf, and even less good judgment. Seems as if there's enough trouble going on here at Windmill Farm. I would think you would give your poor father a break."

"My sentiments exactly," Sadie said, poking a finger at M.K.

Amos raised an eyebrow. "I'll go talk to the old Swartzen-truber fellow. Plan on them starting next Saturday."

M.K. sighed and Jimmy blew air out of his mouth. Edith spun on her heels.

"Jimmy! Come along!" His mother's voice sailed from the buggy.

Jimmy leaned close to M.K. and squinted at her. "You're making those big words up."

She squinted back at him. "What big words?"

"No lo contend and feet accomplished. You were throwing them around awhile ago."

"They're in the dictionary," she said sweetly. "Right in front of the word *snitch*."

8

During breakfast the next morning, the baby woke up and started to wail. The entire family covered their ears as Sadie tried to settle him down.

"You know," Amos said, "I hadn't thought about this for years, but Menno used to yell like that."

Sadie's head jerked up. "Really?"

"Yes, just like that. As if someone was pinching him." He smiled wistfully. "He had colic. We tried everything. Even tried all kinds of formulas—just like you're doing."

Fern leaned forward in her chair. "Did anything work?"

"Let's see. It was awhile ago, you know." Amos looked up at the ceiling, as if watching a memory pass overhead. "Goat's milk." He looked pleased. "Worked like magic." He snapped his fingers.

Fern looked at him as if a cat had spoken. "And you're just thinking to offer that up now?" She reached over and scooped the baby out of Sadie's arms. "Go to Ira Smucker's right now and get fresh goat's milk."

Sadie hesitated. "Let M.K. go."

Fern sighed. "Fine." She turned to M.K. "Get a couple of clean jars from under the sink. Lids too. Tell Ira you need the freshest milk he's got. See if he'll even milk a goat for you while you watch. And then bring that milk back here. No lollygagging." She gave M.K. a gentle push in the direction of the kitchen.

M.K. huffed. "I don't lolly and I don't gag."

The baby took a few gulps of air and started to wind up again, like a siren. M.K. grabbed the jars and lids and darted out the door.

Not thirty minutes later, Ira Smucker returned with M.K. in his flatbed wagon, with large containers of sterilized goat's milk, still steaming, and a goat. Fern and Amos went out to meet them.

"It's nothing," Ira told Fern when she thanked him for being so thoughtful. "This goat is a good milker and has a sweet disposition too. Goats can be pretty ornery." He sneezed a loud sneeze, whipped out his handkerchief, and covering his nose, honked once, then twice.

"That's good to hear. I had a very unpleasant experience with a goat once." M.K. nodded in solemn agreement.

Ira put the handkerchief back in his vest pocket. "If the milk agrees with the baby's digestion, I thought it'd be easier to have a goat here, rather than having to keep sending M.K. trotting over the hill for fresh supplies." He led the goat off the wagon and handed the rope to M.K.

"Take her to that far pasture," Amos said. He turned to make sure M.K. was headed to the right pasture and was surprised to see her losing a game of tug of war with the goat. The goat had dug in its heels and wouldn't budge, despite

M.K.'s efforts to pull it forward. Amos went over to help her and M.K. thrust the rope in his hands, scowling.

"I never did like goats." Suddenly her attention was riveted to the wagon where Fern and Ira were standing. "Would you look at that? Who would have believed it?"

"What?" Amos looked to where her eyes were fixed.

"Why, Ira Smucker's ears are burning up red. Redder than a beet."

Ira sneezed again and honked into a handkerchief.

"Well, maybe he's sick," Amos said.

"Oh no. It's just like Gid. His ears go as red as a tomato every time he gets around Sadie. Like father, like son."

They locked the goat into the pasture and M.K. went skipping off to the house. Amos turned back and watched Fern and Ira talking. She was laughing at something he said. What could he have said that would be funny? Ira wasn't funny. Not funny at all. Rather serious and somber, especially since his wife passed on. It would appear that Ira was smitten with Amos's housekeeper. The thought nettled him. He walked over to join them.

Ira swallowed, his Adam's apple bobbing up and down. "Would you mind if I saw the baby?"

Amos's mouth dropped open. Snapped shut. Since when was Ira Smucker interested in babies?

Fern lifted her chin to Ira and narrowed her eyes. "Are you catching a cold? You shouldn't be around the baby if you've got a cold." She lowered her voice. "Or Amos, for that matter. He shouldn't be exposed to a cold. With his heart trouble and all."

Amos stiffened. Fern treated him like he was a six-year-old!

"No," Ira said solemnly. "Hay fever. I get it every year about this time."

"A farmer with hay fever?" Fern frowned. "Never heard of such a thing."

"Runs in my family," Ira said sadly.

"Well, since it's allergies, I suppose it would be fine to see the baby." She turned to Amos. "Would you mind bringing in those milk containers while I show Ira to the house?"

And off the two of them went, with Fern chattering away to Ira all about the baby as they walked. Amos was left to haul in the milk containers.

He reached to pick up a container and hoist it to the ground, feeling strangely left out. *And just what is that all about, Amos Lapp?* he asked himself. *Are you feeling like a scorned teenager because you think you might have had a claim on Fern Graber? Do you honestly think you stood a chance with her? Well, think again.*

Amos knew he wouldn't exactly be a woman's dream man. What woman would want to marry a man who took twenty-seven pills a day to keep his body from rejecting his heart. It always, always came back to that.

Sadie was at the end of her rope. The baby seemed to be in agony. He stiffened, his back arched, and let out a whopper of an ear-piercing scream which sent M.K. flying out of the house to find Will Stoltz.

Sadie was a little annoyed that M.K. kept fetching Will from his important bird business whenever the baby started to holler, but he didn't seem to mind. He would arrive at the house with a pleased grin on his face, head straight to Sadie, and take the crying baby out of her arms. And the baby would settle right down, relieved, as if he knew he was in the hands of a professional. Sadie was relieved too. Will had a knack for soothing this baby.

All morning long, Sadie had been walking the baby around the family room, through the kitchen, and back again. A big circle, around and around, trying to lull him to sleep. When she made a pass through the kitchen, she noticed Fern and Ira heading toward the house. As Ira drew closer to the house, Sadie saw his head jerk up in alarm as he caught the first sound of the baby's screech. Ira doubled over and Sadie thought he was going to drop to the ground in horror, but then she saw he was merely overcome by a big sneeze. Then another and another. It was quite a dramatic fit of sneezing. Finally, he wiped his nose with his handkerchief and strode a few steps to catch up with Fern.

Sadie pushed the squeaky kitchen door open with her knee and handed the baby to Fern, completely exasperated. "I can't do a thing with him."

"Ira brought some fresh goat's milk to try," Fern said, talking over the baby's wail.

Ira remained on the porch, gripped by another sneezing fit.

"Hay fever," Fern said, letting the door close. "He'll come in when he's ready."

Sadie watched him for a while. "Gid gets hay fever like that too." She tilted her head. She went into the kitchen and opened a cupboard, took out a container, and opened it. Inside was a chunk of honeycomb from one of M.K.'s hives.

Sadie picked up a knife and cut off a section of honeycomb. She put it on a napkin and took it outside to Ira.

"Chew this," she said, handing him the napkin. "Some folks say that chewing honeycomb every once in a while will relieve hay fever and stuffy noses."

He sneezed again, honked his nose again, sneezed, honked, and decided to give the honeycomb remedy a try. Sadie watched him earnestly as he chewed. And chewed. And chewed.

"Do I spit out the wax or swallow it?"

"Chew and chew, then spit out the wax."

Behind him, Amos climbed up the porch with the goat's milk container and handed it to Sadie. She went to the kitchen and took out a clean bottle, filled it with the warm goat's milk, capped the bottle with a rubber nipple, and held it out to Fern. She shook her head and handed the baby to Sadie.

Sadie sat down in the rocking chair and fed the baby. The baby gulped and coughed and spit at the strange taste, but then he settled down to suck. Sadie looked up at Fern.

"Don't get too hopeful," Fern said. "It's not the eating part that troubles him. It's the digestive part." She turned to Ira. "Would you like some coffee? I can brew a fresh pot."

"Thank you, Fern, but I should get home." Ira walked up to Sadie and put his hands on his knees to bend over and peer at the baby. "Well, with that coloring, there's no doubt who he belongs to."

Sadie looked up to ask, "Who?" just as the baby took in too big of a mouthful and started to choke. She held him up against her chest, the way Will had shown her, and jiggled him, patting his back. Dandling, Will called it. When the baby stopped sputtering, she tucked him back in her arms to feed him.

Ira clapped his hands on his knees and straightened up. "Amos, would you mind walking me out? Something I'd like to discuss with you."

Sadie opened her mouth to ask Ira who he thought the baby resembled, when he spun around, his face brightened. "Why, Sadie Lapp! I haven't sneezed once since you gave me that honeycomb!" He scratched his head.

"Chew on a little each day and see if it helps," Sadie said.

"My sister sent me some honeycomb from Indiana," Ira said. "I'll give hers a try."

Sadie shook her head. "It needs to be local honey. It's the pollen that you're allergic to. I'll give you a chunk to take home."

"I'll get it," Fern said, hurrying to the kitchen to wrap up the honeycomb. "I always said Sadie was a born healer." She put the honeycomb in a Tupperware container and handed it to Ira.

In a low voice, Ira said to Fern, "I'll see you on Saturday, then," and she nodded and smiled in return.

Sadie wondered briefly why her father was scowling at Ira, but then the baby started to choke and sputter again. She blew air out of her cheeks. Fern was right. Babies were a heap of trouble.

Amos walked Ira out to his wagon, chatted for a while, waved goodbye to him, and practically bumped right into Fern as he turned around to head to the house. Where had she come from? A gust of wind swept in and knocked his hat off. As he bent to pick it up, he remembered something he hadn't thought of for a long while. As a child, he thought of the wind as a person with many different voices, somebody you never quite got to know very well because it would arrive without warning and then leave just as suddenly. A lot like Fern. "Oh, didn't see you there. Sorry about that."

"What did Ira want to talk to you about?"

Amos frowned. "Fern, if Ira wanted the world to know what was on his mind, he would've just stayed in the kitchen."

She ignored him. "Was he asking about Gid and Sadie?"

Amos lifted his eyebrows. "How did you know that?"

"He's talking about Gid and Sadie getting married, isn't he? And soon."

How did Fern seem to know things without being told? It was unnerving. Nailing shingles to a twister would be simple compared to understanding Fern Graber. "Maybe."

Now it was Fern's turn to frown. "Well, Gideon Smucker better have himself another think." She turned and looked at the house. Will was following M.K. up the porch steps and into the farmhouse.

Amos was annoyed. Fern thought she knew his own daughter better than he did. "Sadie is too young to be thinking about marriage, but Gideon Smucker is a good fellow. He's crazy about Sadie. Always has been. And last fall, Sadie didn't seem to mind having Gid around here."

"That was then and this is now," Fern said enigmatically.

Amos sighed with the old frustration of this conversation. It bothered him when she spoke in puzzles. Why couldn't women just say what they meant? Be clear and to the point.

Instead, he often felt like he was chasing a tumbleweed on a windy day.

She turned and looked right at him. "What kinds of things were you going to have the bird boy do around the farm?"

"The bird boy? Oh, you mean Will. Plowing, mostly. Help with chores, I suppose."

"He doesn't have any farm experience."

"What makes you say that?"

"His hands. Too soft. They're not even calloused."

Amos looked down at his own hands. Rough, large, a few small scars.

"You've got to get that bird boy busy."

"He is busy! M.K. keeps dragging him into the house to settle down the crying baby. And he seems to be the only one who can do it."

"That's not the kind of busy I mean. You've got to keep him outside, away from the house."

Amos heaved a stretched-to-the-limits sigh. "Fern, what exactly are you getting at?"

"Have you seen the way he looks at Sadie? He's paying too much attention to her."

No, Amos hadn't noticed that. A more mismatched pair than Sadie and Will would be hard to imagine. He hardly knew Will—he had given his permission to let him stay at Windmill Farm solely because of the game warden's request. But he didn't think Will was untrustworthy, the way Fern assumed all English to be. Maybe a little immature and misguided, according to what Mahlon Miller had told him, but not a bad apple. And as for Sadie having more than a casual interest in Will? Well, Amos had faith in his daughter's judgment. "Sadie has a good head on her shoulders. Surely, she wouldn't be drawn away by this boy."

Fern gave him a look as if he were a very small child. She spoke slowly and carefully. "Have you seen the way she blushes when she's around him?" She shook her head. "Sparks are starting to fly."

"What?"

"Whenever you see a person's face turn red, you know something is up."

Would that also pertain to Ira Smucker's ears? he wanted to ask. *And what did Ira mean about seeing you on Saturday?*

The kitchen door opened, squeaking on its hinge. Their attention turned to see Sadie and Will, laughing over something.

Fern stepped forward, arms akimbo, like a teapot with two handles. "Keep that bird boy busy."

Could Fern be right? She usually was. He worried suddenly that Sadie might have so little experience with men that she would be easy prey for somebody like Will. He would have to keep an eye out. But then again, she might be misreading the situation. He knew Fern was suspicious of all English folk. Maybe she was just overreacting. Amos watched Fern pass Will, talk to him for a brief moment, point to Amos, then head to the house.

Will walked up to him. "Fern said you wanted to talk to me."

Amos blew air out of his mouth. Ah, Fern. She had a way of making things happen. "Will, have you ever plowed? With a horse, I mean. Not with a tractor."

Will's eyebrows shot up in alarm. "Plowed? Uh, no. Not with a horse. Not with a tractor, either." His smile drooped.

Amos put a hand on his shoulder. "Well, Monday morning, first thing, you are going to learn. Meet me at the north pasture at dawn. The soil will be just right after last night's drenching rain. Moist, but not too wet."

"Dawn?" Will scratched his head. "That's actually the time of day that's best for birding. The game warden wants a list made up of all invasive birds on the property."

Amos nodded. "As soon as you're done with your bird list, you come find me and we'll get you started." He patted Will on the back and strode off to the barn, enjoying the startled look on the boy's face. If Will Stoltz thought his Sadie was a girl to pursue, he needed to think again. Then his grin faded as he pondered Fern's comment that Sadie would turn down Gid's interest. And that she might be growing sweet on this English boy. Why were women so complicated?

It was a miracle. As soon as the baby drank his first bottle of goat's milk, he stared at Sadie as if he couldn't quite believe she had taken so long to figure that one out, then he finished the bottle, closed his eyes, and fell into a deep, restful sleep. Sadie gazed at the sleeping infant—the perfection of round cheeks, peach fuzz on his head, minuscule ears. She touched the bottom of a tiny foot, and the toes curled. "Really, he's a beautiful baby when he's not doing all that wailing."

"I made another list of name suggestions, Sadie," M.K. said, coming over to Sadie with two still warm-from-the-oven chocolate chip cookies in her hand.

Sadie broke off half of one cookie and took a bite. "No more palindromes."

M.K. shook her head. "Even better. Onomatopoeia—call him Ono. Allegory—we can call him Al. Hyperbole—shorten it to Hi."

"Joseph," Sadie said decidedly. She reached out to break off another piece of cookie.

M.K. tilted her head. "Menno's middle name?"

Sadie took another bite of cookie. "We can call him Joe."

M.K. put the cookie in her hand on the table and stooped down to peer at the baby in the basket. "Joe sounds too old. Can we call him Baby Joe? Or Joe-Jo?"

Sadie put a hand out to grab the cookie and Fern covered her wrist, holding it there until she released it.

"Joseph it is," Fern said. "And now, Sadie, you need to get back to work. Whenever you start eating nonstop, it's your stomach's way of telling your brain that you are fretting and need more on your mind." She pointed to a stack of books on the counter. "M.K. and I picked those up from the library. You've got to keep up your healing work. You don't want to forget all that you learned from Deborah Yoder."

Ever since Sadie had helped cool down an overheated girl at a barbecue, Fern was convinced that Sadie was a natural healer. Gifted, she said, and Fern didn't hand out compliments like candy. Sadie was less convinced of her talent. She had loved working beside Deborah, helping people with discomfort or ailments. She was fascinated by the use of herbs to help people. It seemed to Sadie that God had planned all along for plants to provide gifts of healing, and he was just waiting for someone to discover those secrets. But there was so much still to learn, and being responsible for others was always a worry.

But she couldn't deny that she needed more on her mind. Since the moment she had returned home, she was forever eating or thinking about eating. It wouldn't be long before she gained all of that weight back. Over the last year, she had worked so hard to keep food in the right place in her life—she knew it was a good thing in the right portions, meant to nourish her body, but her mind needed a different kind of nourishment. Fern had helped her to see the difference. Sadie had made such improvements in her eating habits—eating only when she was hungry—yet here she was, right back to fretful snacking.

Sadie ran a finger along the book titles: *Home Remedies, Common Sense Cures.* She slid into a chair and opened one of the books to a page about kidney stones. "Fern, do you think I'm capable of learning all there is to know?"

Fern leaned toward Sadie, her expression serious. "I know you are. But what's more important, Sadie, is for you to know you are. Nix gewogt, nix gewunne." *Nothing ventured, nothing gained.*

Swallowing, Sadie offered one slow nod.

"Ira Smucker didn't sneeze once after you gave him the honeycomb. Early this morning, Orin Yoder saw me at the phone shanty and asked if I knew what to do with canker sores. He said he suffers from them continually. I told him I'd ask you if you had a cure."

"I do, actually. Old Deborah taught me how to treat them. Just make a paste of alum and put it on the sore."

"Well, Sadie. What are you waiting for? I think you have your first client."

A slow exhalation shivered out of Sadie. Ready or not, her healing work was about to begin.

———— ✦ ————

Will felt as if he had been waylaid, a crosscut blow from the front, a kick from the back. He was minding his own business, walking out of the house, and the housekeeper trapped him into attending church. He had barely recovered from that blow when the farmer commandeered him into plowing fields. The invitations were loaded with obvious intention. Will knew the drill. Hadn't he spent years trying to avoid both? Hard work and church.

He let his mind do a rapid rewind, racing backward. He hadn't meant to get sucked into an invitation to church, but Fern caught him off guard. He had been feeling pleased with himself for being so useful as a baby calmer-downer and, suddenly, *wham!* She asked him what church he planned to attend while he was staying on the property. When he gave her a blank look, *wham!* She told him he could come with them and to be ready at 7:00 a.m. Sharp.

He thought he was smarter than these only-up-to-an-eighth-grade-education Amish. Ha! Pride goeth before a fall. It was one of those proverbs that his father told him, a few thousand times. And boy oh boy, was he ever falling a lot lately.

A month ago, Will had just received an acceptance to University of Pennsylvania's medical school—the same place where his father was a teaching professor and had a practice at the university hospital. Will was within a few short months of graduating from college. His future looked bright. It was all going according to plan.

Then it all fell apart. *Whoosh!* One fell swoop.

Two weeks ago, Will had been tinkering around on his computer with Sean, one of his fraternity friends, and hacked into the college's registrar site. Sean was delighted—he quickly got into his files and improved his recorded grades. Will didn't touch his own file, but then again, he didn't need to. He was a straight-A student. He was going to graduate at the top of his class.

It didn't take long for someone in the registrar's office to get suspicious when Sean, a C student, normally teetering on academic probation, asked for his transcript to be sent to Harvard to accompany his application for law school. Sean was called in for questioning, cracked immediately, and sent them off in Will's direction.

Will had been suspended for the semester and lost his acceptance to medical school. Something about ethics. Something about making Will an example to others.

Will had tried to explain it all to his father, but he wouldn't listen to any excuses. His father had always felt Will didn't think before he acted and that was hard to deny. But in this particular case, Will didn't do anything wrong. Sean did. But Will had never been able to win any kind of dispute with his father. Dr. Stoltz owned the truth, pure and simple.

Then his father told him that he had already made plans for Will's spring and summer, that Will needed to learn how to work—to work hard, to fully appreciate the opportunity he had blown. His car would be sold, his monthly allowance cut off. Will was going to be an intern for a game warden in Lancaster County. If Will didn't mess up, then his father might consider paying for that final semester of college so that he could at least graduate and get back on track.

Whose track? Will wanted to shout, but he held back. Even he wasn't that big of a fool as to back talk his father. You didn't do that. No one did.

Still, Will was so outraged by his father's controlling demands that he stormed out of the house. He would move away, get a job, and figure out the rest of his life without a penny from his father! He sought out his fraternity friends for consolation. He spent the evening drinking away his woes with them, and ended the night with an unexpected twist: a brake light on his car was out—the very car his father was going to take back to the dealer in the morning— and he was pulled over by a police officer. Just a routine check, the officer said, but then he sniffed the air and asked if Will had been drinking any alcohol that evening. Will spent the next few hours drying out in the bowels of a Philadelphia lockup. By dawn, Will had made two decisions: one, he was not going to let his father know about this DUI, no matter what it would take. And two, he was going to spend the next few months interning for the game warden.

But he never expected *this*. To be plunked in the middle of an Amish farm. No car. No money. No television. No internet access. Not even a radio. He did have his cell phone, but he had to stand in certain high spots on the farm to get reception.

He gazed around the farm. He was sure the game warden had told his father about this latest development by now. Will could just imagine the delight on his father's face. And what would he do if he learned that Will was plowing fields? Even better . . . he was spreading them with manure! His father would break out a bottle of his finest champagne. He would dance a jig.

Will wanted to quit this ridiculous bird-sitting/field-hand job. He could. There was just that sticky little problem with the law that he needed to keep under his father's radar. He had two options: he could quit, but then he would have to face his father. Or he could stay, but he'd have to figure out how to actually do the job. Like, how to plow a field. And go to an Amish church service.

Hard to say which option was more frightening.

9

The hymn ended on a long note, the voices echoing from the rafters. Then, with a wave of his hand, the Vorsinger brought the singing to an end. Sadie drew a deep breath and sat down, hoping Joe-Jo would sleep through the service. She glanced across the large kitchen to catch sight of Will. He was seated next to Amos, about midway among the men's benches. He squirmed on the hard, backless bench. Their eyes met, and he silently mouthed, "How long does this last?"

"Three," she mouthed back.

He couldn't understand her so she held up three fingers.

His eyes widened in alarm. "Three hours?" he mouthed.

She gave a slight nod of her head, just as Fern jabbed her in the side with her pointy elbow.

From her other side, M.K. jabbed her. "Don't look now, but Gid's watching you."

Of course, Sadie's gaze shifted immediately to Gid. He was squinting at her as if he wondered what was going on in her head. Could he tell? She had no idea. Her thoughts and emotions were all over the map, like they didn't know where to land.

He had a look on his face that touched her. It was so sweet and so sad and so filled with love. She melted like butter. Then she stopped herself. *Don't you go soft on him, Sadie Lapp,* she told herself. *He's the one who believes the lies about me.* She turned her head and lifted her chin, a silent signal to him that she was still upset. She knew Gid was sensitive enough that he would feel her emotion, as real as if she had shouted.

Sadie sensed, more than saw, an icy glare aimed in her direction. Out of the corner of her eye, Esther, the deacon's wife, was watching her. With her salt-and-pepper hair and delicate features, Esther could have been pretty, but there was something off about her. Her mouth, Sadie decided. She looked like she'd just spit out something that tasted awful.

The baby let out a yawn. One eye was open in a squint, like a pirate, as if he was halfway in between waking and sleeping. That worried Sadie and she shifted him in her lap, which caused both of his eyes to pop open.

Fern glanced at the baby, then at Sadie. "If he starts his yammering, take him outside."

"Can't you do it?" Sadie whispered.

"No," Fern said, her eyes fixed on Ruthie's father, the new minister, who had just stood up to preach after a long and quiet interchange among the ministers and bishop as to who would begin.

Joe-Jo let out a squeak and Sadie sighed. Ruthie's father took his new responsibilities very seriously, especially preaching. In just a few months, he was getting a reputation of being the most long-winded, dry-boned preacher Stoney Ridge had ever heard.

Sadie turned to M.K. "Will you take a turn with the baby?"

"Not a chance," M.K. whispered. "Babies don't like me."

The baby's face turned red as he started to strain. Oh no. This was worse than Sadie had feared. Sure enough, Joe-Jo's lower regions emitted a horrible gurgling sound, then a sour tangy odor wafted around her. The women in the bench in front of Sadie turned back to look at her as if they had never heard a baby make such noises. M.K. pinched her nose. Worse still, the baby let out a howl. Once, then twice.

Sadie jumped up and scurried out the side door with him, then rushed to the barn, far from the house so the baby wouldn't disturb the service. Inside, she plunked down on a bench against a wall. Sadie searched the barn. A row of cows munched contentedly from hay boxes, and a bird peeked over the edge of a nest snug against the rafters. Other than that, the barn was empty.

As she was rooting through the makeshift diaper bag to find a fresh diaper, she heard a door slam shut. She leaned forward on the bench and looked out through the open barn door. Will strode down the porch steps that led out into the sunshiny yard and straight toward her. A cat trotted ahead of him, tail sticking up as straight as a poker. The cat glanced back now and then as if to make sure he was still following. Sadie couldn't help but smile.

Will came into the barn and blinked rapidly as his eyes adjusted to the cool, dim light. He grinned broadly when he spotted Sadie, snatching off his hat to reveal a thick thatch of sun-streaked hair. "Thought you might need some help quieting the baby," he said cheerfully. "Is the goat's milk helping with his colic?"

"I think so," Sadie said. She felt her cheeks start to pink up and tried to will them to stop. She glanced over at the farmhouse, hoping that no one in the house could look out the window and see them. "He hasn't had a big crying jag since yesterday morning."

He patted the gray mare that stuck her head over the stall for affection. "Is this service really going to last three hours?"

She nodded. "Fern should have warned you."

Will grinned. "I have a feeling she intentionally kept that to herself."

No doubt, Sadie thought. Fern seemed to have taken an instant disliking to Will, and Sadie wasn't sure why.

"And it's all in that language?"

"Two languages, really. The preachers preach in Penn Dutch, but when they quote Scripture, it's in High German."

"So you're fluent in three languages?" He let out a whistle. "I can barely manage English."

She smiled. "All the Amish know three languages." She put a blanket down on the bench and placed the baby on top to start the preparations to change his diaper. She hoped Will would take the hint and go back to the farmhouse before someone noticed them.

He didn't. He sat across from her on a hay bale and stretched one long leg. "Sure is a beautiful day. I'd just as soon pay my respects to the Almighty outside than in a stuffy house." He grinned at her. "Did you see that mouse scurry along the walls? My mother would have screamed to high heaven if she saw that." He started in on a rambling story about going to church as a child, and at some point Sadie stopped listening and just started to change the baby's diaper.

If the smell and sight didn't bother him, then she wouldn't let it worry her. She was rattled enough by the presence of Will. She knew she shouldn't pass more time with him, especially here, at Sunday church.

They'd scarcely met, yet she felt . . . tingly. Confused. Undeniably impressed by his strong presence and protective ways. His thoughtfulness. And, she admitted, his deep voice and warm looks disturbed her in a thrilling way. Was this how it started? You fell for someone because of the tilt of his smile, or because he could make you laugh, or in this case, because he made you feel as if the two of you shared a special connection. With a jerk, she stopped herself from that line of thinking. *Oh, Sadie Lapp, this isn't good. This isn't good at all*. She was *not* starting anything with Will Stoltz.

She wrapped the yucky diaper in a plastic bag and stuffed it into the diaper bag. Then she brought out the bottle of goat's milk.

Will, still talking, stopped midsentence. "Want me to feed him? I'm not so good with diapers, but I can feed a baby." He reached out his hands for the baby.

"Will," she started, then hesitated. "You should probably get back into the service."

"Why?" he asked, looking genuinely surprised. "I thought I'd keep you company."

Sadie winced. "It doesn't look right for us to spend time together."

Will scoffed. "That's ridiculous! We're just two friends, talking on a spring morning."

How could Sadie phrase this in a way a non-Amish boy could understand? "It's not just a spring morning. It's a

Sunday morning. A churchgoing morning. The best day of the week. A morning of worshiping God, an afternoon of friendship. Heart and soul—Sundays are meant to fill you up. And the young men don't talk to the young women. At least not until later in the day, after lunch."

Will was stunned. "You're pulling my leg."

She shook her head.

"And lunch too? So we're not just heading home after the three hours?"

He looked so woebegone that she nearly laughed out loud. Some of her shyness left her.

"You'll enjoy the lunch."

"Will you sit with me?"

"Oh no! No, no, no. You'll eat with the men. The men eat first. The women and children eat later."

That shocked him even more. "So . . . many . . . rules."

"Oh, you don't know the half of it!"

"Does it bother you? All those rules?" He lifted his knee. "Rules bother me."

Somehow, that didn't surprise her. "When you grow up with these rules, you don't even think twice about them. It's just the way it's always been."

He looked at her. "Maybe that's the problem. Folks don't think enough about the rules. Maybe the rules need to be streamlined a little." He made an axing motion in the air. "You know, simplify things."

A male cardinal whistled from a branch on the tree outside the open barn door, catching Sadie's eye. The little bird was strutting along the branch, hoping to woo a mate. "I suppose our life may seem complicated to an outsider, but to us, the rules are supposed to create simplicity. We don't have to worry about what to wear or what fancy car to buy."

"You don't get many choices, though."

"No, but we don't have as many problems that come with choices, either."

"Like what?"

"Like . . . debt."

He jerked his head toward her, as if she hit a sore spot. "Touché." He stood up to leave. "Well, I'd better get back inside so I don't tarnish your sterling reputation." He winked at her and sauntered back to the house, slow and easy.

Her sterling reputation? She supposed it might seem that way to him, but from the cool reception she received this morning from some of the women, it didn't feel like a sterling reputation. She felt quite tarnished. On an ordinary morning before the church service started, Sadie and her friends clustered to share the latest news. Over by the horses, the young men clumped together, smacking one another on the back, shifting their gaze toward the girls, bragging about the number of calves or lambs or pigs born on their farm since last Sunday's church.

Today, however, Sadie was not welcomed into the circle like she usually was, like she hoped to be after returning home from a long stay in Berlin. A few faithful friends ventured over to get a glimpse of the baby. No sooner did they ooh and aah over the baby but their mothers captured their arms and escorted them straight up to the farmhouse without giving them a chance to say a word. Her throat tightened, recalling the embarrassment of those moments when a few others sent supercilious looks of disapproval her way. She felt the needles of a hundred eyes on her, and every whisper held her name. How could things have changed so quickly? For the first time in her life, she knew of no rule that could tell her how to behave.

A plain brown female cardinal flew close to the red male, clearly intrigued. The male did a little smug hop, drawing closer to the female. That boy got just what he was after, Sadie realized, with his dashing red feathers and bold whistle.

Will returned to the farmhouse and tried to slip back to his seat on the bench next to Amos and Hank without being too obtrusive, but he moved a hymnal to sit down and accidentally dropped it. He was sure that every single person in the room turned to look at him, stunned. Was he the first person to ever drop a hymnal?

The preacher was still preaching, in a language Will couldn't understand, and he didn't know how he was going to be able to sit still for at least two more hours. Maybe he shouldn't have asked Sadie how long this service lasted. Maybe it would be better not to know. He glanced at others around him and wondered who they all were, what their lives were like. Did they act this pure and pious all the time? The woman in the far corner on the left with those two daughters—did they ever fight? Did her husband ever forget her birthday? Did he ever make harsh, sarcastic remarks to their children?

He watched the minister wave his arms expansively as he delivered his sermon. He gazed meditatively at the church members, first the men, then he turned to face the women. Did that minister enjoy a good joke? Had he ever gotten drunk and given anybody a black eye? Cursed? Did he ever have a lustful thought?

Or what about the plain little man sitting in front of Will? He looked pretty timid, but maybe he drank and smoked on Saturday nights. Across the room, next to Fern, was a woman with three young children. The little boy, probably one or two years old, had received numerous pokes from his sisters seated on either side. Now he moved over to sit on his mother's lap.

Will looked at Mary Kate, whose chin was lifted high and eyes were darting around the room. He wondered what went through that busy mind of hers. Sadie told him he had no idea how many rules governed their lives. How could someone like M.K. ever be satisfied with this strict Amish life? It seemed to him that every day looked like the day before, and the day after.

After a while, Sadie came inside and wedged between M.K. and Fern. The baby must have fallen asleep, because Will saw Sadie tuck him into the basket by her feet. He watched her for a while, mesmerized. The more time he spent with her, the more attractive she became to him, with her soft light hair, the long neck, those eyes the color of an azure sky. Will wondered if she knew she was pretty. He doubted it. She seemed terribly naïve. How would someone as pure and innocent as Sadie ever survive in the cruel world?

He almost smiled at the irony of his thoughts. From one family came M.K., who seemed like the type who would want to push every envelope: Draw a line and watch me cross it! And then there was Sadie, who saw the rules of the church as comforting, the way a snug seat belt in a car is meant for your protection. How could two sisters begin at the same spot but end up as such different individuals?

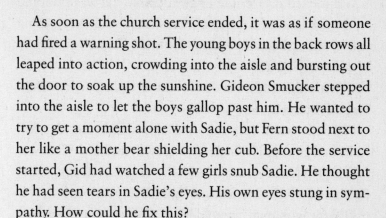

As soon as the church service ended, it was as if someone had fired a warning shot. The young boys in the back rows all leaped into action, crowding into the aisle and bursting out the door to soak up the sunshine. Gideon Smucker stepped into the aisle to let the boys gallop past him. He wanted to try to get a moment alone with Sadie, but Fern stood next to her like a mother bear shielding her cub. Before the service started, Gid had watched a few girls snub Sadie. He thought he had seen tears in Sadie's eyes. His own eyes stung in sympathy. How could he fix this?

When their eyes met, she grew flustered and pivoted away. He tried to draw near to her as she was heading to the kitchen to join the women. He raised his eyes and let himself feast on her for just a few seconds. Strands of loose hair fluttered across her cheek. He could hardly resist touching her cheek and smoothing back a wisp of hair. Twice, he opened his mouth to speak; both times, words failed him. *I love you, Sadie!* he called out silently. *Do you love me? Just a little?* But, of course, she didn't hear him. And after that, Sadie avoided looking at him. Discouraged, he decided he would just make up a feeble excuse about needing to get home and skip lunch altogether.

"Gideon Smucker! You hold up there a minute."

Stifling a groan at the sound of Fern's voice, Gid came to a halt just as he reached the door.

Fern's stern frown sent folks scuttling out of her way. "I

need your help with something. There's a young fellow staying at Windmill Farm to babysit the falcons. His name is Will
Stoltz and I want you to sit with him for lunch."

Gid looked over at the English fellow. He was standing
on the outskirts of a group of Amish men who were milling
about, discussing the weather. "He looks like he's got plenty
of company."

"That's the truth. He does seem to make friends easily.
Sure does buzz around Sadie."

Gid had noticed Will Stoltz had hopped right outside when
Sadie had gone out from the service with the baby. What was
Fern trying to say—that Will Stoltz was interested in Sadie?
Or could Sadie be interested in him? Not possible!

"I'll eat with him," he told Fern. *I'll keep him away from
Sadie*, was what he meant. He slammed his hat onto his head
and charged out the door.

The lightning bugs were out in full force. Sadie sat on the
swing in the backyard and listened to the night sounds. The
last few nights, after settling the baby down, she had started
coming outside to pray. There was something about being
under the open sky, she found, that made it easier to put her
thoughts into prayers. She had a lot to pray about these days.
She felt an urgent decision bearing down on her. "Lord, this
can't all be for nothing," she cried aloud.

"What's for nothing?"

She spun around and saw a flicker of light from the far end
of the back porch. The flicker became a glow, accompanied
by a ribbon of aromatic smoke. Uncle Hank's deep chuckle

resonated in the night. He smoked a pipe every so often, but rarely before witnesses. "Did you think it was the Lord Almighty answering you back?" Another chuckle. "Well, Sadie, come on over here and join me since you're up."

Sadie made her way to the edge of the porch, where Uncle Hank sat in one of two rickety straight-back chairs. Sadie sank into the second chair, smiling when a barn cat stretched out her paws and meowed in greeting.

A thin band of smoke circled Uncle Hank as gentle puffs rose from the pipe's bowl, flavoring the air. The smoky scent was sweet, earthy, manly. Uncle Hank took a draw on the pipe, creating a soft glow in the bowl, and blew the smoke toward the ceiling. "I'm quitting soon. Real soon. Maybe tomorrow. Maybe next week. But in the meantime, I'd appreciate it if you didn't tell Fern about this. You know how she thinks I'm going to burn the porch off the house one of these times."

"Your secret is safe with me," Sadie said.

"Want to tell me what's keeping you awake?"

Sadie let out a deep sigh. "If you don't mind, I'd rather not." She didn't have to say anything. He knew. People underestimated Uncle Hank, and he liked to keep it that way—he often said it was comforting to have such low expectations placed on him—but Sadie knew he grasped the heart of important matters in a way few others did.

"Don't take a few mean-spirited remarks to heart, Sadie. NOSIR. There will always be folks that behave like a flock of chickens, peckin' on the one they see as the weakest."

Sadie nodded. She had witnessed the hens' ill-treatment of one poor bird in the coop—the one M.K. named Toot. Sadie's heart stirred with pity each time she glimpsed that bedraggled, skinny hen huddling in the corner of the coop. She had tried to rescue it and raise it as a pet in the barn, but Toot kept escaping and heading right back to the coop. In a way, Sadie thought she understood Toot's logic. That poor hen would rather be with her friends, pecked at and heckled, than be without them.

— 10 —

Will Stoltz had never worked so hard in all his life. On Monday morning, Amos set him behind two harnessed-up chestnut Belgians with white manes. They carried the odd names of Rosemary and Lavender, the gentlest, biggest beasts known to mankind. When he asked how the horses got their names, Amos said that he always allowed his children the privilege of naming the animals. Julia named the cats, Menno named the dogs, M.K. named the chickens, and Sadie named the horses. All of the horses had names of herbs or spices, he explained, because that was Sadie's main interest. The newest buggy horse was named Cayenne. Now, that was a name that needed no explanation. Will had already noticed Cayenne, pawing away in her stall like she was trying to break free.

Amos promised him that plowing the field would be as easy as dragging a spoon through pudding with the help of these two mighty Belgians. "You'll have it done in no time!" he said, patting Will on the back as he turned to leave him. Rosemary and Lavender dragged the plow back and forth, turning the ground over, exposing rich, dark soil. Thick as it was, only the horses' combined strength made the task bearable. After turning the plow in the opposite direction, Will's arms felt shaky. Like they might rattle right off. He was pretty sure his arms would go completely numb before he finished this field. If, that is, he ever finished. He might expire right here, in the middle of a field, and not be found until the buzzards circled over him.

But there were worse things than having to deal with two gigantic horses and a plow all day—like having to deal with his own problems. He couldn't believe it when he heard his cell phone ring in his pocket. He groaned, recognizing the ringtone he had set for Mr. Petosky—a startling alarm. How was it possible to get extremely sketchy service on this farm, but whenever Mr. Petosky happened to call, he seemed to be in just the right spot for it to come through? He stopped the horses and sat down on the plow to answer the phone. "I thought we had an agreement that you would wait until I called with updates."

"So sue me," Mr. Petosky said. "Any activity with those birds? Are you scouting them out?"

"Yep, morning, noon, and night," Will said. He looked up and saw Adam fly over the cherry orchard, off in the distance. Or was it Eve? It was hard to spot the difference in size without his binoculars. "Look, you're going to have to be patient. You can't rush nature."

"Think it's going to work?" Mr. Petosky asked. "Are they sticking around?"

"I think so. The falcons like this farm. The female is staying close to the scape. Wouldn't surprise me if she lays her clutch this week."

"Good. Good. Keep an eye on those birds."

Will had sensed from the beginning that Mr. Petosky had a lot more interest in these rare birds than he let on. "That's what I've been doing, Mr. Petosky," he said, his voice thin on patience.

"Well, I'm just trying to give you some tips, that's all," Mr. Petosky said. "How do you like living out there in the boonies?"

"It's not the boonies." Will looked around, praying no one would come by.

Mr. Petosky snorted. "Don't tell me you're starting to enjoy living with those kooks."

"They're not kooks, Mr. Petosky. They're a very nice family." Probably the kindest people Will had ever met. "They're not like you think."

That only got Mr. Petosky laughing out loud. "Imagine that! Will Stoltz, trust fund kid, bound for medical school until he gets himself kicked out of college—"

"Suspended. There's a difference."

"—trying to pay off his lawyer to get rid of his DUI before his old man hears about it—imagine a kid like you wanting to be Amish."

"I never said I wished I were Amish. I only said these are nice people." Will was irritated now. "Look, Mr. Petosky, if there's nothing else you need from me right now, I really need to get back to work."

"That's fine, kid. Just remember that June 16 is right around the corner."

Will heard the click of a hang up.

Rosemary and Lavender looked at him with their big brown

eyes and long eyelashes, wondering what he wanted. *What do I want?* he thought as he shook the reins to get the gentle giants moving. *What in the world do I really want?* Life here was nothing like Philadelphia, but he felt just as lost.

When Gid returned to the house after school let out on Monday, he wasn't surprised to find the deacon, Abraham, sitting on the back porch with his father, sipping iced tea. That sight was nothing new. The ministers and bishop and deacon often had church problems that needed discussing. Long conversations, looking at the problem from every angle, trying to find solutions that were fair and just and pleasing to God. So as to not interrupt them, Gid went through the side door and washed up at the kitchen sink. The back door was left open and he heard Abraham say, "This is on shaky ground, Ira. There's no real cut-and-dry answer."

"But you wouldn't ask him to quit, would you? If he married her in six weeks' time?" He heard his father let out an exasperated sigh. "He loves teaching, you see."

Gid grabbed a dishrag and took a step closer to the door.

Abraham took awhile to respond. "I heard of one community that let the fellow continue teaching because the pupils wouldn't have to shun him, seeing as how they aren't baptized." Gid heard Abraham settle back in his chair. "But most would make him stop until he was a member again in good standing."

Gid leaned against the door. He thought something like this might be stirring after receiving a few chilly receptions in church yesterday. Before lunch was served, he had walked up to his friends, deep in conversation, and they suddenly stopped talking, looked uncomfortable, and the circle broke up. If this was how he had been treated, how must Sadie be feeling? His heart went out to her. He wasn't going to let her face this alone. He threw down the dishrag and went out to the porch.

Abraham looked up when he saw Gid and smiled, standing up to welcome him. The deacon was shorter than Gid by several inches. He reached out and gripped his hand firmly. "Have a seat, please," Abraham said, and he waited until Gid had sat down before he took the chair facing him. Gid was reminded of how he felt when he met with the ministers about becoming baptized, and in a sense he supposed that was what this was all about.

Abraham steepled his fingers together, as if praying before he began to speak. "I take it you heard what we're talking about?"

Gid nodded.

"A child is always a good thing. We thank God for bringing this little boy into our lives. But we need to make things right for this child." He glanced at Gid. "Just because a marriage starts off on the wrong foot doesn't mean it can't find its right path." The deacon crossed one leg over the other and set his Bible on top of his thigh, both hands resting on it. "So, your father tells me you are willing to make a confession that you have sinned. Is that true?"

Gid nodded. He could make a confession like that. He definitely could. He knew he was a sinner. Didn't his thoughts often wander down slippery paths?

Abraham clapped his palms together, pleased. "So then, I will ask the bishop if we could let you keep on teaching."

Ira asked Abraham a question and the two went back and forth for a while. Gid was beginning to breathe more easily now that he realized that he probably wouldn't be called on to do much talking.

Abraham turned to Gid. "And after six weeks' proving time, then the bann will be lifted, and you can marry." He clapped his hands together. "And then . . . a fresh start!"

Ira gazed at Gid, waiting for him to respond to Abraham. But what could he say? If he objected to getting put back or marrying Sadie so quickly, he would be betraying her. "What I mean," Gid started, "is that . . ." but then he couldn't think of what to say or how to say it. This was what he hated so much about conversations in which he was forced to participate. He could never end his part right. He was always trailing off lamely and leaving thoughts unfinished. Maybe he should suggest using pencil and paper for a conversation sometime. He was sure he could come across better if he could write his responses. Or better still, if he could find the words in the works of Shakespeare or Wordsworth, and they could speak for him. But that wouldn't really be addressing the heart of this dilemma. He didn't need Shakespearean language for that.

There were a few things Gid knew for certain about himself: He wasn't the life of the party. He didn't enjoy casual conversations, like striking up conversations with people standing next to him in a grocery line or at the hardware store. In fact, he couldn't remember ever doing such a thing. He didn't make friends easily or quickly. He knew those things about himself. But he was loyal to a fault. When he loved someone, he would stick by to the bitter end.

Abraham was waiting for his answer. Fumbling to speak, he blurted out, "I want to make things right for Sadie."

Abraham stood. "Well, then. I guess that's that." As he passed Gid, he placed a hand on his head like he was giving him a blessing.

Gid looked at his father. "That's it?"

Ira leaned back in his chair and sighed, relieved. "That's it."

Will Stoltz felt muscles he never knew he had. After putting the plow upright in the barn with the other tools, Amos told him that now he should spread manure from the compost pile over the field he had just plowed. Shoveling manure atop the field took the rest of the afternoon. Oh, how his father would relish that sight! The way Will's luck was going lately, he was surprised the game warden hadn't dropped by to check on the falcons while Will was knee-deep in manure.

Thinking of the game warden reminded him that he had better hurry to go observe the falcons at dusk. He hadn't spotted any eggs in the scape, but any day now, he was sure one would appear. Hopefully, more than one. A niggling doubt poked at him, but he pushed it away. He *wasn't* doing anything wrong. Not technically.

As he left the barn, he saw a horse and buggy pull up the drive. He shielded his eyes from the western sun and thought he saw Sadie in the driver's side. He smiled. His luck was turning.

Will met Sadie as she pulled the buggy to a stop. He opened the door to help her down. "Where have you been?"

"To the store. I left a few things there." She reached into the backseat to get a couple of packages of cloth diapers. "And Fern says it's time to switch this baby from paper diapers to cloth." She wrinkled her nose. "I was a little disappointed to hear that." Then she got a whiff of Will. "Why, you're as dirty as a peasant in a mud puddle. What have you been doing today?"

"Your dad got me plowing." Will pointed over to the field. He was proud of his work. Palm on his forehead, he heaved a mighty sigh. He opened his palm and looked at it. His hand was filled with blisters. So was the other hand.

"Oh no! Will, didn't you use gloves?"

"Believe it or not, I did."

"You've got some serious blisters there, and more coming."

"They're not all that bad. I was just pouring some water over them when you arrived. They actually feel much better now." More likely, his hands had lost all feeling. His arms hadn't lost that shaky feeling, as if he were still plowing.

She looked at him as if she didn't believe him. "You'd better come up to the house. I'll fix something up for those poor red hands of yours. I have just the thing to speed up their healing." When he hesitated, she added, "You'll be sorry tomorrow if you don't let me help you now."

"I've got to get out to the falcons before the sun sets." He looked down at her. Strands of hair fluttered across her cheek. Automatically, he reached over and used the back of his fingers to tuck them behind her ear. A slight blush stained her cheeks, which charmed him. She was so unlike the girls he had known. "I'll stop by later, after you all have supper, if that's okay."

Side by side, they strolled toward the house. Mouthwatering aromas wafted from the house and Will's stomach rumbled. Sadie glanced up at the house, then back to Will. "Join us for supper."

Will winced. "I'm not so sure your housekeeper would want that. She isn't too fond of me."

"Don't mind Fern. At first, she can be as prickly as a jar of toothpicks. It takes awhile for her to warm up to folks. But she does love to feed people. We eat at six."

His stomach rumbled again, louder this time. Sadie's lips parted and laughter spilled out of her.

Will smiled. "Then I'll be back in an hour."

Amos barely had one leg out the door of the Mennonite taxi as Fern peppered him with questions about his appointment with the cardiologist. This was exactly why he refused to let her accompany him to the doctor, even though it was clear he had ruffled her feathers. She promised she would stay in the waiting room, but he knew she would somehow worm her way into the doctor's office with a laundry list of questions. He was a grown man, for goodness' sake!

"So what did he say? Is there trouble brewing?"

She had such a worried look on her face that he felt himself softening. It was nice, really, to have someone fuss over him. He closed the car door and waved goodbye to the driver. "Everything's fine, Fern. Just fine."

"Fine, as in Fern Graber's version of fine, or in Amos Lapp's version?"

The sweet moment between them fizzled. What was *that*

supposed to mean? "Fine as in everybody's version of fine."
He started to walk toward the house.

She caught up with him. "Did he give you every test for
rejection? Stress tests, biopsies?"

"He gave me every test known to man. I have no blood left.
I've been completely drained by those sharp needles. And it
took all day long!" That's what annoyed him about being
sick, most of all. Losing time for his farm. He glanced over
at the field he had put in Will Stoltz's care. He cocked his
head and squinted his eyes. The furrows should be straight,
like a ruler; Will's furrows wove like a ribbon of rickrack.

"If everything is so fine, then why are you feeling so tired
and wrung out?"

Amos glanced at her. Should he tell her? She was peering
into his face, concern written in her eyes. She was waiting
for him to explain. He looked past her to the setting sun,
dropping low behind the pines that framed the house to the
west. "The doctor thinks my problem is I haven't grieved
for Menno."

She tilted her head.

"He thinks so much happened, so fast, that I just put off
my grieving for my boy. And now, it's catching up with me."
He missed his son in a way there wasn't words for. He clung
to the past so hard it was like leaving an arrow embedded
instead of pulling it out and letting the wound bleed clean,
then heal.

"I've wondered the very same thing." She nodded solemnly.
"He's a good doctor."

He turned his head sharply toward her. "Then why didn't
you say something? You could have saved me a doctor's visit."

"You were due in, anyway. Besides, you're not exactly the easiest man to try to tell what to do, you know." She folded her arms against her chest and held her elbows. "So what did the doctor recommend?"

Amos felt a surge of stung pride, recalling the doctor's advice. He had told Amos there were some interesting facts about heart recipients that weren't true for other organ recipients: 75 percent were male, 25 percent were female. In addition, he said, most of the transplant cardiologists and surgeons were men. And yet, the doctor explained, men have a harder time coping with the surgery than women do. More depression, for example.

"Why would that be?" Amos asked him.

"My theory is that men are uncomfortable with the idea of accepting someone else—heart, spirit, or piece of meat, whatever way you want to view your donor heart—into their bodies and their being. Simply put: receptivity is not easy for men."

Amos would never tell Fern *that* particular piece of information. He could hear her response now: "Amen to that. Amen!"

Amos waved a pamphlet in the air. "He wants me to go to a grief support group." He set his jaw. "But I'm not going."

"Now I see where M.K. gets her famous stubborn streak." Fern took the pamphlet from him and skimmed it. "Wouldn't really hurt to talk to somebody about your grieving."

"I'm not talking to a bunch of strangers."

She closed the pamphlet. "Maybe not. But you could talk to somebody. Somebody caring and understanding. Somebody you trust."

"Like who?"

She paused, tilted her head, and Amos watched her expression go from hopeful to saddened to resolute. Then it passed and her brow wrinkled as her eyes traveled over the field with the cockeyed furrows. "Maybe like Deacon Abraham." She pointed to a horse and buggy driving along the road. "He's coming up here, now. Probably to talk about Sadie." She took a few steps toward the house, then stopped and swiveled around. "Ask him to stay for dinner."

"Fern, hold up. Why would Abraham want to talk to Sadie?"

She took a few steps back to him, with a look on her face as if she thought he might be slightly addle brained. That look made him crazy, especially because he often felt addle brained around the females in his household.

She tilted her head to the side and plunked a small fist on her hip. "Have you noticed how quickly rumor becomes fact in this community?"

Her frown grew fierce—a ridiculous expression for someone who could be pretty when she smiled.

"Here they come. Looks like Esther's with him." She took a few steps toward the house, then stopped and swiveled around again. "Send Esther up to the house. You be sure to tell Abraham about what the doctor said. About grieving for Menno."

Did that woman ever stop handing out unasked-for advice? What irked him all the more was that she was usually right. Under his breath he muttered, "Yeder Ros hot ihr Dann." *Every rose has its thorn.*

She spun around. She had heard him. She heard everything. "Ken Rose unne Danne." *There is no rose without a thorn.*

Impossibly weary, Amos sighed and went to meet his friends.

"Abraham," Amos said, shaking the man's hand after he'd tied up his horse to the hitching post.

Esther went up to the house to visit with Fern. The two men walked together, away from the house.

Abraham couldn't keep a grin off his face when he heard Amos tell the story of the visiting bird boy and surveyed the cockeyed furrows. "Well, wheat seeds can grow and flourish and reach for the sky whether the rows are straight or crooked. Maybe there's a lesson in that for us, eh, Amos?" He gripped his hands behind his back. "But I can tell there's something you want to tell me."

Why, Abraham was as prescient as Fern! It baffled Amos that some people seemed to be able to see what wasn't visible. He was a man who relied heavily on his sight and hearing. He looked into his dear friend's kind brown eyes. "I just came from the doctor. I thought that I was having heart trouble again. But the doctor said my heart was fine, that the problem was I hadn't grieved for Menno. I buried it, he said, amidst all the busyness of the heart transplant and trying to get well. Grieving has caught up with me."

A flicker of surprise passed through Abraham's eyes. He stroked his wiry gray beard, deep in thought, and gave a sad half smile. "So, in a way, you are still having heart trouble. The kind that can't be fixed by doctoring."

Out of the corner of his eye, Amos peered up at the male falcon, soaring over the fields, hunting for an evening meal to bring to his mate. He was the size of a crow, with a three-foot wingspan, a dark head with a pale breast cross-barred with dark brown. "What do I do with that information, Abraham? I can't switch feelings on and off like a diesel generator."

"You're not new to grieving, Amos. I remember how it was when you lost your Maggie. You didn't heal from that loss overnight. Grieving takes time. It can't be rushed."

How well Amos remembered what it felt like when Maggie had passed. It was like a limb had been torn from him, with no anesthetic. The pain was so deep then, he wondered if it would ever lessen. Just yesterday, his thoughts had drifted back to a lazy Sunday afternoon, long ago, when the children were playing in a tree fort in the backyard while Maggie and he sat on a wooden swing nearby beneath the canopy of a maple. He thought those days would last forever.

"God's ways are not ours, Amos. As much as we rejoice that our loved ones are in God's holy heaven, we miss them." Abraham looked into the sky to see the falcon swoop down on an unlucky bobolink flying low in the field. "Memory is a strange thing. At times, so sweet. At times, so painful. But it's what separates us from fish and fowl and beast. God wants us to remember his gifts and blessings." He put a hand on Amos's shoulder. "There's a difference between keeping memories alive and using them as an excuse not to start living again." He pulled his hand away and crossed his arms against his chest. "My advice for you is to talk about Menno. Remember his life. Celebrate the gift of a son God gave you, even if it was for a brief time. I think, by remembering, it will allow your grief to surface. And, in time, to heal." He patted Amos's back. "Talk, Amos Lapp. Talk and remember."

Abraham made it sound so simple, but Amos knew it wasn't. Grief was a hard, lonely thing to bear.

Suddenly, he realized that Abraham had something else on his mind.

Abraham's eyes were fixed on the farmhouse. "And now I'd like to talk to Sadie. Alone."

— 11 —

Sadie saw her father and Deacon Abraham talking outside her bedroom window, over by the field Will had plowed. If, that is, you could call it plowed. It looked more like a giant hand had scooped down from the sky and raked its fingers haphazardly through the dirt. The sight of the wiggly furrows made her smile. Any eight-year-old boy in her church could have done a better job, but, of course, she would never tell Will that. He had seemed so pleased with his efforts.

She studied herself in the mirror as if seeing herself for the first time. Usually, she only looked to see if the knot she wore on the back of her head caught all the strands, even the one that always seemed to work its way loose. Now she pulled out the pins that held her hair and let it tumble. She shook it free and studied her face like it was the map of some unknown country. Was she pretty? She shook that thought off, as quickly as it came. That was vain, and mirrors don't tell everything.

Her thoughts traveled to the conversation she had with Will, just a short while ago, and to the way he brushed back a swoop of her hair that had come loose.

It still shocked her that she talked to a stranger, a boy

stranger, the way she talked to Will just now. But there was something about him that made talking so easy and natural. She'd never felt so comfortable around a boy before, around most people, and certainly not an English boy. It was nice to be able to share her thoughts with someone outside the church, someone who had a different point of view, who saw things more objectively and didn't layer a situation with shoulds and shouldn'ts.

A door banged open and Sadie heard M.K.'s voice yell out, "Saa—ddeee! Dad wants you to come outside and talk to Deacon Abraham!" followed by Fern hushing M.K., scolding her that she would wake the baby.

Sadie took a deep breath. She had expected this visit. Maybe not today, but soon. This had just turned into a horrible day. The worst day of her life.

Sadie had thought by the time she had reached her late teens, she would be able to speak her mind, but she had yet to figure out a way to quell her constant need for approval.

Fern had told her once that she needed to be bolder, that there was a time for submission, and a time for boldness. But Sadie wasn't a naturally assertive person. Even horses took advantage of her. Just today, the buggy horse—her father's oldest nag—wanted to go right when she wanted it to go left. They ended up going right and she had to go far out of her way to get to the Bent N' Dent. Right turns only.

Enough. She had had enough of getting walked on and pushed around, even by an old horse! Enough! She would face this ridiculous accusation head-on.

Sadie twisted her hair into an orderly arrangement. A half-dozen pins slipped into place, and her hair and prayer cap assumed its normal style. She blew air out of her cheeks. If only she could discipline her mind and her heart as efficiently.

Outside, as Sadie passed her father, he gave her a light squeeze on her shoulder. Did he know what the deacon wanted? She had seen them talking together for quite a long time. But her father didn't say anything to her, didn't give anything away with his eyes. She steeled herself and went out to meet the deacon, patiently waiting by the fence. When she reached him, Sadie had to hide her hands behind her so that he couldn't see how much they were trembling.

Abraham was a kind man, and he looked quite sad. "Sadie, I just came from having a long talk with Gideon Smucker. He admits that he's the father of this baby. He's willing to go before the church in two weeks' time, and confess to all. And then he wants to marry you, after the proving period, in six weeks' time."

"Is that what he said?" she asked in a shaky voice.

The deacon nodded. "He said he wanted to make things right for you. He didn't want you to have to face this alone."

Sadie discovered she was clasping her hands so tightly her knuckles ached. She relaxed her grip, flattening her palms on her thighs.

"So, Sadie Lapp, I'm here to see if you are willing to confess as well, to have a time of proving, then to marry Gid and make things right."

Sadie's lips quivered. Her chest grew tight. How dare Gid let others believe he was the father of that baby! And by doing so, he let others believe it was Sadie's baby. Gid had actually contributed to the spreading rumors . . . not through a lie, but through his omission of the truth. And wasn't that a lie? What you didn't say could be just as damaging as what you did. On top of it all, Gid had the unmitigated gall to look as if he was rescuing Sadie from a troubling fate. Tears clouded her vision, but she kept blinking them away. Once she was out of sight, she could fall apart—but not in front of the deacon. What a fool she had been to care about Gid, to think he was someone she might love one day. She wanted to escape to her room, bury her face in the pillows, and cry this intense hurt away.

Minutes ticked by while the deacon waited for a response. Sadie was terrified: like the first time she jumped off a diving rock at Blue Lake Pond, like the night she knew Gid was first going to kiss her, like the day when the bear came up to the house and poked its nose at the window. She had trouble getting a full breath, and then she felt a little dizzy.

Off in the distance, Sadie heard M.K. shout, "She's going down!"

Sheer horror shadowed the deacon's face, and then it was like someone pulled the curtains. Everything went dark. The next thing Sadie knew, she was getting scooped up in Will's strong arms and pulled so tight against his warm chest that she could feel his heartbeat.

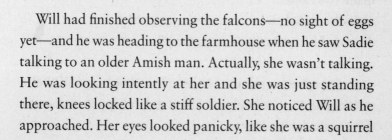

Will had finished observing the falcons—no sight of eggs yet—and he was heading to the farmhouse when he saw Sadie talking to an older Amish man. Actually, she wasn't talking. He was looking intently at her and she was just standing there, knees locked like a stiff soldier. She noticed Will as he approached. Her eyes looked panicky, like she was a squirrel caught in traffic—too frightened to move. Then he heard M.K. give a shout from the farmhouse porch and Will bolted to catch Sadie, just as her head was about to hit the fence post. He lifted her in his arms like she was a bag of feathers and rushed to the farmhouse with her, the Amish man following close behind. Will laid Sadie gently on the couch as Fern and M.K. fluttered around her.

"What happened?" Fern asked.

"We were having a talk and she just . . . fainted," Abraham said, visibly upset. "Dropped like a stone."

Sadie's eyes fluttered open. She looked bewildered as everyone crowded around her. M.K. brought a cold, wet cloth and slapped it on her forehead.

Fern intervened just as Amos opened his mouth to say something. "Why don't you take Esther and Abraham outside and give Sadie a moment to pull herself together."

It wasn't posed as a question, Will noticed. It was an order. Fern ushered everyone out the door. She held the door open and pointed to M.K. "Your hens require your attention." Her gaze turned to Will next, and he knew he was about to get ordered out, but the baby let out a healthy squall and Fern's attention was riveted to the basket in the kitchen.

"You all right?" he whispered, leaning close to Sadie. "What made you faint?"

Sadie pulled the dripping wet rag off of her face. "The deacon. He was laying a sin on me."

"You could never sin!"

Sadie pulled herself up. "No one is without sin, Will." She put her hand to her forehead. "But I didn't happen to commit this particular sin."

He glanced in the kitchen and saw Fern jiggling the baby, trying to settle it. It was the first time he felt grateful for the baby's loud cry. It provided a moment of privacy. "What particular sin was he trying to lay on you?"

Sadie rubbed her face with her hands. She let out a deep sigh, and then, to Will's surprise, poured out the story of how people assumed the baby was hers—when he wasn't!—that the quiet guy he had lunch with at church yesterday—Gideon Smucker—didn't deny he was the baby's father—which he wasn't!—and that the deacon was expecting Sadie and Gideon to marry and set things right.

Will was outraged. He made sure Fern was out of hearing distance and leaned close to Sadie. "You need to stand up for yourself. I know about these kinds of people—they will wear you down and plan out your entire life. You've got to have a backbone."

She hugged her arms across her middle, as though she were cold. "How can you be so sure of that?"

"Because I've been in your shoes. This type will run roughshod over you if you don't open your mouth and speak up."

"Will Stoltz." Fern eyed him from the kitchen. "Come and make yourself useful. Get this baby to stop his yammering while I tend to Sadie."

Will rose to his feet. "You gotta learn to speak your own mind. Otherwise, you'll get swept along like a twig in a creek. You'll wake up one day and wonder whatever happened to your life. If you have strong feelings, Sadie, now's the time to say so."

Sadie went very still.

M.K. ran to the feed room in the barn, filled up the container with cracked corn, and flew to the chicken coop like she had wings on her feet. The chickens lived penned up in a coop on the far side of the barn. Downwind. After Julia got married and moved to Berlin, charge of the chickens was handed to Sadie, who promptly turned the responsibility over to M.K. Chickens and Sadie didn't get along. If she had to keep them, she said, she'd as soon not eat them. But M.K. had a hand with fowl. She named them too, every chick of them, before they feathered out. Fern said better not name anything you're fixing to eat. But M.K. went right on naming them.

The last hen pecked at M.K.'s bare toes as she tossed cracked corn inside the chicken coop. "Try being mean like that again, Kayak, and I'll have Fern introduce you to the inside of a pot." Holding the corners of her apron, she hurried Kayak into the coop with the other chickens and locked it tight for the night. She didn't want to miss a minute of excitement going on inside the farmhouse. She saw Uncle Hank come out from his buggy shop and waved her arm like a windmill. "Uncle Hank! Hurry! Hurry! Hurry! Sadie's got the vapors!"

They rushed over to the farmhouse and found Sadie, upright and talking, with color back in her cheeks, sitting at the kitchen table with Amos and Abraham. Will was walking the baby and Fern was at the kitchen sink, looking like she had a kernel of popcorn stuck in her back molar. But then, that look on Fern was not unusual. She was scraping carrots like they had done something that made her mad. She wasn't idle. She didn't know how to be idle. Daylight never caught Fern sitting down.

They stopped talking for a moment as Uncle Hank and M.K. came in and sat themselves at the table. "Maybe we could finish up this conversation tomorrow, Sadie," Abraham said.

"No," Sadie said. "We can settle it now, Abraham." She looked around the room at everyone, then her eyes rested on the baby in Will's arms. "I have something to tell you. Something I haven't wanted to say until I knew for sure. But I think the time has come to tell you everything I know about the baby."

In a clear, calm voice, she explained about the baby in the bus station to Abraham. M.K. was amazed, watching her sister talk to the deacon with such confidence.

After she finished, Abraham let out a long breath. "Sadie, why didn't you just tell me that in the first place?"

"But you didn't ask, Abraham. You just told me what I had to do to make things right. You never asked me for the truth."

Nose in the air, Esther huffed. "Such disrespect!"

For a span of a heartbeat, no one said anything. For an instant, Sadie felt free. She'd told the truth. Then she felt dreadful. "I'll agree with you there, Esther."

Esther's tiny mouth was pursed full of triumph as she looked around the room.

"It's disrespectful to assume the worst about someone. It's disrespectful not to hope the best for another." Sadie turned to Abraham. "I'm not trying to be rude to you, Abraham, but no one has ever asked me for the truth. Not you, not Gideon, not my friends and neighbors. Love is supposed to think well of others. Not tell tales and gossip."

Struck dumb by Sadie's lengthy, emphatic speech, M.K. could only stare at her in amazement.

Abraham looked at Esther. "Did you not tell me that you talked with Sadie about the baby at church yesterday?"

"She talked *to* me," Sadie said quietly. "She never talked *with* me."

Esther narrowed her eyes. "You could have offered up the truth. You never said a word."

M.K. exchanged a glance with Uncle Hank. There was so much electricity charging the air, she wondered if she'd be hearing a thunderclap soon. The tension in the air practically sizzled.

Abraham lifted a hand. "You're right, Sadie. I hope you can find it in your heart to forgive me."

Sadie reached out and covered his hand with hers, a silent offering. The baby let out a wail and Abraham glanced at him.

"Well, one problem is taken care of, yet we have another. What shall we do about this little one? Babies just don't appear out of thin air."

"This one did," M.K. offered. "We think an angel brought him to Sadie." Everyone sent startled glances in her direction, as if they'd forgotten she was there.

Abraham smiled. "Even a baby brought by an angel needs a family."

"Two parents," Esther added. "A real family. Children are a blessing and a responsibility. He's not just a doll for you to play with, Mary Kate."

Red heat swept through M.K. She forgot that she was a child and Esther an adult. She forgot it was the deacon who sat before her. She barely felt Fern's fingers digging into her arm. "You can't just take a baby and give him to this or that person like he's no more than a stray dog!" She wasn't exactly yelling, but she was very close.

"You Lapps have your hands more than full already," Esther pointed out, her voice sounding shrill as a pennywhistle. She turned to her husband. "I can think of a few families who would welcome a child."

M.K. was shocked. "But the angel brought him to us!"

Esther frowned at her.

She knew she was pushing it, but she couldn't help herself. It wasn't fair! "How about for the baby? What's fair and reasonable for him? Or for the rest of us?" She was on the brink of bursting into tears. She looked up at Sadie, expecting to see her sobbing right along with her.

But she wasn't. Sadie rose from her chair, standing tall and straight, calm and serene. "This baby does have a family," Sadie said firmly. She bit on her lips, as if bracing herself. "There's something else about this baby, something I haven't wanted to say until I was sure." She went over to the trunk that held her mother's quilts and lifted it open. On top of the pile lay a yellow and blue crib quilt. She picked it up and brought it to her father.

"Your mother made that," Amos said. "All of you babies slept under it."

Sadie took a deep breath. "I think this baby belongs to Annie." She turned to Abraham and Esther. "She's the young Swartzentruber girl who lives with her grandfather." As everyone started murmuring, she held up a hand. "Let me start at the beginning. It was really M.K. who gave me an idea. She suggested we find out who made the baby's basket."

M.K. beamed at that remark. Her detective skills were paying off.

"Until M.K. mentioned that, I had forgotten that Annie

was a basketmaker. On a hunch, I went to visit her grand-father last Friday while M.K. was having that buggy race with Jimmy Fisher. He seemed pretty confused—at first he thought I was Annie. It seemed like he was waiting for her, but I could tell he lived there alone. I made some supper for him because he said he was hungry. I could tell that someone had been there pretty recently—there were some casseroles in the freezer with last week's date on them—the day before I found the baby at the bus station. And I found this quilt, folded, in Annie's bedroom. The dog I brought home—that's our Lulu's pup, all grown up." Sadie took a deep breath. "I think it was Annie who saw me sleeping in the bus station and left the baby with me." She lifted her eyes to look at her father. "She must have had the quilt because Menno had given it to her. He must have known about the baby. Do you remember how he told Julia he wanted to marry Annie? But then . . . he died. And Annie was left to have the baby alone. I think Annie left the baby with me because the father of the baby was Menno. Our Menno."

Everything slowed. Fern stopped peeling carrots and froze. M.K. felt frightened by how quiet the room got, and she didn't scare easily. She didn't know how Sadie got through that brave speech without her voice breaking in two.

It was Uncle Hank who broke the ice. He rose to his feet and strode to Will, taking the baby out of his arms. Tears streaming down his face, he gazed lovingly at the baby. "THIS IS WONDERFUL NEWS! I knew there was something grand and glorious about this little one the very first time I laid eyes on him. God has given us a great gift, Amos. Our Menno has left us with a child."

After Abraham and Esther's buggy rolled out of the drive-way, Amos stood for a moment looking up at the stars through the treetops. He tried to absorb all that had happened today and it felt mind-boggling. He felt a flood of feelings, at the top was sorrow over his Sadie. How could anyone accuse Sadie of such a sin? His soul told him to forgive, but his heart ached with the unfairness of the situation. And on the heels of those feelings came another, one of awe and wonder. There was this child in the house, one of his own. He lifted his head and saw that more and more stars were now visible in the bruised sky. A chilly breeze blew and a few night birds twittered.

"Heaven's dazzling us with stars, like thousands of angels winking at us," Fern said.

Amos jerked his head down. Where had she come from? She was as stealthy as a cat on the prowl.

"Did Abraham have anything else to say?"

Nosy. Fern was downright nosy. "He said he would write some letters to the Swartzentruber colony and see if he can find out how to locate Annie." He kicked a dirt clod on the ground with his boot. "And he said that if I felt the need, it would be all right to have the baby's blood tested. To make sure he's a Lapp."

"So what did you tell him?"

"I told him it wouldn't matter what the results were. The baby is one of ours."

She smiled at him, and he couldn't help but smile back.

"I suppose you, in your infinite wisdom, knew Abraham

stopped by to talk to Sadie about this . . . this ridiculous gossip."

She gave him a sweet look then, as if he were a naïve child. "Did you not notice how a few people treated Sadie at church yesterday? Like she might be contagious."

No, he didn't.

He had been so preoccupied with worry over his heart—convinced his body was starting to reject it—that he was hardly aware of anything yesterday. He couldn't even say what the sermons were about. Or whom he sat next to for lunch. His body might have been at church, but his head was elsewhere. A blanket of guilt covered him. He had been so focused on himself that he hadn't even thought about what might be going on in his daughter's life. What kind of a father was that? "Surely not everyone treated her that way."

"No, but it felt like everyone to Sadie. You know how sensitive she is. She felt as if she had to protect Menno."

"I can't bear the thought that anyone would think ill of Menno." He wiped his face with his hands. "He's not here to explain or defend himself, or even to confess."

"Amos, Menno was God's special child. No one will accuse him of anything."

He sighed. "If some folks were so quick to accuse Sadie of sin, what will they be saying about Menno?" He glanced at her. "I know that's why Sadie didn't want to tell us about the crib quilt. Or who she thought was the baby's father. Menno meant so much to her. She knows folks will talk."

"If folks want to say hurtful things, that's something God will have to deal with." She put a hand on his arm. "There's good in all of this, Amos."

160

"Like what?"

"Just today, your doctor told you to talk about Menno, to get your grieving out. Maybe this little baby is part of God's healing for you." She looked down at the ground. "He even looks like Menno, with that thatch of unruly hair. Menno never did comb his hair."

Remembering his son's wild hair, a slight smile tugged at Amos's lips. He felt a stone lifting from the pile weighing on his heart, shucking off into the newly plowed field. The tightness in his chest eased a bit.

"And did you see how Sadie stood up for the truth? Maybe God is using all of this gossip nonsense to help her become a strong woman." Fern looked over at the house. "When I first arrived here, she was afraid of her own shadow. Today, I saw a girl become a woman."

Amos mulled that thought over. It was true, what Fern said. Sadie was showing more backbone than he ever thought possible. He was grateful to Fern for those encouraging words, and tried to think of how to tell her that he appreciated it. That he appreciated *her*. That his feelings for her were growing in ways he had never, ever expected, that she filled his thoughts more and more each day. She turned to him and their eyes caught and held. Amos leaned closer, so close that the space between them felt intimate. *Something was happening.* His heart pounded like he was a seventeen-year-old boy again, an odd staccato that echoed in his ears. He cleared his throat.

"Fern, I find that I have grown rather fond of you," Amos had intended to say, but for some reason the words came out as, "Fern, dinner was good."

She tilted her head as if she hadn't heard him correctly, then she squinted her eyes as if he might be sun-touched.

Dinner was good? *Dinner was good?* Nice work, Amos Lapp, he chided himself. Just what a woman wanted to hear.

But the moment had passed and Fern turned to leave. Over her shoulder, she tossed, "Amos Lapp, has it occurred to you that you're a grandfather?"

Back at the house, M.K. took care of the baby while Sadie and Will gathered dishes from the table and set them in the sink to soak. Uncle Hank sank into his favorite chair by the woodstove. He was into a sack of pecans Sadie and M.K. had gathered last fall. In a litter of shells he was trying to pick out nutmeats. Sadie seemed to see for the first time how twisted and knobby his hands were. Arthritis had gotten to his joints, and he had pain he never spoke of. Tonight, Sadie thought, she would mix up a special tea to help him with the pain.

As Sadie went back and forth from the table to the kitchen, she was glad to see her legs were holding her up, solid and sure, though she prayed her trembling wasn't still noticeable. She had never been so bold in all her life as she was tonight. She actually said some things she wanted to say. But the thing was, she wasn't sure if it made things better or worse.

Sadie's conversation with Abraham had ended on a sweet note, as he took her small hands in his large, calloused ones. "You've reminded me of an important quality of love today, Sadie Lapp," he said. "Love believes the best in others."

Sadie readily forgave Abraham. How could she not? Yet she couldn't quite keep her hands from shaking. It occurred to Sadie that she had actually confronted Esther—one of the most intimidating women in their church. Some would say the most intimidating woman. Which proved to Sadie that she could confront people when push came to shove! That little epiphany made her day.

But all of those thoughts would need to be sifted through later, when she was alone. As for now, Will Stoltz was waiting for her to bandage his blistered hands. She filled a bowl of water for him to soak his hands, first, and ended up sloshing the bowl of water onto the table hard enough to spill some water on the floor. She wiped it up and fetched another clean towel from the hall closet, then poked her head around the edge of the doorjamb to find Will waiting for her in the kitchen, a patient look on his face. The very first time she saw Will she had the vague thought that he looked sad, but the second time she realized it was mainly the shape of his eyes. Everything else about him looked pleasant enough, handsome, but his eyes, even when he smiled, pulled down a little at the corners. His jawline was square, and his thick hair had just the slightest hint of a wave in it. Not fair! Not fair that a boy had such thick, wavy hair. She would have loved such hair.

She took a deep breath and squared her shoulders. *Watch that line of thinking, Sadie Lapp,* she told herself. *Jealousy will only take you down wicked and twisted paths.* "Come to the table. After your hands soak for a while, I'll put some healing salve on them."

Will smiled, sat at the table, and held his hands out to her. She plunged his hands into the bowl of water. Dirt was caked into the blisters and Will winced as the water hit the open sores. She made a mental note to get to work on expanding her herb garden with a variety of herbs that Old Deborah had taught her about, if only to keep some healing remedies handy. She moistened several diamond-shaped pigweed leaves and placed them, one at a time, on the tender, reddened flesh on Will's palms. "Leave them sit a spell. You'll still blister some more, but not as bad. You'll heal quicker too."

"That feels much better. Thank you. The sting is almost gone."

She glanced at his face. "Your hands looked as dirty as if you'd been digging for worms."

"Now there's an idea. Digging for worms sounds like a lot more fun than plowing. Do you like to go fishing?"

"No. How did you ever manage to plow a field with those blisters?"

He shrugged. "Just kept at it. Will you go fishing with me?"

Sadie glanced over at M.K. on the couch, feeding the baby a bottle. She knew her little sister was straining to hear every word. "Maybe," she whispered.

She pulled the leaves off his hands and had him rinse in the bowl. She took one of his hands and dried it carefully with a towel. Then she gently spread a salve over it.

Will made a face. "That is vile smelling! What's in it? Kitchen waste?"

"Comfrey." Her lips twisted into a reluctant smile. "It might smell bad, but it will speed up the healing." She bandaged his hand carefully with gauze and snipped off some lengths of adhesive tape to wrap around the gauze.

She dried his other hand and applied the comfrey salve. "You'll need to be careful with these wounds."

"I don't know how to thank you for helping me."

"Keep them covered for now. You don't want them to get infected."

Will caught hold of her hand to keep her from concentrating on bandaging his wound. "It wouldn't be the worst thing I could think of to come back and have you take care of them." His fathomless blue eyes gazed into hers in a way that made her pulse skip more beats than was healthy. "Maybe I can use these blisters as an excuse to spend time with you if you won't go fishing with me."

"I like to go fishing," M.K. piped up. "So does Uncle Hank!" She looked at him happily.

"THAT'S A FINE IDEA, MARY KATE!" Uncle Hank boomed, startling the baby. He put a finger to his lips and whispered, "We'll go tomorrow. First thing!" He scratched his head, remembering something. "No, scratch that. I promised Edith Fisher I'd get her broke-down buggy back to her. Saturday, then. Crack of dawn! We'll take Menno's little one too. Can't start him out too early."

"I can't go Saturday," M.K. said glumly. "I've got community service with that horrible—"

Sadie pointed a finger at her to shut off the flow of words. "Don't start on a list of complaints about Jimmy Fisher. We already know everything."

Uncle Hank kissed the top of M.K.'s head. "I'll make you a deal. I'll help you and Jimmy out on Saturday. Then, if there's time, we'll do some sunset fishing."

Will laughed and Sadie felt herself relax even more around him. He rose to his feet to get ready to go and she was surprised by a tweak of disappointment. Except for those brief times when she thought she saw a sadness flit through his eyes, his heart seemed as light as the breeze, with an ability to absorb all that went on around him and take it all in stride.

So unlike Gideon. It wasn't right to compare Will to Gideon. Comparing a Plain man to an English man was like comparing apples to oranges, deserts to oceans, elephants to lions. But everything felt so serious with Gid. So awkward. But then, she was awkward too. Maybe that was the problem. Maybe they were too much alike. In her mind flashed a vision: she and Gid at a table, surrounded by awkward children. An entire awkward family. She shook her head to clear it of that image. Since when had she ever given serious thought to marrying Gideon Smucker? No! Never! But maybe someday.

Will picked up his cowboy hat and fit it on his head. "Well, Sadie, if you need me to rescue you in the future, just give a holler. I'm right over the hill."

Sadie put one hand up close to her face and gave a tiny slow wave like a shy child. His impish grin put a twist in her heart, and her face tingled with warmth.

12

It was funny what Mary Kate Lapp could do for a room. She burst into Twin Creeks Schoolhouse on a gray, misty Tuesday morning and lit it up. The room was actually brighter when she came inside, Gid thought. It sparkled. She sparkled.

She held out a plate of warm doughnuts, drizzled with chocolate. "I wondered if you've already had any breakfast. You haven't, have you?" M.K. looked at him longingly, with the transparent plea written all over her face: Please say you didn't, that you're famished and were just this minute wishing for some homemade doughnuts.

"Well, I did have a little something," Gid said. "But not enough to satisfy my appetite," he hurried to add when her eyes clouded. Her face crinkled with delight, and she held the plate out farther.

"They're still warmish," M.K. said. "They've been setting on top of the stove."

"I'm sure they'll be good . . . thanks."

"I made them myself. I woke up really early this morning and was just waiting around for something to do."

167

Gid doubted that. Mary Kate kept herself busy. She had more inner resources than any twelve-year-old needed.

"Fern says I need more on my mind so she's trying to turn me into a crackerjack baker. The doughnuts are best with coffee, Uncle Hank said, and he would know because he ate seven this morning—do you have any? Coffee, I mean?" M.K.'s eyes darted to his desk.

"I'm not a coffee drinker. I'm sure the doughnuts will be . . . well, just fine without it . . . the way they are. Thanks."

Gid didn't know what to say, though it didn't seem to matter because Mary Kate was blessed with the gift of conversation. The doughnuts did look good—golden and fried, with just the right amount of chocolate. Though, Gid had to admit, you could never have enough chocolate.

"Go on, taste one," she said, and as he bit into one, her eyebrows scrunched together, and her face tightened.

He nodded his head and smiled. "It's good," he said, talking around the mouthful of chewy, sweet cake. "Very good. It's delicious."

"See? See there? Aren't they good? The best I've ever made." And she clapped her hands together as she laughed.

Then it grew quiet. Gid knew her well enough to know there was something else on her mind. M.K. covered the plate with the foil and set it on his desk. "Well, I might as well just tell you. You'll hear about it soon enough."

This was going to be about Sadie. Gid's stomach twisted. The bite of doughnut in his mouth suddenly tasted flat, gummy, like he would have trouble swallowing it. He set down the uneaten half. "Something's happened."

M.K. told him about last night's revelatory goings-on,

blow by blow, not leaving out a single detail. The longer he listened, the worse Gid felt. As he heard about Will scooping Sadie up in his arms when she fainted—and of course, M.K. had to act that part out with a dramatic flair, swaying like a poplar tree—he had an irrational flash of jealousy in which he imagined himself running that bird sitter out of town, or slinging him into outer space with a large wooden catapult. Just thinking about it felt pretty good. Almost as good as doing it.

For a second he felt guilty as he remembered one of the bishop's sermons about sin and how if a person thought about doing something wrong in his heart it was the same as doing it. But wasn't he talking about big things like murder and adultery? And wouldn't it be good for everybody if the bird sitter were to pack up and head off to wherever it was he belonged?

And then came the shocker. He swallowed and stared at M.K. "This baby . . . you're telling me this is . . . *Menno's* baby? Annie and Menno's?"

"Sadie's pretty confident of that fact. And I don't think my sister is the type to jump to conclusions."

M.K. looked at Gid in pure innocence, but the words she spoke cut him to the core. No, Sadie wouldn't jump to conclusions the way he had, the way others had. It hit him like a right cross, then—why Sadie told him that if he really trusted her, he would never have needed to ask her such a question.

Stupid, stupid, stupid! A large splinter of guilt wedged into his heart. Sadie had hurt him; in return, he'd hurt her. He had wounded the very person he had tried to protect.

The doughnut that he ate felt like lead in his stomach. No

wonder Sadie wouldn't even look at him at church on Sunday. He was the worst person on earth.

As the baby slept, Sadie went into the kitchen to blend some herbs into a remedy that could be brewed as a kind of tea. It was a mixture to break up colds that Deborah had taught her to make: ground ginger and cayenne pepper. A pinch of that, added to a mug of hot water, apple cider vinegar, and honey, sipped throughout the day, could shorten a cold's duration. Sadie sneezed twice as she stirred the mixture. Just sniffing it, she thought, could clear the sinuses. An added benefit to the remedy!

Uncle Hank burst into the kitchen, hopping on one foot. "SADIE! I need your help! I'M DYING! Every move is a misery to me!" He sat on a chair and thrust a bare foot on the table. Sadie went over to see what was causing him such misery and saw a thorn in his leathery heel, imbedded deeply. The area around the thorn was swollen, red, and angry. "How long has this been bothering you?" she asked.

"DAYS! MAYBE WEEKS!"

"Well, why didn't you . . ." She shook her head. "Never mind. I know just how to help." She hurried to the refrigerator, took out some carrots, and grated them into a bowl. She put a towel under Uncle Hank's foot, then applied the grated carrots to the area around the thorn. "You just wait awhile. You'll see. It'll draw the thorn right out." Hopefully, she thought, before Fern came inside and saw Uncle Hank with his foot on the kitchen table. Fern's patience for Uncle Hank always hung by a thread.

Too late. The door squeaked open. Fern's eyes narrowed. "Hank Lapp. You get that dirty foot of yours off my clean table!"

"NOSIR! IT IS AN EMERGENCY!" Uncle Hank roared. "Sadie's doctoring me. We're considering amputation."

While Hank was sputtering away with Fern, Sadie found the tweezers in the medicine box. She brought a warm, wet rag to the table and wiped the carrots away from the thorn. The carrots drew the thorn out and Sadie was easily able to pull it out with the tweezers. She held up the tweezers. "Voilà!"

Uncle Hank turned away from complaining to Fern and looked at Sadie, wide-eyed. He wiggled his toes. "SHE'S A MIRACLE WORKER! First, she cures Ira Smucker of hay fever—"

"Actually," Sadie said, "the rain we had last week cleared out the pollen in the air."

"—and next, she has saved my foot from gangrene! SHE'S GOT THE TOUCH!"

"Not hardly," Sadie said, cleaning up the mess of the carrots. "It was just a thorn in your foot."

"Could've saved yourself a heap of trouble in the first place by wearing shoes," Fern pointed out.

Uncle Hank paid them both no mind. He prided himself on his ability to share news of marvels and curiosities and other odd bits of news that might be of interest to folks. Word of Sadie's healing abilities spread rapidly throughout Stoney Ridge. People came to think Sadie could cure anything and she didn't know how to tell them different.

Uncle Hank said she should hang out a shingle to advertise her healing work, but she didn't. She wouldn't even take any money for helping. That way folks couldn't get mad at her if the remedies didn't work or made them even sicker. That happened once, last fall, when she gave Edith Fisher the wrong remedy. Edith had sent a note to Sadie via Jimmy via M.K., asking for a laxative. At least, that's what it looked like, in Edith's spidery handwriting. So Sadie sent over some slippery elm. It turned out Edith wanted something for insomnia. Edith had to miss church the next day, for obvious reasons, and wouldn't let Sadie forget it.

Gid loped into the kitchen on Saturday morning, freshly showered. His sister, Alice, was taking a batch of corn muffins out of the oven—a complicated thing to do when a person relied on crutches. But at least she was out of the wheelchair and her broken legs were healing and she wasn't grumbling about Mary Kate Lapp quite as regularly as she had been. Amos Lapp had offered to send M.K. over to Goat Roper Hill on Saturdays while Alice recovered from her injuries—a kind of penance—but Alice wouldn't hear of it. After teaching school for seven years with Mary Kate Lapp as a student, Alice was convinced that any interaction with her translated to steady trouble. She was convinced she would end up in a body cast. "She's about as bad as a boy for devilment, with a spark in her eye for warning," she had told Gid more than once. Dozens of times.

Gid thought Alice was slightly paranoid. Personally, he liked the spark in M.K.'s eyes. She was his favorite scholar, and not just because she was Sadie's sister. She was as bright as they come and had the best of intentions, though she rarely thought before she acted. His sister had no appreciation for M.K.'s zest for life. In fact, she was suspicious of it.

Alice had an acute sense of doom and disaster. She even kept a shoe box filled with newspaper clippings of house fires and buggy accidents. Just in case, she always said, if anyone asked why she kept them. And that's when his father would quietly mutter, "And we wonder why she's still unmarried."

Gid took a corn muffin, broke it open, and breathed in the steam. "Mmmm, good," he said, mumbling, and grabbed another. He hopped on the counter, expecting Alice to swat him away, but she didn't seem to mind his company.

"Any improvement in the Sadie Lapp department?"

Gid practically choked on the muffin. Alice pounded on his back.

"I guess not," she said dryly.

Gid swallowed, coughed again. "She's still pretty mad."

"Well, what would you expect, Gid? You assumed the worst about her. A woman doesn't get over that kind of hurt and humiliation easily."

Gid didn't think that now was the time to point out that it was Alice who had told him the baby was Sadie's in the first place. "She's not even talking to me. How can I get her to listen to my apology?"

Alice sighed. "Are you absolutely sure you want to court Sadie Lapp? You know those Lapps are—"

"Alice." Gid's voice held a warning tone. This conversation wasn't a new one.

"Fine. I do happen to have an idea." As she told him about it, he gave her a skeptical look.

"You're sure that Sadie would like that?"

"You can count on it. Jay Glick asked Susie Hostetler to marry him in that very way. The girls are still talking about it. Girls love that kind of thing."

Gid wasn't as confident as Alice, but he had to try something. Twice this week, he had stopped by Windmill Farm in the night and shined his flashlight on Sadie's window. She had ignored it and he had left, defeated. Alice's plan might just work.

Gid stopped by The Sweet Tooth bakery and picked out pink petit fours—tiny little cakes covered with smooth icing. He asked the owner's granddaughter, Nora Stroot, if she would pipe a letter in icing on each petit four—he described it just the way Alice had told him to. Then Nora Stroot told him that would cost an extra fifty cents per letter and Gid gulped. Resigned, he pulled out his money. "Okay. Here are the words I want:

I ♡ U
MEA CULPA

"That's only eleven cakes," Nora Stroot said. "You're paying for a baker's dozen whether you get them or not. But I'll still charge you for the piping."

Gid bit his lip. "Then make it 'Y-O-U.'"

"What does 'mea culpa' mean?"

"It's Latin for 'my mistake.'"

Nora Stroot raised a pencil-drawn eyebrow. "Sure she'll figure *that* out?"

"Absolutely." Wouldn't she? Mary Kate certainly knew it. Of course, Sadie would know it too.

"You must have done something incredibly idiotic." She

waited for Gid to elaborate on his stupidity, but he stood there in stony silence. She sighed, giving up, and turned away to write the letters in white icing on the petit fours, set them in a pink box, wrapped it with a ribbon, and handed it to him. "That will be twenty-five dollars."

Gid swallowed. "Thank you."

He took the bakery box right over to Windmill Farm and knocked on the kitchen door, but no one was at home. The door was unlocked, so Gid thought it would be wise to leave the box of petit fours on the kitchen table so they wouldn't melt in the sun. He saw that someone had left some sandwiches on the table, covered with plastic wrap. He pulled the ribbon off the box and opened it, then grabbed a pen off the kitchen counter and wrote on the top of the box: *To Sadie from Gideon*. Just so there was no mistaking who had brought these little cakes.

He hoped Alice was right about this. He had started to doubt her advice on the ride home from the bakery. What did Alice know about courting, anyway? She had never had a boyfriend. Maybe he should just take the little cakes and go home.

Suddenly, he heard a baby's cry upstairs, then Sadie's voice soothing the baby. She was home! Panic streaked through him. Before he left, he turned the pink box around, lid open, so that she would see it as she came down the steps into the kitchen. He looked at the pink box again, straightened each lettered petit four so it would read just right, took a deep breath, and hurried to leave. Quietly.

This past week, Amos seemed to be feeling more like his old self. He still went about his farm chores slowly and methodically, but he was starting to feel the old bounce in his step. He couldn't even remember when he had last felt a bounce in his step. Why, it had been years!

Amos and Will had spent the last few mornings out in the fruit orchards, trimming dead branches, and moving M.K.'s hives from one orchard to another so the bees could work their magic. Amos's muscles ached from the hard work—a wonderful ache. Will didn't know much about farming, but he was an able and willing worker. He liked to talk too. He asked all kinds of questions about the birds on Windmill Farm and that always seemed to lead to Menno and his birding. Will had a keen interest in birds, all kinds, and Amos was happy to oblige him. Talking about Menno like this, in this way, felt like a healing balm to his soul. Each time they talked, Amos felt the knot in his chest release a little more.

It was past noon and they were famished. At breakfast this morning, Sadie had said she would run lunch out to them after the baby woke up from his nap since Fern was at a quilting frolic, but Amos didn't think they could wait much longer. "Will, if you wouldn't mind running back to the house, Fern left lunch for us on the table. And some iced tea in the fridge."

Happily, Will dropped his gloves and started up the hill. "Bring something sweet too!" Amos called out. As long as Fern wasn't there to monitor his low-fat, heart-healthy diet, he might as well go for broke.

Will stomped off his dirty shoes and walked into the kitchen. The house was quiet except for the sound of water splashing upstairs. Fern was gone, so maybe Sadie was giving the baby a bath. He was a little surprised to find himself hoping to see Sadie for a minute. Or two.

"Your dad sent me to get lunch," he called up the stairs. "He wants to eat now."

"It's on the table," came Sadie's muffled reply. "You can take everything."

He washed his hands at the kitchen sink and filled the cups on a tray with iced tea from the fridge. On the table were a plate full of sandwiches, a bowl of fruit, and a pink bakery box. He put the plate and a couple apples on the tray, then reached across the table to grab the pink box. On top he saw words scrawled: "To Sadie from Gideon." He rolled his eyes. If Sadie didn't want the pink box, then it was clear to Will she had no interest in that hapless schoolteacher.

Will piled the box on the tray, but it slipped and fell to the floor. Will set the tray down. He knelt to open the box and found little cakes, all topsy turvy. Girly cakes! His mother used to serve those petit fours when she had friends over to play bridge. To Will, it was one more piece of evidence that there was something *wrong* with that schoolteacher. He popped a cake into his mouth, then another. Delicious! Will tucked as many cakes as he could on the sandwich plate. He set the pink box on the table. "Thanks for the sweets," he called up the stairs to Sadie. "I took as many as I could and left the rest."

He strained to listen, hoping Sadie might come down to say hello. But he could still hear water splashing upstairs, so he flipped the lid onto the box, picked up the tray, and headed out the door. Amos would get a kick out of those little girly cakes for dessert.

Sadie couldn't believe that a baby could make so much work out of such a little task. She had started to change Joe-Jo's diaper and reached down to get a new one as he released a spray that covered Sadie, her dress, her hair and prayer cap, his own undershirt, the floor, the bureau top. What hadn't been sprayed? She gave the baby a bath, diapered and dressed him—was it the fourth time this morning?—set him in the basket, and stuck her own head under the sink faucet to wash her hair as she heard Will's voice calling from the kitchen. He had come to the house to pick up lunch.

Fern had fixed sandwiches before she left for the frolic. It was good timing to have Will stop in so he could carry everything out, because she didn't know how she would manage juggling the baby and the sandwich tray and the iced tea. She tried to hurry as she rinsed shampoo out of her hair so she could join Will downstairs, but the next thing she knew, he called to say he was leaving, and something about how sweet it was to have things ready on the table.

Wasn't he wonderful to notice?

Five minutes later, Sadie's hair was towel-dried, a fresh cap pinned on, and she was in a clean dress. She took one more look in the mirror that hung on the bathroom wall. She wished so much to be tall and slim that she almost hoped to see a tall, slim girl. But in the glass she saw a small, round girl in a blue dress. Even the face in the mirror was round. Her chin had a soft curve, and her nose was almost right, but her eyes were too far apart, and they didn't sparkle. They didn't sparkle at all. At least her hair wasn't such a bad color. Once, after church, Gideon had told her that the sunlight beamed on her hair and it looked golden. She tipped her head to see if the sun from the window bounced off it. Was it golden-y? Suddenly Sadie realized that if anyone saw her preening in the mirror right now, they would think she was vain! She picked up the baby and went downstairs, stopping abruptly when she saw a pink bakery box. On top it said "To Sadie from Gideon." Inside the box were four little cockeyed tiny cakes. U-L-I-E. Huh? What did Ulie mean? What was Gid trying to say? Then she gasped. You lie.

Tears filled Sadie's eyes. How cruel! How insensitive. How downright *mean*. What was wrong with Gideon Smucker? How dare he accuse her of lying! Then anger swooped in and displaced her hurt feelings. She picked up the box to throw it in the garbage, but thought twice. She might as well eat the little cakes. They did look delicious, even if the message was unspeakably rude. *Then* she would throw the box away.

And she would never, ever speak to Gideon Smucker again.

Will had lied to Mr. Petosky. On Sunday, Eve had laid one egg. He had observed her standing in or near the nest, guarding the egg. Will knew she would lay another egg or two before incubation would begin. On Monday morning, when Mr. Petosky called, there were two more eggs. And this morning, there were four eggs in the dug-out scape.

He had climbed a tree to see the eggs. The eggs were slightly smaller than a chicken egg, mottled with a dark, reddish-brown pigment. Eve would begin incubation now for the next thirty-three days. Once it began, Eve would sit on the nest and rarely leave the eggs unattended. Adam would give her brief reprieves so she could fly off and hunt for food.

And then the eyases would only stay in the nest another four to six weeks before they tried to fledge.

He was going to have to tell Mr. Petosky the news soon. There looked to be four viable eggs in the scape. He just wasn't quite ready to have Mr. Petosky breathing down his neck. He needed time to think. He was pretty sure Mr. Petosky would find a way to confirm Will's findings.

All kinds of things could happen to these eggs. Often, there could be "egg failure." The female would push an egg that has failed to the side of the scape. If an entire clutch was lost, the female may attempt to re-nest several weeks later, often in a different location.

"Nice view up there?"

Will looked down the tree to find Sadie peering up at him. He shimmied down the trunk and hopped off as he neared the end.

She tilted her head when he smiled at her. "Are you all right?"

"Most of the redness is gone." Will wriggled his fingers at Sadie. "The skin isn't as taut as it was before, and the blisters don't appear to be anything that will last more than a day or two."

"I didn't mean your hands, but I'm glad they're doing better." She crossed her arms behind her and leaned her back against the tree. "You had a strange look on your face."

"Me?" Will said, looking straight at Sadie. "Strange? Stranger than normal?"

Sadie smiled, then shook her head slowly. "Don't mind me. Every now and then, I just get this odd feeling that you're carrying around something heavy. But then, the feeling passes and you seem right as rain. Better than rain." She paused. "I might be wrong. Maybe you're not sad or confused about something at all. Maybe I'm imagining things. I've been known to do that."

She wasn't wrong. In fact, she couldn't be any more right. He was sure she had all manners of herbs and remedies for everything else, but what could you do about what was bothering him? He doubted she had herbs for a guilty conscience. Or a concoction for soul sickness.

What was wrong with him—what made him do the things he knew he shouldn't do and what kept him from doing the things he should? Maybe his father was right. Maybe he did have a demon inside him. "My father would say I am suffering from acute laziness."

"What does your father do for a living?"

"He's a neurosurgeon."

She looked puzzled. "What's that?"

"He operates on people's brains."

"So he drills holes in people's skulls?"

"Well, not really. He specializes in endovascular work— the vessels that bring blood to the brain. A lot of problems in the brain occur in those arteries and veins, but there's all kinds of technology that allows him to treat them without drilling open the skull. Much less invasive. No cutting bones or opening someone's head. But endovascular neurosurgery is the most dangerous of all the specialties of neurosurgery. Most of the people he sees have run out of options. They're either going to die, or my dad will operate and save them."

"He must be a smart man. It's hard to imagine having the courage to operate on a brain."

"Dad says the brain is like a melon, with a thick, leathery covering inside the skull—the dura mater—that gets pulled back and the glistening surface of the brain is exposed. He says it's like putting on a diving mask and looking beneath the surface of the water at a coral reef: a whole new world opens up."

Sadie shuddered. "He has such a responsibility. What if he made a mistake?"

"I don't think my father makes mistakes." Will scratched his head. "Ever. He's pretty confident that he's the best neurosurgeon in the country."

"What makes him so sure of that?"

"Everybody tells him so. Other doctors send their toughest cases to him. From all over the country."

She gave him a shy smile. "I can't imagine having that kind of confidence."

"Sadie," Will said, "if you had the kind of self-confidence my father has, you wouldn't be you." He shifted his gaze to a flock of ducks coming in for a landing near the creek. "You wouldn't even be someone you'd like."

Sadie rose and walked down the bank to the creek. He watched her from afar. He noticed a curious stillness about her. She was, at her center, as tranquil as Blue Lake Pond on a windless night. Just being near her had a calming effect. He discovered he was in no hurry to be elsewhere, that his normally impatient, easily bored nature somehow found the patience to stand back and just be.

You're good for me, Sadie Lapp.

For the briefest of moments, Will entertained a fantasy—that he and Sadie were together like this, really together. Caring for a small farm, raising a family.

He chased the fantasy away, swatting it as if it were a mosquito about to bite. He and Sadie Lapp belonged in different worlds. She wasn't his type, much as he wanted her to be.

As he noticed how absorbed she was by the nature around her, it seemed as if she were no mere observer of the world but right in the middle of it. He'd wondered if she knew there was something special about her. Probably not.

Will walked down to join her. There were six ducks, honking and rustling about in the creek. Sounding remarkably similar to last Sunday's long-winded Amish preacher, she called out, "Troubles are often the tools by which God fashions us for better things!"

Blank stares from every last one of those ducks. She sighed. "I'm practicing my newly acquired boldness on them. It doesn't seem to be working."

"Don't take it to heart," Will said with a grin. "My guess is they just haven't been to church lately."

— 13 —

For the first time in her life, M.K. could not imagine life without school and books. She had only one more year of formal schooling ahead of her. After that, it would just be one endless day of chores after another. She was already worried that crotchety Alice Smucker would come back next year and Gid would return to full-time farming with his father. She thought he preferred teaching to farming, though he would never say so. Gid was private about his feelings. He was a first-rate teacher, the best. The very best.

M.K. had always annoyed Alice when she finished her work early and grew bored. Alice would tell her to redo her work for the practice. By contrast, Gid stayed late in the day so that he could give her new assignments the next morning. He always had something new for her to puzzle out and she loved the challenges. Shakespeare for studying the beauty of language, Galileo to read the mystery in the night sky. She had learned the names of all the stars and constellations. She was struggling a little with geometry—she preferred algebra. But today, Gid corrected her paper and handed it back to her with a smile. "You're getting there."

When Gid smiled, his dimples deepened and his eyes shimmered with satisfaction. M.K. had trouble concentrating after getting one of his smiles.

Sometimes, she would stay after class and help him clean up, chattering away about a piece of poetry she had read or an essay, and he would listen carefully. He commented now and then on her thoughts, offered her some suggestions of different poets, and even brought in a book of beginning Latin for her—to help understand the roots of words, he said. He never patronized her, not once.

She watched him work with the second-grade class. He was so handsome! It was a tragedy that Sadie refused to fall madly in love with him. It would be sheer heaven to have Gid as a brother-in-law. She would get to see him every day for the rest of her life. Maybe she could live with them! She planned to never marry because she thought all boys—except for Gid and her father and Uncle Hank—were short on brains and long on foolishness. She had no patience for them.

Gid was playing a game with the second graders—at least, they thought it was a game. It was a clever way to encourage reading comprehension. The three second graders had all read a short story and Gid was quizzing them on details in the story. Each time they answered correctly, they took a giant step closer to the blackboard.

That was what made Gid so remarkable—he was always thinking up ways to make learning interesting. Not too long ago, he had a "100 Days of School" celebration. Everyone brought a collection of one hundred items. Most of the kids brought in pennies or marbles—pretty dull stuff. M.K. brought in one hundred two-week-old chicks. It was great fun until the chicks pecked through the boxes and escaped, scattering around the room. Then Ruthie sat on one and that got her all bug-eyed and tearful. After Davy Mast called her a chicken killer, she couldn't stop crying. She sniffed and sobbed all afternoon until finally Gid sent her home, along with M.K. and her boxes of ninety-nine chicks. M.K. sighed, thinking back on that day. Like many of her plans, this one went awry.

She noticed that Gid dismissed the second graders and brought up the third graders. Now, why couldn't Alice Smucker have ever thought of ways to make school fun? Except for the occasional mischief of Jimmy Fisher and his cohorts, every day with Alice Smucker was identical to the day before. Last fall, as the new school year started, it was almost—though not quite—a letdown that Jimmy had finally graduated eighth grade and was no longer in school.

Almost. But not quite.

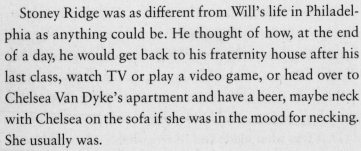

Stoney Ridge was as different from Will's life in Philadelphia as anything could be. He thought of how, at the end of a day, he would get back to his fraternity house after his last class, watch TV or play a video game, or head over to Chelsea Van Dyke's apartment and have a beer, maybe neck with Chelsea on the sofa if she was in the mood for necking. She usually was.

Here, on this Amish farm, he was working himself to the bone. Each night, he trudged back to the cottage and flopped on the bed, exhausted. The next thing he knew, birdsong was welcoming the new dawn. When he heard the sweet music of the birds, a smile creased his face.

Will considered himself to be a closet birder. He never let anyone in his college fraternity, or any girlfriend for that matter, know how he loved birds and spent vacations on bird-watching expeditions. If he were to hunt birds, his friends would admire him. But observe them? Study them? It would be laughingstock, fodder for ridicule.

Bird-watching was the one activity he and his father enjoyed together. Dr. Charles William Stoltz could identify each and every type of the enormous variety of fowl that migrated through southeast Pennsylvania. He was a truly dedicated birder. The birds were proof in some way that Will's father did have a tender side. Most of their good moments together were spent taking long walks through the woods with binoculars hanging around their necks, thumbing through field manuals. Beyond that, Will's study of them gave them something to talk about. His father preferred taking him along on bird-ing expeditions rather than any of his brainy bird-watching doctor friends. Will was quieter, he said.

It was the only compliment his father had ever given him. And Will wasn't really sure it was a compliment. He was quiet around his father because he was thoroughly intimi-dated by him.

Briefly, he thought about wanting to tell his father what Amos had said to him this morning. Amos had pointed out the field he wanted Will to plow under but instructed him to leave the far corner alone because the bobolinks were nesting. "They earn their rent by giving us pleasure," Amos had told him. His father would enjoy that kind of thinking.

Even though the spring morning was raw and bleak, awash in gray, Will was hot. He wiped the sweat from his brow and sat back on the plow, admiring the morning's work. He thought his plowing skills were improving. The furrows in this field weren't quite as wobbly looking as yesterday's, and much better than the day before. He was faster too, which suited him, because he was pretty sure he had felt some rain sprinkles. From the looks of those clouds, he wouldn't be surprised if a drizzle turned into a steady rain.

For now, he needed food. He thought about what he could scrounge up in the cottage when he saw Sadie wave to him from the fence, near the water trough. He led the horses over to the water trough and let them drink their fill. Doozy was chasing imaginary birds on the other side of the fence. He worried about that dog.

Sadie gave him a shy smile and lifted a basket. "I brought lunch."

"Ah! You're an angel."

"Better eat it first, then decide. Dad and Fern took the baby with them to go visit Annie's grandfather—to let him know to expect some help on Saturday. So I made lunch."

Will splashed his hands in the horse trough and hopped over the fence. Sadie was already setting up a picnic under a shade tree. He sprawled on the ground and let out a deep sigh.

She handed him a sandwich. "When will your falcons become parents?"

Will unwrapped the sandwich and took a lusty bite. How was it possible that food tasted better here? This sandwich he was eating, for example. The bread was homemade, the smoked turkey was real turkey, the lettuce was crisp, the tomato ripe. Delicious! "In about a month. Hopefully, they will be good parents too." He glanced at her. "That's not always the case." Not with animals, not with people. Certainly Sadie couldn't understand that, for she'd come from a family where warmth and belonging and love were like flour and sugar, staples in the pantry.

She threw a crust of bread over to Doozy, who pounced on it like a cat. "God seems to give most animals a basic instinct of how to care for their young. I've always thought it's another way he shows us how he loves us."

"Parents—" He stopped, and felt his stomach twist. "I hope God loves us more than parents do. If he doesn't, I'm doomed."

"Your parents weren't loving?" she asked tentatively.

He emitted a bark, humorless mirth. "Not exactly." Love, in Will's family, had always come with strings. It was a reward for perfect behavior. It wasn't handed out for free.

"Some people have a hard time showing love to the ones they care the most about."

He gave her an odd stare. "Do you always see the world this way?"

Sadie reached in the basket and handed him a bright green apple. "What way is that?"

"Always looking for the good in a situation." He took a bite of the apple and chewed. "I can't think of too many girls who would be happy to have a baby dropped in their laps."

"This wasn't just any baby. But this baby—this one is a gift to us. It connects us to Menno." She looked up at the sky. "I think God knew my family needed this baby."

"Life isn't always that way, you know. Some things just don't work out for the best." He took a few more bites of his apple and tossed the core away. Then he tilted the thermos to his mouth and drained it. He felt better now, much better. "The way I see it, I think it's better not to expect too much out of life. That way, you don't get beaten down or disappointed by people. It's better to meet life head-on, eyes wide open, so you're not blindsided in the end. Cut off. Left to drift in a canoe without paddles." The last sentence tumbled with a ridiculous amount of emotion. He pressed his fingertips to his forehead and closed his eyes, embarrassed. They had drifted way too far into personal issues, and he thought he might be making an idiot of himself.

"The Bible says that for those who love God, things will work out for the best. Like the way the baby worked out to be the best." She glanced at him. "Don't you believe in God's goodness?"

They locked eyes.

"I believe in you, Sadie Lapp, and your goodness." He'd only known her for a week now, but he could tell she was a genuinely kind, genuinely good person.

"But I'm not, Will. No one is truly good. We're all on the same level in God's sight. We're all sinners in need of his mercy. But the amazing thing is that God loves us anyway. And he can straighten us out and smooth out all the wrinkles and put us to use again."

Will opened his mouth but nothing came out. He was seized with a sudden curiosity about Sadie. What would she have been like as a child? What did she want her life to look like in five years? In ten or twenty? There was so much about her that he didn't know. He raised her hand and impulsively pressed a soft kiss on the back of it. "Thank you for lunch." He jumped up and hopped over the fence to get back to work. Before he climbed back on the plow, he tipped his cowboy hat to her and grinned.

The week dragged by interminably—but finally it was Saturday. M.K. charged into the kitchen, her very being radiating sparks of excitement. She had a plan all worked out for today. The most brilliant plan she had ever come up with! She knew Fern wondered why she was so especially cheerful, but she would have to wait to find out.

Edith Fisher and her son Jimmy pulled up to the house at eight o'clock sharp, as expected. Uncle Hank and M.K. were waiting for them, arms filled with tools and gloves and hampers filled with groceries. From the backseat of the buggy, M.K. directed Jimmy to drive to a tired-looking house on a tired-looking lane. She hadn't been there since before Menno had passed, and it had looked bad then. Knee-high weeds filled the front yard. Spiderwebs hung from every corner. The old man was sitting in his rocker on the front porch, like he had been expecting them. Then she remembered that he might be, since her father and Fern had dropped by earlier in the week to let him know they were coming today. Fern had taken him a casserole and come home clucking with disapproval that an elderly Amish man was living alone. "What is the world coming to if the Amish aren't caring for their own?" she muttered all afternoon.

M.K. would never say it aloud, but sometimes she thought that Fern sounded downright prideful about being Amish, as if they could do no wrong, unlike the English, who could do no right. Such thoughts were best left unsaid, she decided, and felt that it was a sign she was growing up. She was starting to have a filter—just like Fern always said she needed—and it amused M.K. that the filter was being used for Fern!

When the Swartzentruber colony decided to up and move to Ohio, Annie and her grandfather stayed behind. Amos thought it might have had something to do with the baby's arrival, though Fern chimed in that she was pretty sure Annie had taken pains to hide her pregnancy. There weren't many signs of a baby in that house, she pointed out. "Certainly no signs that a baby was going to be staying."

Amos said he had tried to encourage Annie's grandfather to join up with the Ohio colony, but he refused to leave. He was just waiting and waiting for Annie to return.

Annie's grandfather was really old. So old that the skin on his neck moved up and down like a turkey wattle as he swallowed hard. So old that the veins on his hands stood out like large, blue hoses. When he noticed M.K., he squinted so hard that his forehead knotted up. "ANNIE?"

"No, I'm Mary Kate. MARY KATE LAPP."

The old man crumpled. She nearly fibbed and said she was Annie after the old man looked so disappointed. But Uncle Hank read her mind and elbowed her, nodding his head toward Edith and Jimmy to fob her off. It wouldn't be right to lie, not with Edith Fisher standing right next to her with her can-and-string telephone line, direct to heaven. M.K. didn't think God would mind a little white lie to make an old man happy, but Edith Fisher would think otherwise.

They walked inside the house and found it was worse than

the outside. The kitchen was a wreck—crusty pans in the sink, a sticky floor that needed a good scrub. Smelled bad too, an acrid smell that was worse than Joe-Jo's diapers. They went out to the backyard and couldn't even see the path to the barn, the weeds were so tall. Leaning against the barn was an old buggy—a black top without the reflective triangle on the back—belonging to a Swartzentruber.

"Where do we even begin?" Jimmy said under his breath.

M.K. had no idea.

Off in the distance, M.K. heard the sound of an arriving horse and buggy. Then another, and another. She rushed to the front. It had worked! Yesterday, she had quietly invited all of her friends and neighbors to come to help.

"What is—" Jimmy started to say as he came up behind her and saw the lane crowded with buggies.

"What is going on?" was what he was going to say, M.K. thought, oozing smugness. During Friday lunch, she had one of her brainstorms. It was a bolt from the blue, and not a minute too soon. She felt very proud of herself for coming up with the idea, even though she was a little disappointed that it had taken her so long to think of it. "I invited them. Thirty-three of them." She turned to him. "I figured that if we have to give up thirty-five hours, it would be more efficient if thirty-five people gave up one hour. Then we'd be done with this community service nonsense and I can have my Saturdays back for fishing with Uncle Hank."

Even Jimmy Fisher couldn't hold back a grin of admiration on his handsome face. "Bischt net so dumm wie du guckscht." *You're not as dumb as you look.* "Think it'll work?"

M.K. looked up at him. "Absolutely!"

"Graeh net zu gschwind," said a familiar voice from behind her. *Don't crow too soon.*

The wind went out of Mary Kate.

Fern! So meddlesome!

Jimmy started laughing so hard at M.K. that he had to double over.

Combining double bossy powers between Fern and Edith Fisher, folks were organized in groups of two or three and given tasks to complete. M.K.'s plans for the day fizzled as she finished a task and was given another one, again and again. And again.

By midafternoon, the work crew had made a serious dent in the transformation of Annie's grandfather's house, inside and out. There was food in the cleaned-out refrigerator, fresh linens were put on his bed, rugs were beaten, floors swept and wiped down, windows washed. Outside, the weeds had been mowed. Fern had even brought some potted flowers for his porch. "To cheer him up," she said, "while he waits for Annie."

"She's never coming back," M.K. said. "She gave us that baby because she's never coming back."

"You can't be so sure of that," Fern told her. "A mother has mighty strong feelings for her baby."

"Not so strong that they stopped her from abandoning the baby," M.K. said.

"She didn't really abandon him," Fern said. "She put him in Sadie's care for safekeeping. She must have been awfully scared and overwhelmed."

"Then she should have just married someone."

"Marriage isn't always a solution to a problem." Fern

smoothed some stray hairs off of M.K.'s forehead. "Things in this world aren't always so white and black." She picked up a broom and a pail filled with dirty rags and headed out to the porch.

"Well, at least we have Annie's grandfather set up so he'll be all right by himself," M.K. said hopefully.

Fern eyed her over her shoulder. "We have him set up so that you and Jimmy can come each Saturday and keep up with the housework and bring him fresh food." Out loud, she subtracted seven from thirty-five. "Let's see. Just four more Saturdays."

"That many?" M.K. asked in a puny voice.

Fern wasn't listening. "Don't you agree, Hank?"

Uncle Hank was helping Annie's grandfather into his chair on the porch where he liked to sit and watch the world go by—not that much of the world was going by this little dirt lane. He lifted up the old man's feet and placed them on a pillow. "You betcha! I might even come with you two next Saturday. I'll bring my checkers."

Annie's grandfather brightened at that thought. But it worried M.K. Since when did Uncle Hank volunteer for work? Ordinarily, he woke early and tinkered with a few buggies that were sitting in his buggy shop, since he was up at that hour anyway. But then he figured he'd done his day's chores and off he'd go to fish at Blue Lake Pond.

"What would you say to that, Edith? You coming too?" Uncle Hank looked over at Edith and winked, which flustered her. Edith Fisher never flustered.

Edith looked away, and her hand crept up to the knot of hair on her neck. "We'll see." A rosy blush crept over her face.

Their eyes met.

M.K. and Jimmy exchanged a dark glance, a rare moment when they saw life from the same vantage point.

What was happening to the world? Everything was upside down.

— 14 —

Weeks passed, and life at Windmill Farm fell into a routine. With the weather growing hotter and more humid, the family tried to rise early in the morning and do chores before the worst of the day. The baby slept for longer stretches now and was putting on weight. Now and then, he would have a colicky day, but the goat's milk had helped considerably.

Sadie loved the baby's soft, round cheeks best of all. She couldn't stop kissing those fat cheeks. She wondered how long it took for a baby to become yours, for love and familiarity to set like mortar in bricks. Maybe that was the process described as bonding: knowing a child so well you knew him as well as you knew yourself.

As she cradled Joe-Jo in her arms, she thought about her neighbor Mattie Riehl, who had been a foster mother for a baby girl and had hoped to adopt her, but then the birth mother changed her mind and refused to relinquish parental rights. Afterward, she remembered Mattie saying that life felt overturned, like freshly plowed earth. Life had to start over.

At least every other day, someone stopped by Windmill Farm to seek Sadie out for a remedy or advice. She felt encouraged to keep going, to continue learning about healing herbs and offer remedies to people for minor ailments, aches, and pains. She loved helping others, but she assumed that she was making little difference in the day-to-day lives of most people. She rested in the knowledge that she had given them all she could to make their lives a little better.

Deacon Abraham stopped by one sunny morning to ask Sadie if she would pay a call on his wife, Esther, who suffered from persistent headaches. "She's been to every doctor and chiropractor she can find, had every treatment and test and scan imaginable, and they can't find anything that's wrong."

This was just the kind of ailment that worried Sadie. The very reason she didn't charge people for her remedies. If the best medical minds of Lancaster County couldn't help Esther, what could she possibly do? And on top of that worry bounced another one: Esther frightened her. Sadie had never seen a smile rise all the way to her eyes.

Abraham sensed her hesitation. "Just . . . go talk to her, Sadie. For my sake."

So Sadie went to Abraham and Esther's farm. The brick house lay nestled amidst a sea of carefully tended greenery and neat outbuildings. Chickens clucked in a fenced yard, and a cow lowed from a small pasture. Esther's mare stood within the buggy shafts, her head low, apparently dozing. Sadie drew her buggy alongside Esther's and the mare stirred, nosing the visiting gelding. He nickered in reply.

Leaving the horses to get acquainted, Sadie walked stiffly across the yard to the house.

Esther met her at the door. "Now's not a good time for a visit, Sadie. I've got a frightful headache today."

"Abraham asked me to come by." She held up a little bag. "I brought some special tea that might help."

Esther looked suspiciously at her. "I suppose it couldn't hurt."

She opened the door and led Sadie to the kitchen. As Sadie brewed the tea, Esther told her all about the headaches. When they started, how often she had them, how they made her head pound as if a woodpecker were hammering away at her. How incompetent doctors couldn't find any reason for them. She left nothing out, filling the air with blame for others, as if they had given her the headaches. Did Esther always look for the dark side of things and judge?

Before Esther could start on another grievance, Sadie handed her a cup of tea, and she sipped it, then made a face. "It tastes like tree bark."

"It is. It's made with the bark of a willow tree." Sadie sat down beside her. "So you say the headaches started a few years ago?"

Esther nodded.

Sadie felt a strange stirring in her heart. "And the doctors can't find anything wrong?"

"No. But that doesn't stop them from taking my money." That thought inspired her to launch into another tirade against modern medicine.

Sadie wasn't really listening to her. She had traveled back to a time when a woman arrived at Old Deborah's door. The woman's face was tight and pale, riddled with anxiety. Old Deborah listened to her ailment—Sadie couldn't exactly remember what it was but thought it was something like neck pain. Similar to Esther, this woman had spent a fortune on doctors and treatments and tests and scans—without any relief. Old Deborah listened carefully in that wise, knowing way she had. Then she took the woman's hands in hers and told her what she thought the problem was. At first, the woman was shocked, angry even. Then she cried. But when she left, she was a different person. Calm, at peace, and as far as Sadie knew, her neck never bothered her again.

Sadie had the strangest feeling that the cause of Esther's headaches was the same as that woman with the neck pain. As Esther kept talking, Sadie was praying, and waiting for an answer, listening for God's voice to speak to her heart. She had learned that the most important part of her prayers was the waiting and listening. *Go ahead*, she heard God whisper. *It's okay to speak the truth in love.*

Sadie's lips quivered. Her chest grew tight. She was clasping her hands so tightly her knuckles ached. She forced herself to relax her grip, flattening her palms on her thighs. She knew one thing—she had to be willing to speak up, regardless of the response she might get. *Please, Lord God, give me boldness.*

"Esther, there is something I'd like you to think about. Emotions can affect the health of our bodies, for good or for bad. Stress, anger, and resentment can have powerful negative effects. Those bitter feelings are like an acid that eats away at its container."

Esther looked at Sadie as if her barn was short a rafter.

Sadie's heart was thumping so loudly, she was sure Esther could hear it. Why did she have to say anything like this? She could have just given Esther the willow bark tea and left it at that. That's all Abraham had asked of her.

For a brief second, Sadie thought about running. Just dropping everything and bolting. No explanation. But what would that serve other than to confirm to Esther that Sadie Lapp was crazy? This made no sense! Still, she felt that strange inner stirring to keep going. *Oh Lord God, please help!* "Is there anyone in your life whom you have not been able to forgive?"

Esther's face frosted over. Minutes ticked by while Sadie waited for Esther's response. She opened her lips, but no sound came out.

Sadie was scared. Deborah had always said that some health problems were spiritual and emotional in nature, but she didn't tell Sadie which ones. What right did Sadie have to ask someone such a personal question? Especially someone like Esther!

Sadie studied Esther carefully. A vision popped in her mind of watching a cobra puff up, fangs glittering, preparing to strike. Sadie scooted her chair back a little, just in case. But after a few more long, painful seconds, Esther suddenly deflated like a balloon in her chair, dropping her head to her chest. She uttered a name that Sadie would never have expected to hear from her.

"Emma."

For a moment Sadie thought she had misunderstood Esther. "Excuse me?"

"Emma. My daughter. For leaving the church, like she did. With that man. Steelhead."

Sadie had forgotten that Esther's daughter had left the

church. It had happened years ago, when Sadie was just a little girl. "Do you want to tell me about it?"

Without hesitation, Esther began to talk, describing how Emma had eloped with an English man—a former convict, she hastened to say, wrinkling her nose. "Emma works in a quilt shop in town. Right in Stoney Ridge! And never comes by to see me, not ever. Not once."

"Have you ever invited her to come for a visit?"

"Of course not! Emma is shunned. I'm married to a deacon. I'm held up as an example to others. Emma is the one who chose to leave. There are consequences to that decision. There are reasons for shunning. Sin endangers us all."

"I understand your feelings," Sadie said. "It's clear that you feel stress over Emma."

Esther held her hands tightly in her lap, so tight that her knuckles had turned white. But she wasn't ushering Sadie to the door, as Sadie had thought she would.

"You feel as if you've lost a daughter."

"I *have* lost a daughter."

Sadie nodded. "Maybe you even feel that she's rejected you, as well as our church. But, Esther, this bitterness toward Emma might be hurting your health and stealing joy from your life."

She paused for a few moments to see how Esther was responding. Her eyes were downcast, fixed to the tabletop, but her hands were tight fists in her lap.

"Jesus said that if we forgive others, he will forgive us. But if we don't forgive others, God will not forgive us." She reached out and covered Esther's hands. "I think you need to forgive Emma."

Esther looked genuinely surprised. "I don't know . . . how I can do that."

As soon as the words left her mouth, she began to weep. Sadie got up and scrambled to find a box of tissues.

This was new territory for Sadie, but she had an idea of what needed to come next. "If you're willing, we can pray, right now, for your heart to be changed."

Esther was crying so loud that Sadie handed her the whole box of tissues. "I'm going to pray now."

Esther gave a brief nod.

"Lord God, Esther chooses to forgive Emma for the things she did that hurt her. Now you continue, Esther. What do you want to forgive Emma for?"

Esther took a deep, shuddering breath before she spoke. "I forgive Emma for making poor choices. I forgive her for thinking only of herself. I forgive her for breaking her vows to you."

"Is there anything else you need to forgive Emma for?"

"I forgive Emma for . . . for . . . choosing Steelhead over her own mother." The words whooshed out of Esther, as if she had been waiting to say them for years. That confession started Esther on another round of weeping, but Sadie didn't mind so much. She had the most wonderful feeling that God was doing some housecleaning in Esther's heart.

"Esther, we all need to be forgiven. Each one of us. Would you like to ask God to forgive you for holding these feelings of resentment and bitterness against your daughter?"

Esther was so ready that she didn't wait for Sadie's words but offered her own. "God, please forgive me for holding this bitterness toward Emma. And . . . Steelhead, for taking her away." It was as though a long silence between Esther and God had been broken. A sense of relief came over the room as Esther wiped her eyes and nose.

As Sadie got ready to leave, she thought that Esther hardly looked like the same person. Sadie had actually observed a calm wash over her, like an ocean wave. Her countenance had gone from austerity to softness.

Two weeks later, Sadie saw Esther at church. Esther lowered her voice and whispered, "I stopped by the quilt shop and saw Emma." She squeezed Sadie's shoulder. "Of course, we'll just keep that between ourselves."

Abraham found Sadie, after lunch, and thanked her for the herbal tea she had left for Esther. "Her headaches are so much better that she hasn't needed any of her pain medication. Sadie Lapp, that tea of yours really worked."

"It's always God who does the work," Sadie said.

Sadie had never seen anything have such a transforming power. Asking God's help to forgive had turned a harsh woman like Esther into a kinder, gentler person. The result was amazing. Forgiveness, Sadie decided, was the best medicine of all.

Amos had been filling the lawn mower with gasoline and spilled it on his shirt. He went to the house, gave a wave to Fern in the kitchen, and bolted up the stairs to get a fresh shirt before she smelled the gasoline on him and chewed him out for ruining a good piece of clothing. At the top of the stairs, he stopped suddenly. It was a miracle, one he hadn't even been thinking of lately. He had walked up the stairs—upstairs!—without having to stop halfway, without gasping for air. Why, he had practically taken the steps two at a time, like a young colt!

He changed his shirt and passed by Sadie's room, where the baby was starting to stir in the basket. Joe-Jo was nearly outgrowing it, and they should be thinking about getting a crib soon. Amos listened to the even rhythm of the baby's breathing. He picked him up and held him close, as close as he could. He put the baby's tiny hand over his heart. "Do you feel that, little one? That's your father's heart, beating away."

When he turned, he saw Fern standing at the doorjamb with a soft look on her face.

He felt a little sheepish. "At my last appointment, the doctor said that I should stop referring to it as Menno's heart and call it mine. He said it would be better for me to think of it as mine as I take all the drugs to fool my body so it doesn't reject it." He kissed the baby's downy head. "But I can't seem to think of this heart as belonging to me."

"Doctors don't know everything. He didn't know that Menno had the biggest heart in the world." Fern walked toward him and put a hand on the baby's back. "I can't think of anyone's heart I'd rather have than Menno's."

Amos watched her for a moment as she stroked the baby's back and he thought it was a shame that Fern wasn't a mother. Though, he quickly corrected himself, in a way, she was everybody's mother. Someday, maybe soon, he would have to tell her how much he appreciated her. How much they all counted on her. What a difference she had made in their lives.

Of course, she had no way of knowing what was running through his head. She turned to go. At the door, she stopped and quickly reverted to her starchy self. "Where did you hide that shirt with gasoline? It's going to take all afternoon to get that stain out."

Caught red-handed! "Under the bed."

As he heard her hunting for the shirt in his room, he leaned his chin on the top of the baby's head and nuzzled him close. What was it about Fern that made a person feel like he was out on a snowy night and had just turned the horse and buggy down the lane that led to home?

Blessed. He was a blessed man.

One morning in the middle of May, Sadie was in the kitchen getting a bottle of goat's milk ready for the baby as Will knocked softly on the kitchen door and waved through the window. He had started a habit of popping in for a cup of coffee after he did a dawn check on the falcon couple.

Fern opened the door for him and said, "No secret what you're after." She tried to sound gruff.

Will gave Fern a kiss on her cheek. "Can you blame a man? There's no better coffee on this green earth."

Fern huffed, pleased. She handed Will a mug of hot, steaming coffee with two spoonfuls of sugar already mixed in, just the way he liked it. Little by little, day by day, Sadie had watched Will win Fern over with his easy charm and smooth compliments.

"No eyases to report yet," Will said. "But it wouldn't surprise me to find a chick or two has hatched any day now." He walked over to where Sadie was sitting with the baby.

The baby opened his eyes and blew a spit bubble. "Isn't

he wonderful?" Sadie's voice held awe. "He hardly ever cries anymore, and I think he knows me more than anyone else."

"I'm counting on the first smile," Will said, watching the baby over Sadie's shoulder. He finished off the last sip of coffee and put the mug on the kitchen table. "I'd better get back to Adam and Eve. Since it's Saturday, the bird-watchers will be out in full force."

"Don't forget about the gathering tonight!" Sadie called.

Will grinned and waved to her through the open window.

"Sadie, don't tell me you asked Will to the gathering." Fern frowned.

"Why not? You invited him to church and he's come twice now. Same thing." To be fair, Sadie knew it wasn't the same thing. She knew Fern wanted Will at church to see how very different a world he was entering.

"It's not the same thing. Not at all." She wagged a finger at Sadie. "I've warned you to not get sweet on him. A boy like that—he thinks he can talk any girl around to his side with a smile and flicker of his eyelashes."

Isn't that exactly how he got you in his corner? Sadie wanted to ask but knew enough not to.

Sadie couldn't begin to explain how she felt about Will Stoltz. She couldn't truthfully deny Fern's assumption. A tiny piece of her was, as Fern had put it, sweet on him. How could she resist? Will had openly sought snatches of time with her, moseying by the garden when she was picking vegetables or appearing in the barn when she was preparing the horse for the buggy. She had recognized his ploys and managed to remain kind but cool in the face of his attentiveness, accepting his assistance without encouraging him to pamper her.

Will *was* charming. He was also handsome and funny and unpredictable and . . . oh how he made her laugh! Of course, there was always that other complication . . . he was English.

But if he weren't—if there wasn't a caution, an invisible boundary about the English that had been drilled into her as a child—Sadie would be falling head over heels in love with Will Stoltz.

Then there was Gid. Many times now, he had come over late at night and flashed his beam up at her window, but she ignored it and didn't go down to meet him. Compared to Will's silver tongue, Gid was . . . solemn as an owl. Lacking passion. He had little to say, and when he did say something, it seemed to come out all wrong.

Life was so complicated. A few months ago, everyone would have assumed that she and Gid would end up together one day. But Sadie had never felt absolutely convinced of that. She wasn't sure what held her back from wholeheartedly returning his affection until she had started spending time with Will. In just a month, she felt as if she knew so much about Will—little things, like the fact that he hated tuna fish but loved sardines, or the reason he wore a cowboy hat was because he thought his head had a funny shape. It didn't. His head was beautifully shaped.

And she knew big things about him too—there was pain in his eyes when he spoke about his father. He felt as if he couldn't do enough to make his father proud of him. When Sadie held up her gentle and good father next to Will's, she knew that her childhood was one long sunny spring picnic in the country compared to his.

Her thoughts traveled to Gideon. What could she say about Gid? She cataloged everything she knew about him:

He was almost twenty years old.

He had red hair.

He had a passel of older sisters who were married and raising families of their own. All but Alice. Oh, and Marty too.

He had a widowed father.

He was a schoolteacher.

He suffered from hay fever every spring.

He wore glasses.

He liked to read.

These were facts that everyone knew about him. Although they had grown up together, she was realizing that she hardly knew him, not really.

Gideon Smucker spent most of Saturday afternoon washing and polishing his buggy, thinking up what he would say when he stopped by the Lapps' to see if Sadie wanted a ride to the gathering. It had to be executed very carefully so that it would seem like a casual thing and not so he would appear to be desperate or cloying. No, never that. He didn't want Sadie to feel smothered. Girls didn't like to be smothered, he had heard one of his sisters say.

More than a few times, he had gone over to Windmill Farm late at night to try to talk to Sadie. He flashed the beam of light against her window, but there was no response. Either she was sound asleep, not in her room, or most likely, she was ignoring his signal.

She was mad at him. Steaming mad. By now, he would

have thought she might have forgiven him for assuming—like many others had—that she had a child out of wedlock. Yet she seemed far more angry with him now than she had weeks ago. Was that typical of females? For anger to multiply, like yeast in dough?

It was certainly true of Alice. She hadn't lost a bit of her anger toward Mary Kate for the sledding accident. If anything, she did her best to try to convince Gid that Sadie's indifference to him was a gift. A heaven-sent opportunity to avoid being permanently connected to the crazy Lapp family. "Take it and run!" Alice told him at least twice a week. But he would never do that.

Mary Kate had given him an idea at school last week. She mentioned that the baby was growing out of his basket. He would make the baby a cradle! Sadie couldn't stay mad at him if he gave the baby such a gift—something the baby could use every day. It would be a way to show Sadie how he felt. It was always easier for Gid to show love than to say it. Trying to put what he felt for Sadie into words was impossible. To even say it out loud—those three little words—diminished it somehow, the way a firefly lost its spark in a jar. Simple syllables couldn't contain something as rare as what Gid felt for Sadie.

He had spent the next few evenings in his dad's workshop, cutting and sanding and staining, then placing pieces in a tight metal vise to let them dry, before coming back to stain and sand some more. He rubbed his hand along the narrow rails. They were like butter! When it was completed, he stood back, pleased with his work. Not a single nail was used. Every joint fit together like a glove on a hand. Ideally, he would have liked to wait one more day, for the glue to cure in the joints, but he really wanted to give the cradle to Sadie tonight.

At four o'clock, he set the cradle carefully in the backseat of the buggy, covered it with a blanket, and went off to Windmill Farm, reviewing again what he would say and do when he saw Sadie.

First, he would surprise her with the cradle. Then, he would offer to drive Sadie to the Kings' for the singing. They would have time alone and he could finally explain and apologize for deeply offending her. She would forgive him and things could go back to the way they were, before she left for Berlin.

That was the plan. Ironclad! Foolproof.

As he drove up to Windmill Farm, M.K. flew out of the house, baby in her arms, to greet him before the buggy even reached the top of the drive. He barely hopped out of the buggy as she handed him the baby.

"Isn't he precious?" she asked.

Gid looked down at the little face peering up at him. He had held his nieces and nephews and felt fairly comfortable with babies. This little one was cute, with round dark eyes and a headful of wispy hair. He held out a finger for the baby to grab. "They start out so sweet and innocent and trusting," he said. "So full of awe at anything new, which is almost everything." The baby was smiling at him now, really smiling. A big gummy grin.

Mary Kate leaned over and softly said, "You got the first smile! Wait until Sadie hears this. She's been hoping for that first smile."

Gid looked up at her. "Let's not tell her, okay? Let's wait for her to get the first smile."

Mary Kate was lost in admiration. She gazed at him in such a way that he blushed. He actually blushed. It wasn't like he was a hero or anything, but that was the way she was staring at him. As if he saved someone from getting hurt by a felled tree, or as if he stopped a runaway buggy. It embarrassed him.

"Is Sadie here?" he asked, handing the baby to M.K. He reached into the back of the buggy for the cradle.

"She left over an hour ago with Will. She wanted to show him Blue Lake Pond."

He spun around. "The bird sitter? Blue Lake Pond?" All of his wonderful plans drifted away like smoke from a chimney.

She was staring at the cradle. "Gid, did you make that?" She bent down to rub her finger against the satin finish. "It's beautiful. It's the most beautiful cradle I've ever seen."

He put it carefully on the ground. "Don't use the cradle until tomorrow. Everything needs to set."

She looked at him as if he hung the moon. "This will definitely butter Sadie up. To think *you* made a cradle for our baby."

Gid was mortified. Was he that transparent? Now without a doubt Sadie would be convinced that he was desperate . . . Which he wasn't! He definitely wasn't. "Not a big deal. I was in the middle of making a cradle for my sister's baby. When you said the baby was growing out of his basket—I just thought I'd give you this one. I can always whip up another one for my sister's baby." And now he was a liar. He hardly ever lied! Whenever he did, even a small one, he imagined the devil himself dancing with delight.

She gazed at him with clear, blue-gray eyes, their directness telling him precisely what he did not want to hear—she was probably thinking the same thing. He was a liar of the worst sort.

She sighed. "If this doesn't convince Sadie to start talking to you again, well, then, I don't know what will."

15

Could it have been only a little more than a few weeks since Will had first met Sadie? It seemed that he had known her for years.

He was sitting on the bank of Blue Lake Pond with Sadie, watching the water lap onto the sandy shore. The lake was quiet, still, the surface so glassy—so smooth the sun shined off it like a mirror. The water rolled out in a reflection of the sky, uneven at the edges where it touched the shores, weaving into cliffs and crevices, hiding pitch-black under the shadows of overhanging trees. At times like this, with a beautiful lake looking so calm, without another human in sight, it was hard to believe there could be anything wrong in the world.

A whip-poor-will called in the distance, and from the tangle of branches, its mate trilled out a reply.

Afterward Will couldn't say how it had happened, but as they sat there in the peace of that moment, he started to tell Sadie things about his family that he had never told another living soul. Ordinarily, Will deflected any discussion about his family. He'd always made a point to keep his issues to himself. He wasn't sure if it was Sadie's low musical voice or easy, nonjudgmental manner, but it all worked together to loosen his tongue. Will was astonished to hear himself describe the last time he had seen his father—when he had told Will to pack his bags and leave the house.

Sadie's knees were bent and her elbows rested on top of them. "Do you think he really meant it?"

"He meant it. In the next breath, he told me where I was expected to go—to report to the game warden in Lancaster County. It's like . . . my dad is a barbed-wire fence—the same kind that I put up around the falcons' scape. That's what our relationship feels like. The only thing that holds us together is rusted, sharp, twisted."

Sadie drew a line in the sand with her finger. "And those barbs keep catching you?"

"Yes. Exactly! That's what he did with Mahlon and this internship—it's like he caught me."

"Maybe his barbs are meant to hold you close, not to let you go. Maybe he just doesn't know how to be close to you. Maybe he's afraid he'll lose you. Maybe barbs are all he knows. Fear makes people hold a little tighter than they should."

Will thought about that for a while. He couldn't imagine that fear of losing Will could be his dad's problem. But what if it was? He never knew anything about his father's family. Charles Stoltz had a habit of brushing aside any questions about his childhood. His mother didn't have much to add to the story, and she looked uncomfortable when Will pressed for more details. "I met your father when he was a resident at the hospital," she said. "He was estranged from his parents and put himself through medical school."

Sometimes, he wondered how well his parents really knew each other. Even now, they lived side by side, amicably. They gave each other a lot of space. But they never laughed with each other, or sat around the dinner table, lingering the way the Lapps did, playing board games or working on jigsaw puzzles by the flickering firelight. He thought of the talks he and Amos had in the barn, how much Amos had told him about Menno, his son with special needs. Whenever Amos spoke about Menno, it was always about something he had learned from him. Patience, kindness, or how Menno helped Amos's faith grow.

The world outside Windmill Farm would have looked at Menno Lapp as a problem to be dealt with, a burden to be endured.

Windmill Farm considered him to be a gift from God.

Will looked up at the sky. He had thought more about God in the last few weeks than he had in his entire life. Just last night, Amos pointed to Adam, soaring on thermals, and quoted a Scripture. Something from the book of Isaiah, about how a "youth can grow tired and weary, can stumble and fall, but those who hope in the Lord will renew their strength. They will soar on wings like eagles." It spoke to Will, deep down, in a way he couldn't explain. It felt so right, so appropriate. This spring, he had felt weary. Not physically, but mentally. Weary of his father's endless pressure, of never succeeding or pleasing him. And Will had stumbled and fallen.

Something was changing inside of Will this spring, something was softening. What a fluke! To end up on a quiet Amish farm and find himself reenergized, renewed, inside out.

But it didn't feel like a fluke. It seemed that this place,

Stoney Ridge and the people here, had been prepared for him, designed ahead of time as a nurturing nest, a soft place from which to grow new wings.

He looked over at Sadie. "Your parents loved each other very much, didn't they?"

The corners of her eyes crinkled. "Yes, they did. They built a life together. It was a good life, and they were happy."

He slapped his hands on his thighs. "Sadie . . . I'm going to follow your example. I've decided no more resentment."

Her smile faded. "It's really not something you can do without God's help, Will. Only God is the true healer of hurts."

Only God is the true healer. That was a phrase Sadie often said, especially when people came to her for remedies, which they were doing more and more. Hardly a day went by when someone wasn't seeking her out for help. Will worried they were taking advantage of her because she didn't charge them, but she said it brought her pleasure to help others. And then she would always say, "After all, only God is the true healer."

What would his father, the brilliant neurosurgeon, say to that? He would probably be outraged. He believed that a good surgeon shouldn't go into surgery unless he believed he was the sole instrument of healing. But then, his father would scoff at Sadie's remedies too, saying that they were merely anecdotal and that she used unproven, unscientific methods. "My dad wants me to follow in his path and go into medicine." He wasn't sure why he admitted that to her.

"Have you considered it?" Sadie said.

Will lifted a shoulder in a careless shrug. "I considered nothing else. I even got accepted to medical school—assuming that I would be graduating this spring." He took in a deep breath. "So what did I do? Nine weeks shy of graduating with honors, I get myself suspended by doing something stupid."

That was only half the story. He then did something even more stupid, but he just couldn't tell her about the DUI. There were only three people aware of that little problem—Will, the police officer, and his lawyer, Mr. Arnie Petosky, found at four in the morning through the yellow pages at the city jail. This particular lawyer was the only one who answered calls in the middle of the night and took credit cards for payment of criminal defense. "It's your first offense, Will. Sure, you came up a little high on the blood alcohol concentration—and that can usually mean a little jail time—"

Will's eyes went wide.

"—plus a $5,000 fine—"

Will's eyes went wider.

"—plus your license could get suspended. But this was a routine traffic stop. No doubt your constitutional rights were violated—"

Will scratched his head. The police officer had actually been pretty nice to him.

"—we might even end up with a claim. Money back."

Will doubted that. He really just wanted it all to go away. Will was trapped. Up a creek without a paddle.

As the calming water lapped against the shore, Will found himself telling Sadie about hacking into the registrar's office, about losing his acceptance into medical school. He wondered what she thought of him. He was telling her things that shamed him. She didn't say anything for a long while. Sadie was one of those people who knew the virtue of quiet patience.

"So you thought it would be easier to just walk away from

your future, from your father, than to try, didn't you?" Sadie spoke quietly, and when he lifted his head, he marveled again at the piercing depth in her blue eyes.

She tucked in her shoulders, like she was embarrassed to have brought up something painful. "I'm sorry. I didn't mean to—"

"It's okay," he said, and he felt her hand slip into his, small and warm. Her face turned upward, her eyes dark like liquid. Slipping a thumb under her chin, he tilted it upward, looked into her in a way he never had looked at a girl—all of the girls he'd dated but never got too attached to. With Sadie, things were different in some way he didn't even understand yet.

He leaned over and kissed her, because they'd talked long enough.

Gid wondered what was wrong with him as he turned right onto the dirt road that led to Blue Lake Pond, through a thick canopy of pine trees. He shouldn't be spying on Sadie like this! This was wrong, wrong, wrong. Unspeakably wrong. But still, his hands didn't seem to get the message from his brain to pull back on the horse's reins. Not until he saw Sadie and the cowboy sitting on the shore. Then, he stopped the horse abruptly.

He watched them for a moment or two, trying to decide if he could interrupt without looking like a fool.

Though the distance was enough that they didn't hear his horse and buggy approach, Gid tried to make sense out of Sadie's expression when she looked up at the cowboy. Was it gladness or dismay? Shyness? Or maybe just plain amusement?

The cowboy said something to make Sadie laugh. Gid heard

laughter floating on the breeze, the cowboy's deep and husky, Sadie's light and young.

Suddenly something clicked in Gid's mind. He couldn't believe he hadn't figured it out sooner. No wonder she had been ignoring him. A dark thought suddenly began to take form in Gid's mind—he had always felt a tweak of concern that the cowboy was sweet on Sadie, but now he realized that she was growing fond of the cowboy! Gid saw Will's head dip toward Sadie. Quickly. Briefly. Not so briefly he couldn't have kissed her in that time. And Sadie made no move to shove him away from her.

Pain streaked through Gideon. He turned and left.

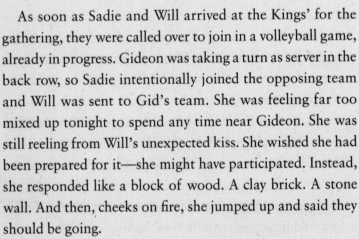

As soon as Sadie and Will arrived at the Kings' for the gathering, they were called over to join in a volleyball game, already in progress. Gideon was taking a turn as server in the back row, so Sadie intentionally joined the opposing team and Will was sent to Gid's team. She was feeling far too mixed up tonight to spend any time near Gideon. She was still reeling from Will's unexpected kiss. She wished she had been prepared for it—she might have participated. Instead, she responded like a block of wood. A clay brick. A stone wall. And then, cheeks on fire, she jumped up and said they should be going.

But she was not going to let her nerves get the better of her. She was an adult now. Fern had said so. Tonight, she was going to act like she was kissed by handsome cowboys all the time. Practically every day of the week except for Sundays! The truth was, it was only the second kiss from a boy she had ever received. The first one was from Gid and it had made her knees go weak. Today's kiss from Will felt sweet and gentle. Nice. Maybe it would have made her knees go weak if she had been ready for it.

She cast a furtive glance at Gid, but he wasn't looking at her. He was talking to Will, tapping the ball delicately into the air, to show him how the game was played. Will waved Gid off, telling him he had played plenty of volleyball in his day. He threw his cowboy hat off to the side and winked at Sadie. She looked away, embarrassed.

Gid went back to the service line. He cracked his neck on each side, like the prizefighters did at the county fair as they prepared to head into the ring. He was staring at the back of Will's head like he was boring a hole through it. He tossed the ball in the air to serve, and instead of the ball arcing through the air, sailing over the net, it was launched like a rocket, straight at Will's head. Will fell to the ground, face-first.

Every place on a farm had its own sound, if you stopped and listened. Will liked to identify those sounds as he walked through the fields each morning before dawn to check on the falcons. The streams that crisscrossed through Windmill Farm had a soft, gurgling sound. The crops in the fields had a rustling sound, like they were whispering. The trees had a sound—pine needles dropping as the branches waved in the wind. The rocky ridge on the northern edge of the farm had a sound—pinging sounds that echoed.

Will climbed a tree to watch the falcons with a telescope just as the sky began to brighten. Adam flew off the edge of the scape and circled overhead. Will watched him glide on the warming air currents, stretching his wings in the mist. Eve remained in the scape, as he expected, incubating her brood.

Sure enough, a whitish down head with a disproportionately large beak poked around Eve's body. The first eyase to hatch! He expected the next one to hatch today or tomorrow, with the other ones to follow. He watched the small chick until the sun had emerged on the horizon, filled with wonder and awe. It was times like this that he thought Amos Lapp might be right, that God had a plan. It was a phrase Amos repeated often, especially when he told Will stories about Menno as a boy. It seemed as if he always wrapped up a memory of Menno with that phrase, "God has a plan," like it was a benediction. An "Amen."

Will rubbed the back of his head, feeling the goose-egged lump from yesterday's surprising encounter with a volleyball. When he had come to, twenty Amish teens were staring down at him with deeply concerned looks on their faces. Sadie fussed over him the entire evening, bringing fresh ice for him to hold against his head and checking the pupils of his eyes for signs of a concussion.

"I'm fine," he kept reassuring her. She wanted to take him home but he insisted on staying. To be honest, he enjoyed the attention he was getting from everyone. It felt like he had finally broken through that invisible wall that separated him from these Amish people, the wall he felt whenever he was at their church service. All but with that Gideon guy, the one who whacked him with the ball. Sadie was furious with Gideon. He offered up a weak apology to Will, something lame about how a bee landed on him just as he was serving up the ball.

"There was no bee," Sadie whispered loudly, after Gideon sauntered off. She glared at his back with a look he wasn't accustomed to seeing on her sweet face. Like she was about to go after him with a shovel as if she was killing vermin.

He wouldn't have missed the barbecue for anything. The food was the best grilled food he had ever eaten, bar none—chicken and steak, smothered in thick sauce, spicy baked beans, coleslaw that was nothing like the soggy mess his mother served, three kinds of pie for dessert. And still, everyone kept fussing over him like he had suffered a mortal blow! Hardly that. His head was harder than a pileated woodpecker's, his father often told him.

Now, if Sadie had insisted that they leave before the singing, it wouldn't have been hard to be persuaded to go. He hadn't realized there was singing involved—she had just called it a youth gathering. But after his third helping of pie, she seemed confident that he was fine and didn't ask him again if he wanted to leave.

Afterward, he was glad they stayed. The singing was different from those long, lugubrious hymns sung during the lengthy Amish church service. For one thing, the host asked others to call out requests to sing. Like eager bidders at an auction, several shouted out song titles. Unlike Sunday church, they sang only one stanza of each, and it was easy to tell these were favorites. Also, unlike church, these tunes were quick, with a beat. The boys took a turn alone, bellowing the melody like they were a marching band made up of tubas and trombones, trying to impress the girls with their deep, honking voices. Then the girls took a turn at it. It had struck Will that the sound of women's voices had a tinny sound—nothing that came anywhere close to raising the roof like the boys did. The girls sounded like a little choir of flutes and piccolos. Except for Sadie's. Her voice rang the truest.

He had a surprisingly enjoyable evening, sore head and all.

The ringing of his cell phone cut off Will's wandering thoughts and pulled him back to the present. He set the scope in a nook on the tree and looked at who would be calling him at 5:34 a.m. Mahlon Miller, the game warden. Will sagged.

"Morning, Mahlon," he said as he answered.

"Have any hatched?"

Not even a hello. Or, how are you, Will? Need anything? Like, food, money, clean laundry, transportation? "First one. I'm watching it now. Looks like a viable eyase."

"Good. As soon as the clutch is hatched, I want you to think about how you're going to band them."

Will was silent for a moment.

"You've banded before. Your father told me you had. He said you had volunteered at a raptor rescue center and banded hundreds of birds."

Aha! Will's father was behind this. "Well, yeah, I've had a little bit of experience with banding. But not out in the wild. Not when the parents were hovering nearby." At the raptor rescue center, Will had become so good at banding that he was dubbed the Band-Aid. Banding birds provided important information on the birds' movements and habitat needs year-round. These metal bands on the birds' legs were uniquely lettered and numbered by the government so that if the birds were observed later, or found injured or dead, they could be identified. "Don't you have an expert bander in the office?"

"Nope. Well, we do have a guy who usually does banding,

but he's out on paternity leave. He said you just gotta act quick so it reduces stress on the birds."

What about the stress on the unpaid intern? Act quick so that he didn't get his eyes pecked out by Adam and Eve. Quick so that they didn't try to strike him with their powerful feet. Quick so that they didn't carry him away with their razor-sharp talons and drop him, like a stone, into the field.

Banding a falcon chick was serious work. Adam and Eve would turn into threatened predators if anyone—or anything—messed with their clutch. Just a moment ago, he watched Adam capture, in midflight, a menacing crow that flew too close to the scape. Eve was provided with fresh crow for breakfast. "I thought that fell under game warden duties."

"Nope. It's part of your internship duties."

Will doubted that. "Do you have suggestions?"

"Well, I'd recommend you wait until the parents are away from the scape." He snorted a few times, as if he had made a funny joke.

Will rolled his eyes.

"Timing is critical. Besides watching out for falcons, that's another reason I put you out there on that farm. There's really only one day that is the ideal point to band—the foot is small enough for the band to go over the toes, but not too small that the band falls off. They can start fledging at three weeks—especially the males, and they'll begin to leave the scape for short times." Mahlon took a long slurp of coffee. "As soon as you tell me how many eyases are in the clutch and what sex they are, I'll put in a request for the bands and drop them off next time I see you. You'd better start figuring out how you're going to do it." And he hung up.

Will stared at the phone in his hand. Broken connections—wasn't that the story of his life?

Passing over him, Adam cried out a complaint, letting Will know he was horning in on his territory. As a serious birder, Will knew it was ridiculous to attribute human characteristics to birds, to any animals. Anthropomorphism, such foolishness was called. But still, he talked to wild things like he expected them to answer. He cupped his mouth and shouted at Adam, "I'm not doing anything to hurt your babies. If anything, I'm helping them." Adam circled near him again, uncomfortably close, as if he knew exactly what Will was talking about. He let out a *cack cack cack cack*—one of a wide range of sounds he made. As if he wanted to taunt Will by saying, "Who do you think you're fooling?"

16

Off-Sundays had their own feel. On Sundays without church, everyone was allowed to sleep in and start the day slowly. M.K.'s father was the only one who would rise early, feed the stock, but then he would head back to the couch in the family room and lie down. "Just resting my eyes," he would tell M.K., if she tried to stir him. The only part of the day M.K. didn't like was that Fern didn't make a hot breakfast like she normally did—today's offerings were cold cereal or toast. She said it was her off-Sunday too.

On this morning, M.K. felt as jumpy as popcorn in a skillet, waiting to hear the first sound of Sadie stirring upstairs. She had the cradle hidden in a corner of the family room, covered by a blanket. She knew Sadie would be home late from the gathering last night, and she didn't want to miss seeing the look on her sister's face. She knew better than to wake Sadie up. Even she wasn't that big of a fool.

Finally, M.K. heard Sadie's door open and her light steps come down the stairs. Fern was in the family room, feeding the baby a bottle. Her dad was in his chair. reading the Bible and sipping coffee. Sadie went to the kitchen and poured cereal into a bowl.

Perfect. The moment was perfect.

M.K. cleared her throat to get everyone's attention. "I have here a lovely gift to present to you, made by Gideon Smucker himself, to show Sadie how deep are his affections."

When M.K. was satisfied that everyone's attention was on her, she whipped off the blanket to reveal the cradle. Sadie gasped, and Amos jumped up out of his seat to see it.

Holding her cereal bowl in one hand, Sadie came over to look at it. "Gid made it? Why, it's beautiful!"

M.K. pushed one side of the cradle, to show Sadie how it could rock, but didn't realize how close Sadie was standing to the cradle. When it knocked Sadie's knee, her cereal bowl dropped into the cradle. The bottom of the cradle fell out, clattering to the ground. M.K. grabbed the side of the cradle to hold it in place, but the top rail came apart in her hands. One by one, the dowels popped out like springs. They watched, amazed, as the entire cradle began to collapse, side by side, piece by piece.

Amos bent down and examined a joint. "He must have forgotten to glue the joints."

"Glue?" M.K. said in a small, squeaky voice. "It needed glue?"

"*Forgot* to glue them?" Sadie shook her head. "I doubt it. Oh Gideon. You have sunk to a new low."

Fern blew air out of her cheeks. "That boy. He needs to shake the snowflakes out of his head."

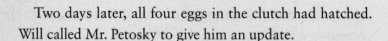

Two days later, all four eggs in the clutch had hatched. Will called Mr. Petosky to give him an update.

"That's good. That's very good news. Have you told the game warden there are four?"

"Not yet."

"Good. Don't tell him."

"I don't have to. There are ten avid bird-watchers staked out who've already spotted them."

Mr. Petosky sighed. "Look, I'm going to need two of them."

"What?! But you only said one. One is reasonable. It won't raise any red flags. We always talked about one."

"That was before we knew there were four viable eyases. It's not a big deal. The game warden will never get suspicious. I'll get you the bands this week so you can just switch them out with the warden's bands. You know as well as I do that the chance of all four eyases making it to the fledgling stage is very unlikely."

"Yeah, but—"

"Stuff happens in nature. All the time. He knows that."

Will didn't respond. He couldn't deny that truth.

"That's what happened to me. Nature took a swipe—just like it took on you with that nasty DUI. I'm just trying to recoup." The hard edge of Mr. Petosky's voice softened as he added, "Look at it this way, Will. This is good for the falcons. A very good thing. To take a falcon chick or two from the wild and allow it to breed in captivity—it strengthens the entire species. This is a good thing for the falcon, it's good for my breeding stock, and it's good for you."

Will heard the click of Mr. Petosky's phone as he hung up. What was it he had learned in an ethics class last fall? Opportunity + pressure + rationalization create a fraud triangle.

Of all the lawyers Will could have found, he had happened

upon a falconer. That fact had come up when the lawyer had called Will to tell him his credit card payment had been declined—the very day he had started his internship and discovered the falcon pair. Mr. Petosky had called Will as he was out stocking trout in the creek near Windmill Farm and recognized the shrieking sound of the falcons in the background. They had a very nice conversation about falcons and that was when Mr. Petosky told him not to worry about the legal fees. They could work something out.

And so he did.

The next day, Mr. Petosky showed up at the game warden's office. Will walked him to his car, away from Mahlon Miller's listening ears. Mr. Petosky told Will that he had thought of a way to help Will. He had a little side business of falcon breeding. This spring, a virus had run through his hatchery and wiped out his stock. He just needed a little bit of help to rebuild. A fledgling here, one there, and he would be able to supply his customers and stay in business. Will knew how ethical falconers were—it was a cardinal virtue. And the offer from Mr. Petosky came at a moment when Will was desperate. Mr. Petosky offered to take care of all of his legal bills associated with the DUI. Down to the penny, he said. "The entire unpleasant business will go away, like it never happened." He snapped his fingers to illustrate his point. "You'll be back on track. I'll be back on track. Everything can get back on track." By June 16, the day Will was due in court.

Gid loved this time of day. It was after four and the last scholar had finished up and gone home. A satisfying day of teaching, followed by the gentle slant of the sun as it reached the westward facing windows. The last thing he needed to do was to erase the blackboard. He picked up his glasses and rubbed the bridge of his nose, stood, stretched, and started to wipe the board clean.

"Gid?"

Sadie Lapp was standing three feet away from him.

The tips of Gid's ears started to burn. "Sadie, what a nice surprise." Could she hear his heart? Because it sounded like a bongo drum was in his chest. *Bah-bum . . . bah-bum . . . bah-bum . . .*

Sadie had a way of holding her hands at waist level, close to her body, fingers tightly interlaced. She stood that way, just a short distance from Gid's desk, and took a quick breath as if to say something, but stopped. She shook her head and frowned.

Something was on her mind to say and he thought he might as well help her out. He had to lick his lips because they were so dry. "Did you know that penguins don't have ears?" Oh smooth, very smooth, he told himself. Rule number one, whenever you can't think of the right thing to say, just start spouting pointless trivia. That should warm the heart of any woman.

Sadie looked confused. "I didn't know that."

"Oh. Mary Kate did a book report on that very thing today. About penguins not having ears. She wondered if they realized that they have wings but they can't fly. That they were birds . . . but not really. That got an interesting discussion going in class . . ." His voice trailed off as he caught the baffled look on Sadie's face. *Let's try this again.* "Did you like those little cakes?"

She looked up at him in surprise. "Like them?"

"Was it . . . too hard to understand?" Maybe Mrs. Stroot was right—maybe Sadie didn't know what "mea culpa" meant. He shouldn't have used Latin. Stupid, stupid, stupid! Why did he have to make things so complicated?

"Oh no. You were very clear."

This wasn't going well. Sadie was looking at him as if he were an ax murderer. What had he done wrong? Let's try this again. "Did the baby fit in the cradle?"

"How could he?" She put her hands on her hips and looked—well, an awful lot like her housekeeper, Stern Fern. "Have you completely lost your mind? Why would you try to hurt a baby? An innocent little child?"

"What?!"

"The cradle fell apart. Like dominoes."

Gid was stunned. He thought he had tested every piece of that cradle. He should have held off another day, just to make absolutely sure all of the glue in the joints had dried. He had been so eager to take it to Sadie on the night of the gathering that he didn't want to wait. He never would have given Sadie a cradle that wasn't sound. Stupid, stupid, stupid!

She frowned at him. "The other night, you aimed that volleyball right at Will's head. Don't tell me you didn't. You're much too athletic to not have controlled that serve."

How could he defend himself against that? It was true. Sports had always come naturally to him, and generally, he always held back a little, even as a child on the school playground. But he had never considered himself very competitive. Until now.

She folded her arms against her chest. "And besides, I saw that evil look in your eyes just before you served it."

That was also true. When Gid saw the cowboy kiss Sadie, he was surprised at how suddenly and violently his anger was aroused. When the opportunity presented itself to wallop Will Stoltz in the head with the volleyball, Gid took it.

It was a warm afternoon, thick with humidity, and Gid suddenly felt so closed in that he wasn't sure he could even frame a complete sentence.

"Why would you do such a thing? Then . . . you left those horrible little cakes!"

He blinked twice. "But I thought—" He had tried so hard to get it right! Why were they horrible little cakes?

"What kind of a message is *that*: 'You lie.'"

What?! But that wasn't the message he had left for her! How could this have happened? Confusion swirled through his head like gray fog.

Sadie's controlled calm was gone as her voice snapped like a twig. "How dare you say something like that? Why would you do such a thing?"

A protest sprang to his lips. "But that's not . . . ! Someone must have rearranged the—"

"Oh sure . . . blame others."

His mind, so nimble in front of a classroom of twenty-five scholars, was absolutely paralyzed. He needed to let his mind stop racing long enough to relax, so that he sounded like a normal person, but there was no time! He couldn't seem to string two words together. All that ran through his head was how hurt Sadie must have felt when she saw the little cakes. They *were* horrible! *No wonder she's been avoiding me.*

She was mad now, really steaming. "I thought . . . I thought I knew you, Gid." Sadie's blue eyes were boring into his, glowing with anger, waiting for a reply. "Don't you have *any-thing* to say for yourself?"

He had plenty to say for himself, but it was hard to get the words organized when she was staring at him as if he was the scholar and she was the teacher. *I'm so sorry, Sadie. For not trusting you. For misunderstanding. For being a clumsy oaf. For everything.* The words were in his mouth, smooth and round like marbles, but what came out was this: "You let him kiss you."

She didn't move. She didn't speak. A slow flush creeping up her throat to her cheeks was the only indication that she might have heard him at all. "I didn't let—"

"I saw it, Sadie. You were at Blue Lake Pond, and he kissed you."

"I . . . he . . ." She sighed. "Yes, he kissed me. I didn't expect it."

"You didn't seem to dislike it."

Between collar and hairline, her neck turned rosy pink. "I was . . . surprised by it."

As fast as a comet streaking across the heavens, Gid's holy outrage passed. She was so lovely; of course another man would court her. He couldn't blame Sadie for seeking someone else. He hadn't trusted her.

But he didn't know how to say all of this to Sadie, and she was growing impatient with him.

"It's none of your business who I kissed or who I didn't. You and I might have kept company in December, but that's all it was. Just a few rides home from youth gatherings now and then."

That's all he was to her? A ride home now and then? That

was the sum of what he meant to her? Gid felt as if he was suddenly smaller, deflated. "Not any of my business? None of my business?" For some reason Gid couldn't stop there. Words kept pouring out. "Sadie, ever since you got back from Ohio . . . it seems like you're slipping away."

She didn't answer. Instead, she went to the door and brought back a bag of books. She set it on a desk. "These are all the poetry books you sent me while I was in Ohio. I know you wanted me to read them. I'm sorry to tell you this, but I didn't read any of them."

"Not one?" All of those little notes he had placed so carefully in the margins?

She shook her head. "The truth is, Gid, I don't like to read. Not unless I have to. I know that's a disappointment to you. I know you've wanted me to be a person who liked stories and poetry and enjoyed long discussions about them. But that's not me." She gave Gid a long look. "I'm just not sure where what you want for me ends and what I want for me begins."

Those words hung between them, suspended, waiting for Gid to respond. Struck dumb by her lengthy, emphatic speech, he could only gaze at her in wonder. She'd always been pretty to him. Now, with the sun pouring through the window, gilding her skin and reflecting off her hair, her looks held something more, something deeper than beauty—strength. He read it in her broad cheekbones and determined chin, the firmness of her mouth and set of her shoulders.

A bead of sweat rolled down his back, awakening him from his stupor. As Sadie turned toward the door, his mind struggled frantically for the right words, the ones that would free his speech.

"Sadie, I didn't send you these books because I wanted you to be a different person. I wouldn't change anything about you. Not a thing. You're yourself, and that's what I love. What I've always loved. I wish I had learned long ago how to put into words the feelings that I have for you. Instead, I've only known how to use what others have written. I sent those books to you so that they could tell you what I couldn't—to tell you how much I care for you. That I love you. Just the way you are."

But by the time he got the words out, it was too late. Sadie was already halfway down the road to Windmill Farm.

The thing about a rainy day that Amos liked was that it gave a man a chance to catch up on indoor chores. Amos had been hammering new boards in Cayenne's stall after the horse had kicked holes through the wall. He wondered if he should consider selling that hot-blooded mare. Fern and Sadie wouldn't get near her. He and M.K. handled her well, but it didn't seem right to have a buggy horse that took such serious managing.

"Amos?"

Amos spun around to find Ira Smucker standing behind him. "Ira? What brings you here?"

"My love for Fern. It brings me here."

Such a revelation didn't surprise Amos. It was clear that Ira Smucker was very interested in Fern. Amos still felt the shock of it, though, that Fern, whom he thought was a mature, intelligent person, seemed to be responding quite warmly to Ira's poky and cautious method of courtship. Here was just more proof of the great mystery—how could you ever figure women out? He was fifty-one years old and he still didn't understand women.

Then Amos chastised himself for thinking uncharitable thoughts about his friend. A minister, to boot! It's just that Ira was so deliberate in pace, so measured and careful—identical to Fern's nature—that Amos was certain nothing so seemingly passionless could qualify as real love.

Amos looked at his friend. "You love Fern."

"Yes. I do. I would be a happy man to have her as my wife."

Amos's stomach tightened. "Have you asked her?"

"No." Ira's chin lifted. "I thought I should be asking you." His eyes turned to a barn swallow, flitting from rafter to rafter. "There was a time when I thought you might be fond of Fern, yourself. I would never take her from you, Amos. I'm asking you plain, are you wanting Fern for yourself?" Ira searched his face.

Amos looked away. What could he say? If Fern wanted to marry Ira, he would never stand in her way. He couldn't answer Ira's question. "So, you're asking me for Fern's hand?"

"No." Ira shook his head. "I'm telling you I'm marrying her. I'm seeking your blessing, though."

Will couldn't sleep. He threw the covers back and went outside to look at the moon. It was full tonight, pocked with craters. He listened for a while to the sounds of the night: the howl of a coyote, the hoot of an owl.

He couldn't wait to tell Sadie about the hatched chicks. Imagining her catching a breath and looking so pleased when he told her there were four eyases now, all hatched out and healthy. It crossed Will's mind that he was thinking about Sadie again. He shut down the conversation in his head as soon as he realized what he was doing. It wasn't like him to have his mind linger so long and so often on a girl.

Unsettled. That's how he felt after he spent time with Sadie. He remembered what he thought when he first met her—that if he walked into a room, she wasn't the one he would have noticed. But oddly enough, long after he left the room, she was the one he kept thinking about. She was quiet, more of a mystery; her strengths sneaked up on him instead of smacking him front and center.

It amazed Will to see the knowledge Sadie had of healing herbs. Her education was, for the most part, limited to the four walls of a one-room country schoolhouse. And yet, she seemed to have an intuitive sense of what ailed a person.

Earlier today, he had found her out in the enormous vegetable garden, tending to her herbs. "I envy you," Will had told her when she stood to greet him, brushing dirt off her hands.

She looked at him, surprised. "Whatever for?"

"Your healing work."

"But you're the one who is going to be a doctor."

He shook his head. "Not anymore. Besides, even if I were able to talk my way back into medical school, it would only be a vocation. For you, it's a *calling*." He stood up straighter. "I guess that's how I would describe my father's passion for medicine."

Somehow, Will realized, conversations with Sadie wound their way back to his father, even though he didn't intend them to. "He was always at the hospital, never present for any of the events in a kid's life where you'd want a father to be. Not for school plays or birthday parties. We couldn't even count on his appearance on Christmas morning."

"Is he that important of a doctor?"

"Sadly, yes. How can a kid complain about that, either? The guy was out saving lives."

"But a family is important too."

Will shook his head. "I'm only important to him as long as I do everything he wants me to do and wants me to be. The minute I step outside of that line, I'm cut off."

Sadie was quiet for a moment, and then she said, "You need to forgive him."

That was the last thing he wanted to hear. Shouldn't his father be apologizing to him and asking for his forgiveness?

Softly, she added, "Will, I'm sure you've hurt people too. We all have. You need to be forgiven by others. Why shouldn't you extend forgiveness to your father?"

Sadie's words stuck with him all day, like a burr under the saddle. Maybe she was right. Maybe he was having trouble moving on because he wouldn't let his father off the hook. Leaning against the porch post, he said out loud, perhaps to God, perhaps to himself, "Okay. I forgive my dad. I am responsible for my own life. I will stop blaming him." Nothing dramatic happened. No lightning, no thunder, no warm feeling that he had done the right thing. A little disappointed, Will went back inside to try to sleep.

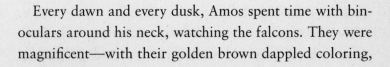

Every dawn and every dusk, Amos spent time with binoculars around his neck, watching the falcons. They were magnificent—with their golden brown dappled coloring, black streaks on their heads. Will had told him scientists had documented that falcons ate a variety of over four hundred and fifty types of birds. He said that they have been observed killing birds as large as a sandhill crane, as tiny as a hummingbird, and as elusive as a white-throated swift, but a favorite treat was bats. The only bird Amos was happy to hear was on that list was starlings. He had no love in his heart for starlings.

He was up on the hillside tonight, watching Adam in a hunting stoop, when suddenly Fern appeared at his side. You'd think he'd have grown accustomed to her out-of-the-blue appearances, but he was always flustered. He watched her as she gazed at Adam. He wondered what she might have been like when she was Sadie or Julia's age. She must have been beautiful. But there was something added to her face that was better than youthful beauty.

She had character.

"I can't help but think how Menno would have loved these falcons," he said, handing her the binoculars. "He would have every fact known to man listed on index cards and read them out to us at supper."

"Better is one day in God's court than a thousand days elsewhere." She held the binoculars up to her eyes. "Menno has a better view of God's magnificent creation than we do, Amos. And he doesn't need index cards to remember anymore." She twisted the knobs for a moment, peered through the binoculars again, then handed them back to Amos and went back down the hill.

He held them to his eyes and discovered he now had a much clearer view of Adam. He watched Fern's receding figure for a moment, then smiled. Fern was always doing that—fixing things that were slightly out of focus.

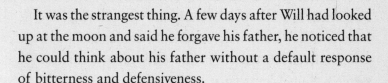

It was the strangest thing. A few days after Will had looked up at the moon and said he forgave his father, he noticed that he could think about his father without a default response of bitterness and defensiveness.

That moment in the night on the cottage porch—something had happened to begin to affect his feelings about his father. He knew it wasn't just a situation of mind over matter. Something—some One—was changing him, inside out.

Questions started buzzing around his mind like pesky mosquitoes: *If this is God's doing, just who is he? What is he like?* When he went into town with Amos that week, he slipped into a bookstore. He told Amos that he was going to get his phone battery charged up and that was true. But he also wanted to purchase a Bible. He ended up buying an easy-to-read translation, small in size so he could keep it in his backpack.

As a freshman in college, he had taken an Ancient Literature class that included some readings from the Bible. The professor had ridiculed the Bible to the class, pointing out all of its inconsistencies. She had been much kinder with *The Odyssey*, he remembered. But that class had shaped his views about the Bible—as an irrelevant, flawed collection of fables and myths. He tried to set that assumption aside and read the Bible with fresh eyes. There was only one question he asked himself: What is God like? That was all.

Over the next few weeks, he alternated between reading the

Old Testament—skipping over the genealogies and lengthy scoldings aimed at the Israelites—and stories about Jesus in the New Testament. He found himself continually surprised by what he had assumed about the Bible and what it actually contained. His appetite for Scripture was growing, and he started to seek out moments when he could read a passage and ponder it. It startled him how often those ancient words seemed uniquely customized to his life.

One afternoon, Amos asked Will to take the sheep to another fenced-in pasture to graze. Sheep were loud with their complaints, day and night, and Will grew frustrated trying to get all of them into the pasture. He chased down one black lamb and carried it over to its mother, bawling at him rudely from behind the pasture fence. A verse he had read that very morning popped into his head: "All we, like sheep, have gone astray." Will settled the lamb next to its mother and looked up at the sky. "Okay, okay. You made your point. The Bible is still relevant. I got that."

He heard a familiar *klak klak klak* sound and shielded his eyes to look for Adam. The tiercel was stooping—diving down to capture its lunch. While stooping, his body hyper-streamlined to achieve high speed, in complete control of the kill. Falcons have been clocked at over two hundred miles per hour. They're the fastest animals on earth; three times faster than a cheetah. As soon as Adam caught his prey, midair, he would pull out of the dive. Karate in the air! The sight never failed to fill Will with awe and reverence—though lately he found that awe didn't end at admiration for the bird but for its creator.

And on the heels of that thought came another out of the

blue. Something inside Will cracked open. He suddenly had trouble breathing. In that moment, all the anger and resentment and frustration he felt melted into one emotion—regret.

He wished he could share the sight of Adam's stoop with his dad. Will missed his dad.

Amos jerked the buggy shafts off of Cayenne so abruptly that the jumpy horse reared up on her hind feet. "Settle down!"

M.K. stroked Cayenne's neck, watching her nostrils flare. "What's got you in such a mood?"

Amos sighed. "Never you mind me." He finished unbuckling the harness's tracings and handed the reins to M.K. to lead the mare to a stall.

If the situation weren't so serious, it might even be comical. Ira Smucker had quietly told Amos that he was going to ask Fern to marry him tonight. And what did Amos do about it? Nothing. Coward! How many times had he had an opportunity to speak to Fern, to express his feelings to her? Hundreds. And yet he said nothing, did nothing. He just watched another man swoop in and make off with the woman he desired, like Adam pursuing prey. Tonight, as Ira had picked Fern up to head to town for dinner, Amos simply stood there, smoldering like a pine log in a forgotten fire pit.

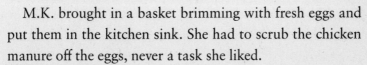

M.K. brought in a basket brimming with fresh eggs and put them in the kitchen sink. She had to scrub the chicken manure off the eggs, never a task she liked.

"Dad's getting crankier than the handle on an ice cream

churn," M.K. said to Sadie. "I don't know what's gotten into him lately. He snaps at me for the smallest thing."

"Fern's gone to town with Ira Smucker tonight, hasn't she?" Sadie said. She had been cooking down a large pot full of plump wild strawberries to make jam. She was ladling the jam into clean jars, then setting them in a boiling hot water bath to seal the lids.

"Yes. They just left a few minutes ago." A light dawned slowly in M.K.'s mind. "Do you . . . are you saying . . . you can't be serious! Dad? Sweet on Fern? Our Fern? Stern Fern?" The thought was too much for her.

Sadie wheeled around from the pot and wagged a finger at her. "You stay out of it. They need to figure this out on their own. There are times to be curious and times to let things be."

Suddenly the thin wail of a baby could be heard, and Sadie stopped the lecture, handed M.K. the wooden spoon, and ran upstairs.

M.K. stirred the jam, watching dark red splatters hit the pot wall. Fern? Fern and Ira Smucker? Fern and her dad? She couldn't get her head around it.

— 17 —

Will was walking along the street that acted as a property line for Windmill Farm, replacing No Trespassing signs that had gotten knocked down in the thunderstorm last night. The wind was the worst part of the storm—branches were down all over the farm. He hammered a nail on a cockeyed sign and stepped back to straighten it.

"Hey!"

Will turned to see that schoolteacher approaching him from down the street. Will raised a hand in greeting. Gideon Smucker stopped, his spine stiffening enough to be noticeable from a hundred feet away. A smile curled Will's lips. This should be interesting. It didn't take a rocket scientist to know how this blustering, tongue-tied man felt about Will—suspicious, jealous, threatened. All because Will was spending time with Sadie Lapp. A great deal of time with her. Probably more time than this schoolteacher had a clue about!

Sadie, the woman Will knew he could never have and yet—

No. He wouldn't think he wanted her. She was a diversion, a spring fling, an excuse to spend a great deal of time at the farmhouse, to eat at the Lapp table and enjoy being a part of a healthy, happy family. After June 16, Sadie could renew her relationship with the schoolteacher, with Will's blessing. Sort of.

Now a yard apart, Gid and Will eyed each other up and down, waiting to see who would speak first. If Will were a cartoonist, he would draw two raptors, one head up, one head down, neither willing to look each other in the eye because that would be considered an out-and-out threat.

Gid was taller than Will, and lankier. With those thick glasses, he reminded Will of Clark Kent, the alter ego of Superman. Bumbling, awkward, ill at ease, but good-hearted. Even Will couldn't deny that. Then his insides tensed at the sight of Gid's large, work-roughened hands. Those calluses would scratch Sadie's smooth skin. Surely she wouldn't let those hands touch her.

"I saw you. Early this morning. Talking to a man in a gray car."

You could have heard a pin drop, a heart beat. A blue jay shrieked overhead, breaking the silence. Another screeched in response.

Will had been careless. The man in the gray car was Mr. Petosky. "I was out this morning, yes. I go out every day to make sure the bird-watchers are respecting the Lapps' property lines."

"He handed you something. I saw it."

Will's mouth went dry, and he couldn't think what he should say. Mr. Petosky had given him the bands for the chicks that he had obtained for his breeding colony—the one that had been wiped out by the virus. But he hadn't bothered to notify the government of that fact. Those bands were treated like gold—all bands were registered with the game commission's office. With a dramatic flair, Mr. Petosky had counted the bands out, one by one, as he handed them over.

Will tried, probably too late, to defuse the situation. "You must be mistaken."

"Something isn't quite right." Gid took a step closer to him and pointed a finger at his chest. "You're up to something." His words emerged roughly, as though each one was formed of grit. "Whatever it is . . . leave Sadie alone. I don't want her to get hurt."

The gloves were off and Will stepped closer. "Seems to me that you've done plenty of that yourself," he snorted.

Gid looked as though he was about to explode. "Leave her be," he ground out between clenched teeth. "She's not a girl to be toyed with."

"Gideon!"

Both Gid and Will spun around to face Sadie, staring at them with a shocked look on her face. They had been so focused on each other that they hadn't noticed she was at the end of the driveway, getting the mail from the mailbox. How much had she heard?

She was indignant, but not at Will. "Gideon, my relationship with Will is none of your concern."

Gid's eyes flashed, hurt. "It's my concern if he's doing something wrong. And dragging you along with him."

Sadie's cheeks turned the color of berries. "Gid, calm down. Will and I are—" She hesitated.

Will held his breath in anticipation of her completed statement as to what he was to her.

"Friends," Sadie finished.

Friends? Just . . . friends? A blast of disappointment shot through Will.

"And he's not dragging me along anywhere."

Gid held his fisted hands at his hips as though ready to strike at any moment. "Then why weren't you at the gathering last weekend?" Gid demanded. "Mary Ruth was counting on your help with the girls' alto section. And yesterday, why weren't you at the workshop frolic at Rose Hill Farm? Bess was looking all over for you when her daughter was stung by a bee."

Will knew the answer to those questions. On Sunday, he talked Sadie into going canoeing on Blue Lake Pond. And yesterday, she was heading out to pick wild strawberries in a secret patch near the woods and he offered to help her. They were having such a good time that they lost track of time and didn't get back until the frolic was nearly over.

Gid glared at her. "What kind of friendship is that, Sadie—when it makes you forget about promises you've made to others?"

Sadie was livid. The way her lips looked at that moment—thin and tight—Will wanted to kiss them again, change their conformation to something much softer.

But Will thought it would be wise to take this opportunity to beat a hasty retreat. "I'll just be on my way." He took off up the driveway before either Sadie or Gid could say another word.

As Will loped toward the cottage, he weighed his options. Maybe he should try to forget about Sadie and concentrate on getting his problem solved by June 16. After all, Sadie had no place in his life outside of this farm, nor he in hers, and he needed to get a grip. Pursuing her the way he had been could bring trouble—he had already created animosity with Clark Kent. And Fern was definitely onto him. That woman scared Will. She watched him like a hawk whenever he was near Sadie, which was often. More and more often.

This was a great example of why he didn't like to complicate his life with relationships. It was like walking on thin ice. You never knew when the ice was going to crack and you were going to fall in a hole. Trouble was brewing, and that was the last thing Will needed this spring.

Still, there was just *something* about Sadie. Maybe . . . he would worry about life after June 16 some other day. For now, he had found a girl who was worth the trouble.

Gid was outside chopping wood when the air began to fill with the smell of rain. Daylight was fading away and the wind was picking up, so he put the ax down and stacked the wood. Before he went inside, he sat on the fence, his head in his hands, berating himself. He was such a fool. Stupid, stupid, stupid! He whacked his hands on his knees so hard that he tipped forward, barely catching himself before he landed, face-first, in the freshly plowed soil. It would serve him right.

Sadie, his Sadie, was involved with another man. An English cowboy. He could see it in her eyes as he confronted her on the road—the way she became so flustered, so defensive.

It was his own fault.

He had bungled things so badly—flown off the handle when he never flew off the handle. He accused her of not keeping promises to her friends. He made her feel guilty because Bess couldn't find her for her daughter's bee sting. It might have been true, but it wasn't as if Bess couldn't manage a simple bee sting. Stupid, stupid, stupid!

He hadn't trusted in the Lord to bring her back to him and had tried to compete for her attentions, her affections. And all he had done was push Sadie closer to the man who was winning her heart.

No wonder Sadie considered him to be untrustworthy. He was.

"God, how can I make things right?" he murmured. "How can I get Sadie to forgive me and trust me again if I behave this way?"

Crows screamed overhead, seeming to mock him with their harsh cawing.

Somewhere, in the deep creases of his mind—the folds where hopes and dreams were caught—he had believed that whatever was wrong between him and Sadie was reparable. When you loved someone, it didn't seem possible to suddenly lose that bond.

"Anything wrong, son?" His father's voice was gentle. "You look like you're not feeling well."

Gid snapped his head up. His father was standing a few feet from him with a worried look on his kind face. "I'm all right." Another lie. He wasn't all right. His head ached. His stomach ached. His heart ached.

"Sadie will come around. Give her time." His father leaned on the top rail of the fence beside him.

"Not as long as Will Stoltz sticks around." Gideon straightened up and looked his father in the eyes. People told him that they had the same blue eyes. His father's were older, though, and crinkled at the edges.

"You know it goes back further than that, Gid." His father's mouth set in a stern line. "You jumped to an assumption about her that was wrong. I'm ashamed to say that I did too."

"No, but I've—" He stopped before he said he'd learned his lesson. He had just proved again to Sadie that he didn't trust her, that he didn't think she had good judgment. Stupid, stupid, stupid! Gid pounded his fist on the rough planks of the fence. "Dad, what can I do? How do I win her back?"

Ira's bushy eyebrows shot up. "You don't. You just keep being the man you are."

Gid stared at his father.

"If Sadie is as smart as I think she is, she'll figure it out."

"What if she doesn't?"

"Well, Gid, the way I see it, there are plenty of other fish in the lake."

Maybe. But none like Sadie Lapp.

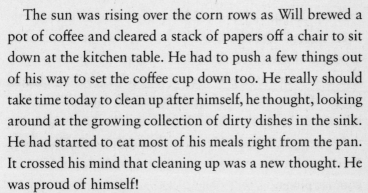

The sun was rising over the corn rows as Will brewed a pot of coffee and cleared a stack of papers off a chair to sit down at the kitchen table. He had to push a few things out of his way to set the coffee cup down too. He really should take time today to clean up after himself, he thought, looking around at the growing collection of dirty dishes in the sink. He had started to eat most of his meals right from the pan. It crossed his mind that cleaning up was a new thought. He was proud of himself!

Suddenly, the door to the cottage burst open. "HELLO!"

Will jumped slightly and spilled some of his coffee onto the table. Hank Lapp stepped into the cottage, carrying his rod-and-reel fishing pole. It looked like he'd been on the lake, or else was headed that way. He strode across the room and handed his rod to Will. Will had patiently untangled the mess of Hank's line one afternoon, and ever since, Hank considered him the finest untangler east of the Mississippi. He was forever hunting Will out on the farm, handing him his rod to repair.

"Well, Hank, you've got a real bird's nest here," Will observed. "I'll try, but I'm not sure I can fix this one."

"DAGNABIT. I was afraid of that." Hank sauntered over to the kitchen table, pulled things off a chair, sat right down across from Will, and eyed his cup of coffee.

"Here, take this. I haven't had a sip." Will pushed the cup on the table in front of him.

"Oh, no thanks. No, no. I didn't come over here meaning for you to offer me food and drink." Hank picked up the coffee cup and took a sip with a loud slurp.

It always amazed Will to see how much space Hank Lapp took up. It wasn't just his Christopher Lloyd–like appearance: ragged white hair, leathery skin, one eye that looked at you and the other that didn't. It was his presence. He had an outgoing, fun-loving nature and a window-rattling laugh. Whenever Hank found him on the farm, Will felt as if he needed to protect himself from the blinding brightness, the piercing loudness. He wanted to shout out: "Warning! Warning! Protect yourself! Get your sunglasses on! Put on your earplugs!"

Hank picked up a cereal box and looked at the cover. "I'm not stopping you from breakfast, am I?"

"No. Would you like some cereal? I don't have milk." Will

didn't have a refrigerator in the cottage, which considerably limited his meal choices—just one of the many reasons he happened upon the farmhouse at mealtimes.

"No milk? Ah well." He reached in the box to grab a handful, as he started talking about a recent fishing trip with Edith Fisher. "I told you about it, didn't I?"

Will was always a little uncertain of how to respond to that question. He couldn't begin to keep straight all the tall tales Hank wove into his fishing stories. Fishermen, in Will's point of view, were pretty much the same everywhere—they talked, they fished, and they talked about fish. It's one of those universal rules.

But there wasn't time to answer. Hank had taken a sip of coffee and started in again. "Now, what was I saying? Oh yes! Edith! It might surprise you to hear that Edith likes to fish. Some of the ladies think fishing isn't ladylike, but Edith isn't one of them. She even makes up her own bait and she's a little secretive about it, which I happen to find appealing in a woman. A little mystery is a good thing, I always say."

With a sinking feeling, Will realized that this didn't have the makings of a short visit. Hank was so easily diverted that Will was afraid he'd never get back to the original point if he didn't stay on task. What was the point of the story, anyway? Maybe there wasn't a point. That was often the case with Hank.

"So the fishing was a little slow the other day. I rigged up a jiggin' hole to trick her. When she wasn't looking, I made a slipknot on her lure and let it go. Looked to Edith like she got herself a fish! She started hootin' and hollerin' 'cause she was sure she had a whopper fish on the end of her lure.

Telling me how she was bringing home dinner! When she reeled it in, she sure was bringing in a nicely prepared meal!" Then he threw his head back and laughed with gusto, stopping with a choking snort. "She reeled in a can of Spam! And here's the best part—she stood up in the boat to scold me—" he wagged a finger at Will to illustrate—"and she fell right overboard!" He laughed so hard that tears ran down his cheeks. "Then, she was so mad that she spent the entire way home drenching me in the mighty flood of her words." That started him on another laughing jag. "She's still mad. Says I should have my fishing license taken away." Finally, he pulled himself together and wiped his face. "If a man can't fish, he might as well pull up the sod blanket, if you ask me."

The story went on, but Will lost the thread of it. He emptied the rest of the coffeepot into Hank's cup.

"Anyhoo . . . Edith won't go fishing with me anymore." Hank ran his knuckles over his bristled cheeks. They'd probably get a shave sometime in the next day or two—for sure before Sunday church. "So I came to see if you might like to go fishing with me. Menno used to be my fishing partner, you see, and M.K. is eager to go but she never stops talking long enough for the fish to get a word in. Sadie's plenty quiet, but she's too tenderhearted for fishing and hunting. She refuses to hook a worm. She carries spiders outside instead of smushing them like the rest of us." He looked Will directly in the eye. "I just thought you might like to give it a try."

Will felt honored. He felt like he had crossed over a bridge and was considered a member of the family. "I would. I'd like that. I know I could never take the place of Menno, but I'd like to go with you sometime."

"No one could take the place of Menno. No one should be asked to. But I can't deny you've been a blessing to all of us, Will. Especially Amos. He's finally got his vim and vigor back. It's been good to have you." Hank looked over at Will swiftly, then stood and looked for a place to put the empty coffee cup. The sink was filled with dirty dishes, as was the counter. He finally put it back on the table. He paused at the door and turned around. "Life's full of turnarounds."

"Yes, I suppose it is," Will said, walking over to see him out.

"But it sure is a blessing to know that the good Lord knows about every single thing that happens to us and has a divine, almighty reason for it all, the good and the bad too."

Will closed the door behind Hank and looked at the kitchen counters and sink. What a mess. It would take half the morning to clean it all up—to get hot dishwater, he had to heat up the water on the woodstove. No wonder he hated to wash dishes. But it wasn't just the mess that troubled him. It was everything, his whole life. That would take much more than half a morning to clean up.

What if these Amish people in this little church district were right? What if every detail meant something? What if the ups and downs and stupid mistakes he had made in the last few months had some kind of specific purpose? What if everything that happened to him ultimately fit together into a plan?

The thought was overwhelming. Terrifying and wonderful.

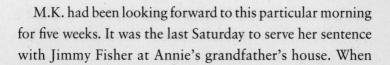

M.K. had been looking forward to this particular morning for five weeks. It was the last Saturday to serve her sentence with Jimmy Fisher at Annie's grandfather's house. When he arrived in his buggy to pick up M.K. and Uncle Hank, he was alone. His mother, he said, was still miffed at Hank for playing a practical joke on her and said she wouldn't be coming today to help.

"You mean, help *supervise*," M.K. said under her breath, and Uncle Hank jabbed her with the pointy part of his elbow.

Uncle Hank begged off. "I better go do some fence-mending with Edith."

M.K. squinted at him. He squinted back. He opened the buggy door and practically shoved M.K. inside. "Now you two work hard and see that old feller gets plenty of loving care." He put Fern's hamper, filled with prepared food for the week, in the backseat.

Jimmy and M.K. didn't speak to each other for the entire fifteen-minute ride to Annie's grandfather. When they arrived, the old man was in his chair on the porch, looking dead, as usual, and M.K. carefully tiptoed up to him to see if he was still breathing.

"GIRL, WHERE YOU BEEN?"

M.K. flinched. He got her every time.

"He forgets," Jimmy said, lugging the hamper past M.K. to take to the kitchen.

"SPEAK UP, BOY! YOU MUMBLE. I'VE SPOKEN TO YOU ABOUT THAT BEFORE."

"I SAID GOOD MORNING," Jimmy said. He lifted the hamper. "BROUGHT YOU GROCERIES."

"COYOTES?" He smacked his lips together. "I AIN'T HAD COYOTE MEAT IN YEARS. GUESS IT BEATS STARVING," he snapped, in his wrinkly voice. "HOP TO IT. STIR YOUR STUMPS."

Jimmy and M.K. exchanged a glance. Jimmy was going to try to fix the sagging porch corner today, so he went back to the buggy to get his tools as M.K. started to unload the hamper. She added some wood to the smoldering fire in the stove so that she could warm up some oatmeal Fern had made for the old man's breakfast. The stove started to smoke and seep soot. "You'd better clean out the stovepipe," she told Jimmy as he passed through, swiping a cookie from the hamper of groceries.

"Me?" He mumbled around a cookie in his mouth. "That'll take all morning. I wanted to get that porch done. I can't do everything, you know."

M.K. held back from giving him a snappy retort. "We can't leave him with a clogged stovepipe. It'll start a fire." M.K. pulled a chair over to the stove. "I'll help."

Jimmy exhaled, a slow whistle. The pipe rose out of the stove and angled at the ceiling. He climbed up on the chair to try to pull apart the lengths but couldn't work them loose. "Botheration! This could take all morning."

M.K. pointed out to him that botheration wasn't a word, but he ignored her. "Sometimes I think you are getting as deaf as Annie's grandfather."

"I hear you," Jimmy grumbled, "but it goes in one ear and out the other."

"Nothing to stop it," M.K. said.

"It's too bad you don't think about things that the average person might actually have to face."

"Like what?"

"Like how to tolerate working alongside one of the most aggravating girls on earth."

It never took long on these Saturday mornings for Jimmy Fisher's manners to go right out the window, which wasn't a long toss. She thought about pushing his chair back so he would fall, but she supposed that might be mean. "And that, Jimmy Fisher, is just one of the many reasons why you don't have a girlfriend."

"Who would want one?" He looked down at her. "Nothing but a nuisance. But if I wanted girlfriends—" he snapped his fingers—"they'd come running."

Sadly, that was true. It was a never-ending mystery to M.K. that so many girls swooned over the likes of Jimmy Fisher.

He hopped off the chair. "I've got a brilliant idea." He reached into a pocket and drew out a metal tin. He opened it and showed M.K. what was inside. "Firecrackers."

It was a well-known fact, to everyone but his mother, that Jimmy Fisher was never without firecrackers. He took three out of the tin. "Just takes a pinch of gunpowder to clear the stove, pipes, and chimney." He snapped his fingers again. "Easy as pie."

For once, M.K. was the one to think twice. "Jimmy . . . I'm not sure . . ."

He waved her off. "Prepare to be swept up in a whirlwind of superior force." He unlatched the stove door, then looked at her and squinted. "Uh, maybe you should stand back."

M.K. went into the other room and watched from behind the doorjamb. Jimmy struck a match to the kindling inside and threw in the firecrackers.

Then quite a lot happened. With an explosion that left M.K.'s ears ringing into the new year, the whole stove danced on its legs. The stovepipe came clattering down from the ceiling, belching a bushel of black soot all over them and the entire kitchen. The windows were covered with coal dust, darkening the kitchen. M.K. thought Jimmy would have been killed outright by the explosion, but he seemed to be still standing. She saw his eyes blinking rapidly in the midst of his coal-blasted face. His eyebrows were missing.

"Maybe one firecracker might have been enough." He spit soot out of his mouth. A burnt-powder haze hung in the room.

It took M.K. a few minutes to get over the shock of it. Then, she roared! "Jimmy Fisher! Er batt so viel as es finft Raad im Wagge!" *That did as much good as a fifth wheel on a wagon!* She stamped her foot and shook a fist at him. Her ears were still ringing. "I won't be hearing right for a week or two!"

"As if you didn't bring this all on yourself."

M.K. and Jimmy whipped around to locate the source of that familiar voice.

Fern! So ubiquitous!

"At this rate, you two are going to be working off your Saturdays for the rest of your lives." Fern said she happened to be leaving the Bent N' Dent when she heard the firecrackers and knew Jimmy Fisher was behind it. So, she decided to check up on them. "Good thing I did," she said, as she folded up her sleeves to set to work. "The two of you without supervision are an accident waiting to happen." She pointed to Jimmy. "Don't look so surprised. A person could hear that explosion halfway to Harrisburg."

"Oh, he's not surprised," M.K. said. "He just doesn't have any eyebrows left."

It took the three of them the rest of the morning to put the kitchen into the shape Fern expected it to be in. By noon, a miracle had taken place. Jimmy scooped a little soot here and there, not much, but at least he fit the stovepipe back together. M.K., naturally, did the work of ten, scrubbing, sweeping, polishing, dusting. The kitchen was restored to its pre-explosion condition. And the stovepipe was cleaned out.

Annie's grandfather slept through the entire thing. When he woke up, he hollered for his lunch.

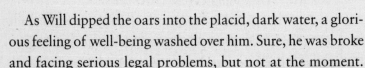

As Will dipped the oars into the placid, dark water, a glorious feeling of well-being washed over him. Sure, he was broke and facing serious legal problems, but not at the moment. At the moment, he was rowing on a beautiful lake with a gorgeous girl seated before him, serenaded by the soft hoots of a pair of screech owls.

Often, lately, Will forgot that he had a job to do and that Sadie was an Amish farmer's daughter. All he could think about tonight, as they set out for a fishing trip to Blue Lake Pond so that he would have some practice before Hank took him out, was how much he wanted to kiss her.

He blamed the soft spring air, the colors of the evening sky, and that strand of sandy blonde hair that kept working its way loose. He blamed the tiny scatter of freckles on her nose and cheeks. He blamed those sky-blue eyes and that rosy mouth. He blamed the way her soft laugh chimed like bells. Granted, today wasn't the first time his thoughts toward her had turned in a romantic direction.

He rowed the little boat out to the middle of the lake. "It doesn't get much better than this—fishing on a warm spring evening!" A mockingbird imitated the call of a dove. A dove cooed in reply, and he figured the mockingbird had a laugh over it. Will slid onto Sadie's seat and put a worm on the hook for her as she looked away. She didn't like anything to get hurt, she said. Even a worm.

He was so close to her that all he needed to do was to tilt his face and he was in a perfect position to kiss her. He slipped a hand behind her head and pulled her face toward his. Then he was kissing her deeply, but gently, as if he had all the time in the world.

After a moment, she pulled away. "That was nice, Will. Very, very nice." She put a finger to his lips. "But don't do it again."

He studied her face for a moment in disbelief, trying to judge how he should respond. Were his instincts off that much? She was always giving him mixed signals—something he found mysterious and compelling. Certain he caught a twinkle in her eyes, he said, "My deepest apologies. The moonlight has made me lose my sensibilities."

The corner of her mouth ticked, but whether it was from amusement or annoyance, he couldn't tell. Then she laughed, a sparkling fall of notes in the still of the evening. He didn't look right into her eyes but rather at those adorable freckles that were sprinkled across her nose and cheeks, like someone dusted her with cinnamon.

But she had a point. They came here to fish, not kiss. He was ashamed of himself. Okay, maybe not at this exact instant, but by tomorrow for sure. His only excuse was that he liked her so much. The more he'd witnessed her caring ways, the more she had gotten under his skin. There were times when he thought he might be falling in love. She wouldn't believe him if he told her, so he didn't intend to. He could hardly believe it himself.

He cast his line out into the lake and watched the gentle ripples undulate through the calm surface. "What would you say if we went into Lancaster for dinner soon?"

Sadie practically dropped her pole. "I can't." The answer was quick, like she didn't even have to think about it. She shifted her shoulder away from his and kept her eyes on the surface of the lake. "Someone might see us."

A laugh burst out of Will. "People around here aren't stupid you know. They've figured it out."

She pulled farther away, looked at him. "Who has? What are you talking about?"

He read the shock in her voice even though he couldn't see her face—just the outline of her hair and prayer cap, lit by the moon around its edges like an angel.

"People know about us, Sadie. They're not blind."

She stood up. The boat rocked dangerously. "Who knows? And knows what? There's nothing to know."

He wished Sadie would quit moving around so much. One slight misstep and they could both end up in the lake. Wasn't this just what had happened to Edith Fisher? He reached up and put his hand on her shoulder, pushing her down on the bench. "You're going to capsize this little boat."

She pressed her palms together, tucked her hands between her knees, and bowed her head forward. "I can't do this, Will," she said, and her words hovered above them for a second. "Will . . . I . . . ." She didn't have to finish the rest of the sentence for him to know he wasn't going to like what was coming next.

Finally, he said it. "You want to just be friends. Buddies. Pals."

Her shoulders rose, then fell. "Exactly."

It was a speech he had given to many girls, but this was the first time he had been the recipient of it. "Is this because of the bumbling schoolteacher?"

She looked at him sharply. "He's not a bumbling . . ." That single strand of hair, pulled loose from the bun at the back of her head, framed her cheek. She guided the lock behind her ear with trembling fingers before answering. "This doesn't have anything to do with Gid." She stiffened her back, lifted her chin. "It has to do with me. And it has to do with you."

"That's the thing I don't get about the Amish. You should be free to choose your life's path, Sadie."

Long seconds ticked by before she lifted her eyes to meet his. "I am free to choose, and I have made my choice. But you . . . are you so very free, Will? It seems as if your life has a giant shadow over it."

Will looked away. He hadn't expected this. His mind spun around and around. This conversation wasn't going at all the way he had planned. He looked back at Sadie, who was still searching his face. He was trapped. He would have to say something. "A shadow?"

"Yes. A shadow. Your father's shadow. Seeking his approval and never getting it." She gave him one of her direct, clear gazes. "So I am going to ask you again: are you so very free?"

The question hovered in the air, and Sadie was still waiting for his answer, stepping into the role of the Almighty, trying to stir up Will's conscience. "You don't know me well enough to figure that out, do you?" The words came out sharper than he meant them to, but he was irritated. He reeled in his line, took the oars, and swung the boat around, then began rowing swiftly toward the shore.

Wisely, Sadie never said another word. By the time they got the boat tied to the dock and started for home, Will was no longer annoyed with her but furious with himself. He never let himself get defensive. He never lost it. He absolutely never lost it. His fraternity brothers called him the Teflon Guy. Nothing ever bothered him.

Why did he have such a strong reaction to Sadie's question? Because she couldn't have been more right.

Sadie was free to choose, and she had made her choice. He was the one who wasn't free. He wasn't free at all.

— 18 —

Amos was often amazed at the overpowering love a father felt for his children. Each one so unique, so distinctive, so special to him. Julia, with her blunt, forthright manner. Menno, who had the biggest heart on earth. Sadie, with her sweet and gentle wisdom. Mary Kate, who was always up to something and he loved her for it.

If you had asked him which of his children most resembled Maggie, his late wife, Amos would have said M.K. Without a doubt. They shared the same sense of mischief and adventure. Life was never dull with Maggie Zook Lapp.

But after Menno's baby arrived, that opinion was changing. It startled him to see how much of Maggie was in Sadie. Even her voice had become like Maggie's. That same rise and dip, the half-amused tone, the way you wanted to keep hearing more, like a favorite melody. Just now, he had passed Sadie's bedroom and glanced in. He felt a tightening in his chest. She was humming to Joe-Jo exactly the way Maggie had always done with each of their babies. Maggie was always humming. Wouldn't she have been pleased to know what a fine young woman Sadie has grown into? A strong woman. A respected woman. Why, hardly a day went by without someone coming to Windmill Farm to ask her advice! He overheard Esther tell someone Sadie was the most respected young woman in the church. Imagine that! His timid little Sadie.

Downstairs, the grandfather clock dinged the hour. One . . . two . . .

So fast, he thought. That was how quickly time could get away from you. One moment your children were babies, and in the next breath, they were grown.

Three . . . four . . . five . . .

You could wake up one morning and find out that suddenly most of your life had passed by.

He heard Fern start dinner in the kitchen. Maggie's kitchen. What would Maggie have thought about Fern? No two women could be any more different. He wasn't sure if they would even be friends. Fern didn't have much patience for daydreamers, and Maggie was a first-rate daydreamer. Maggie might have thought Fern's stern ways were rule bound, legalistic, overbearing. Yet Fern fiercely loved Maggie's children, and for that, Amos had no doubt, Maggie would heartily approve of her.

But what would Maggie think if she knew Amos had grown fond of Fern? Fond wasn't the right word. That was the word used for a favorite horse or dog, not a woman. Dare he say it? Could he be falling in love with Fern Graber?

Such a thought astounded him.

What about Ira Smucker? Fern hadn't said anything after Ira had spoken to her of marriage last weekend, but that wasn't unusual. She was an utterly private person. And he hadn't seen Ira since then. That, too, wasn't unusual. Ira was a busy man.

Wait a minute. It *was* unusual. Ira had been stopping by

on Wednesday nights to play a game of cribbage with Fern. After Ira had confessed his love for Fern to him, Amos had made a point to hang around while they played. He knew it wasn't right—he felt as immature as M.K. when he eavesdropped—but he thought Ira's attempts at conversation were mind-numbingly dull.

Wednesday had come and gone this week, and no Ira. Amos knew it was childish, bordering on sinfulness, but he felt rather pleased.

One late May morning, Sadie went outside to fill Menno's bird feeders. As she poured black oiled sunflower seeds into the opening of the feeder, she thought of her brother without the sting his memory usually evoked. The baby was like a healing balm to the entire family. Even Julia, out in Ohio, wanted to hear every new thing Joe-Jo was doing: his first smile, his first laugh. Last night, her father dandled the baby on his lap and Joe-Jo kept bending his knees and springing up, over and over, like a little kangaroo. The whole family gathered to watch, mesmerized. Sadie thought of the joy of having a baby around—for two months now!—and thanked God for him. For Menno.

Doozy, hanging around by Sadie to lick up fallen sunflower seeds, saw something and woofed. He perked his ears, then flew across the driveway and jumped up to greet a small figure, standing in the morning shadow of the barn. The figure bent down and buried her hands in the fur at his neck. Sadie set down the container of sunflower seeds and shielded her eyes from the bright morning sun. Her heart missed a beat.

She walked down the steps and crossed the driveway. The girl was dressed in English clothes: jeans and a T-shirt that said *Kowabunga!* She wore dime-store flip-flops, and her hair was cut short. But Sadie would know her anywhere.

"Annie," Sadie said.

Annie took a long, shuddering breath. She was thin, so thin, and pale, with dark circles under her eyes as if she hadn't slept in days.

Sadie wasn't sure what to say or how to say it. Annie had come back! A flood of emotions charged through her: sadness, happiness. And anger too. Annie had done a terrible thing. "You probably want to see the baby."

Annie's eyes filled with tears. "I'm so sorry. I didn't trust him with anyone else." Then the tears began, as if she had been holding them back for months now and couldn't keep them contained one more minute.

Sadie opened her arms and Annie rushed into them.

Amos couldn't have been more surprised to come out of the barn and find Annie, weeping in Sadie's arms. They went into the house and Sadie showed her the baby, asleep in the cradle that Gid had made and Uncle Hank had repaired. Annie knelt by the cradle, tears streaming down her face. She watched Joe-Jo breathe in and out, eyes closed. And that was the moment when any judgment Amos might have felt toward Annie slipped away. He saw her for what she was: a frightened young girl, all alone, caring for a grandfather who hardly knew who he was half the time, while caring for a colicky newborn. It was too much.

Amos went into the kitchen to get a cup of coffee. Fern was whipping egg whites for waffles with her lips set in a straight line. Not that he was especially good at picking up what women thought, but her whipping those egg whites into a frenzy wasn't a subtle hint as to how riled up she felt. He thought he knew where her line of thought was traveling.

"It's good that she's here, Fern," he said quietly so that Annie wouldn't overhear. "God always wants to restore his people."

Fern flashed a stern look in Amos's direction. She poured the frothy egg whites into the batter and carefully folded them in. "But is she staying?" She set down the wooden spoon and turned to him. "We have to think of the baby's welfare."

"One step at a time. For now, I can tell you that she's staying for breakfast." He looked over Fern's shoulder to see Annie and Sadie talking in the other room. Annie hadn't left the cradle's side. Amos noticed that she kept glancing at the baby, as if she thought he might disappear. "That girl looks like she hasn't had a good meal in months."

M.K. burst into the house with a basket full of eggs and stopped abruptly when she saw Annie. Her eyes went wide as she took in Annie's appearance. "Annie! You cut your hair!"

Annie put a hand up to her head, as if she had forgotten about her short hair, her absent prayer cap.

M.K. walked right up to her. "Where have you been? We've been looking everywhere for you."

Amos and Fern exchanged a smile. Leave it to Mary Kate to get the answers they wanted.

"I was working as a waitress over in Lebanon. I have a cousin over there."

"Can you believe how big the baby is? Sadie's gotten really attached to him. We all have. We named him Joe-Jo, after Menno's middle name. We're just crazy about Joe-Jo. Even Dad has learned to be a crackerjack diaper changer."

"Only if absolutely necessary," Amos hastened to add.

A light smile fleeted across Annie's face. "You have no notion how much I've ached to come and get him."

M.K.'s eyes went wide in alarm. "But . . . you're just visiting, right? You're not planning to take him away, are you?" She turned to Amos, a plea in her face.

Annie gave the baby a long, telling look and Amos read everything in that gaze. "We'll have plenty of time to work things out," he said. "For now, let's sit down to breakfast and thank God for bringing Annie back to us."

During breakfast, Annie explained that she had returned to her grandfather's house last night and saw that he had been cared for. "The kitchen was spotless."

"That's because of me," M.K. said proudly. "I've been going over on Saturdays and working myself to the bone, cooking and cleaning."

"Hardly that," Fern added primly. "Jimmy Fisher might like some of that credit too. Hank and Edith too. And don't forget that first morning when you talked your entire schoolhouse of children and their parents into working."

M.K. scowled at her and Amos nearly laughed out loud. Fern was always reminding M.K. of her place. His youngest daughter needed constant reminding.

"I figured you all had something to do with it," Annie said. "I have been so worried about Daadi. I didn't want to move to Ohio with the colony. He should have gone with them when he had the chance. I thought if I left, he would go with the colony. I never dreamed he would wait for me to come back."

"Why did you come back then?" M.K. asked, reaching for the jam jar. She took a spoonful of blackberry jam and spread it on her toast, pushing it to the crust and licking the drips on her fingers.

"The baby. I couldn't stop thinking about him, wondering about him. I wasn't worried—I knew Sadie would take good care of him. But I couldn't stay away any longer. I had to come back." She took in a long breath of air. "So I quit my job. I'm here to stay. I'd like . . . another . . . chance at being a mother." She kept her eyes on her lap. "For Menno's sake. For my sake. For the baby's sake."

Amos felt tears prick his eyes as he saw the pain shuddering through Annie.

Annie wiped her face with her napkin. "I won't take the baby from you. I can't be putting my pride before his well-being. I'll wait until you're ready to let me have him." With another long look at the baby's sweet face, she rose. She turned to Sadie. "I'd like to see the baby now and then."

"Of course," Sadie said. "He's a precious little boy. You're welcome to come by any time you like."

"Hold on, Annie," Amos said. "How do you plan to support yourself? And what about your grandfather? He needs full-time care. Our deacon wrote to someone in the colony and they said they would send someone to come get him, after the harvest is in. That's months from now."

Annie nodded. "I haven't worked everything out yet." She lifted her chin. "But I will."

"I'll help," Sadie said. Then, more confidently, "We'll all

help." She looked around the room at her family. Her confidence faltered. "Won't we?"

Fern was quiet for a long while. "I've been needing another good egg basket. The one M.K. uses is falling apart. I should like to order one or two from you."

Annie's face brightened. "I could make you one."

"And Carrie Miller was admiring the baby's basket you made," Fern said. "She's having her fourth baby. I thought it might be nice to get her something new."

The baby started to stir then, and Annie's eyes riveted right to the cradle. Amos noted that her fists clenched tight, as if she was itching to scoop up the baby.

Sadie went over and picked him up, held him close to her heart, then turned and released the baby into Annie's arms. "Have a seat. I'll get a bottle ready. You can feed your son."

Fern hurried M.K. off to school and Amos got himself a second cup of coffee. He leaned back in his chair and studied Annie as she held the baby. He could see that she felt awkward at first, tentative, holding the baby as if he was made of spun sugar. Then Sadie pulled up a chair next to her and showed her how to keep the bottle lifted up high so the milk poured down. Annie's whole being started to relax, and she even giggled at something Sadie told her. For just an instant, she looked like the young girl Amos remembered, the girl who Menno had fluttered around all last summer. It relieved Amos. It gave him hope. He knew she was facing a very long, hard road as an unwed mother.

"I'd forgotten the delicate sound of Annie's laugh," Fern said as she sat next to Amos with a cup of hot tea. "It always reminded me of ice tinkling against glass." She took a sip of tea. "You were right. God wants his people restored." She added a teaspoon of sugar into her tea and stirred it. "The sight of Sadie and Annie and the baby, Menno would be pleased, Amos."

For the second time that morning, Amos's eyes pricked with tears. He looked down to blink them away. To his shock, he discovered that his hand had gripped Fern's, just the way he used to hold Maggie's hand.

The last day of school was right around the corner—just two days away. The scholars had been working hard to prepare a program for the parents. They had learned several new songs to sing. A few students had memorized poems to recite. This was going to be the best program Twin Creeks had ever presented to parents. The children had worked so hard to get everything just right.

Alice Smucker, M.K. thought darkly, had never bothered with doing anything new for the parent programs. Not once. The same five carols were sung for the Christmas program, the same five hymns sung for the end-of-year program. Boring! And poetry, to Alice, was fanciful nonsense. Gideon disagreed. So this year, M.K. volunteered to recite the longest poem she could find: *The Raven* by Edgar Allen Poe. She didn't understand much of it, but it fit in nicely with the falcons living on her farm, and she was determined to memorize it.

Just before Gideon dismissed the class, he mentioned that he hoped they could have a picnic after the program, but a tree limb from the big oak tree had fallen on the playground in last night's rainstorm. "Until we get that limb removed and hauled away, we aren't going to be able to have a picnic like we had planned."

Amidst the scholars' disappointed groans, a crackerjack idea bubbled up inside of M.K. She raised her hand to the ceiling. "We can have it at my house! Windmill Farm is just down the street."

Gideon looked skeptical. "Maybe you should ask your father first."

Ask Sadie, was what he meant. "It's no problem at all! Dad loves having folks over and Fern is a fine cook."

Gid hesitated. "Are you sure, Mary Kate?"

"Absolutely!"

Reluctantly, Gideon agreed. M.K. was thrilled! It would be so much fun to have the entire class, and parents and siblings, to her house for a picnic! Gid dismissed everyone and she rushed out of the classroom, catching up with Ruthie to walk home together. They had plans to go spy on Eve in the falcon scape and see if they could spot her babies.

And M.K. promptly forgot all about the picnic.

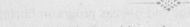

Amos felt like his old, pre-heart-trouble self. So good that he wanted to celebrate. At breakfast, he asked M.K., "After the end-of-year program tomorrow, did Gid make plans for a picnic lunch for the scholars?"

M.K.'s eyes went wide. She grabbed a spoonful of yogurt to plop in her granola, stalling for time. "Actually, I might have . . . possibly . . . volunteered our house for lunch." She gave a sideways glance in Fern's direction at the other side of the table.

In the middle of spooning out a segment of grapefruit, Fern froze.

"That's a fine idea!" Amos said, pleased.

Fern gave M.K. a look. "And when were you going to spring that on me?"

M.K. scratched her forehead. "I guess I forgot to tell you." She dug into her bowl of granola. "Families will bring things! It'll be easy."

Amos rubbed his hands together. "Tell Gid we'll handle barbecuing chickens if everyone else can bring the extras. They can come here right after the program. And tell him Fern will make her good baked beans and coleslaw too. We'll cook everything."

"We?" Fern asked, raising an eyebrow. "*We* will cook everything?"

Amos grinned. "And tell Gid that I'm thinking it would be nice to have a softball game too." He loved playing sports with children. When his children were little, he would tear around the bases with one of them tucked under his arm. Even when his own children had outgrown the crook in his arm, he would find a neighbor's toddler to tote. When he became ill, it was one of the things he missed most.

Fern and Sadie spent the rest of the afternoon cooking up baked beans, preparing chickens for the barbecue, cutting cabbage for coleslaw. Amos and Will cleaned out the barbecue pit, swept the volleyball court, and prepared bases for the softball game. Amos couldn't remember when he had last felt so lighthearted.

The next day, midmorning, parents crammed into the back of the schoolhouse to hear the scholars' recitations and hymn singing. Even Alice, Gid's sister, hobbled in on her crutches and the children politely welcomed her. M.K. kept her distance from Alice's crutches. She was convinced that Alice Smucker had it in for her, and Amos had to admit that Alice wore a pained expression on her face whenever she caught sight of M.K. Especially pained as M.K. delivered her long and unusual blackbird poem.

Afterward, children and parents poured over to Windmill Farm for the barbecue. Fern and Sadie had skipped the program so they could start the chickens on the barbecue. Amos smelled that sweet, tangy smell all the way down the road. He smiled. Behind him, he heard a firecracker go off, which meant Jimmy Fisher was nearby. In front of him, he saw Annie walking up the hill, holding the baby in her arms so that Sadie could cook. Today was a wonderful day.

While everyone ate lunch on blankets on the grass, Amos went to mark out the baselines for the softball game in the gravel driveway. Home base was the tall maple tree in the front yard. The bases were old goose-down pillows that Fern donated to the cause. Gid pitched, Will caught, and Amos helped the six-and-under crowd at bat. When they hit the ball, Amos would scoop the toddler under his arm and run around the bases, pumping and wheezing, red-faced and panting. He was having the time of his life.

Little by little, mothers and fathers made noise about heading home and choring, so the scholars started to reluctantly clear out. Gid remained behind, having a casual back-and-forth toss with Will. They didn't have ball gloves, so you could hear the smack of the ball in the heel of the hand. No one paid them any mind, until the sound of the smack got louder.

Then louder still. The ball was a blur between them now. Gid was red in the face. Will's upper arm strained and glistened.

Then Gid threw a little wild and caught Will's guard down. The ball popped him in the stomach and Will let out a loud "ooof" sound. He doubled over like a deflated beach ball. Then he fell back and splayed as he hit the ground, grinning. The few stragglers who had remained stood around laughing at Will's exaggerated antics.

Will popped up his head and peered at Gid. "Looks like you throw a pitch the way you put together a cradle."

Gid's face tightened.

Quick as a flock of sparrows, the laughs were gone.

Gid took out after Will, sprinting like a panther across the yard. Dust rose behind him. Will had just enough time to make that come-and-get-me gesture with both hands. Then they were squaring off, but not throwing punches yet. Gid pushed Will's shoulders and he fell on the ground.

"Are you crazy?" Will yelled, scrambling to his feet. "What's that for?"

"That's for wrecking the petit fours," Gid growled.

"The what?" Will growled. "I don't even know what petty-fours are!"

Gid grabbed Will in a headlock. "And that's for ruining the cradle."

But Will had a few tricks of his own. He grabbed onto Gid's arm and bent over, heaving him on the ground. "Why would I ruin your cradle?"

Gid leaped to his feet. "Why?" He worked around to swing again and brought a left hook out of nowhere. Will jumped back to avoid it.

Amos would never admit it out loud, certainly not among this small crowd, but he was impressed with this quiet school-teacher's tenacity.

Gid narrowed his eyes. "You'll do whatever you can to keep Sadie and me apart."

Will ducked and danced. "Oh yeah? Well, why would she ever want a man like you?"

The world stopped dead to listen.

Gid was up in Will's face, now pointing a finger at his chest. "You don't know the first thing about being a man."

That did it. Will sprang. Down the two went, rolling in the dirt, throwing punches. Dust whipped into a fog. They rolled one way, then another, and knocked over the blue bird feeder. Sadie gasped as the dinner dish shattered when the feeder crashed to the ground. And still, they kept at it.

M.K. edged around to Amos and tugged on his sleeve. "They're just having fun, right?"

"I think so," Amos said, then frowned. "I thought so." It was hard to tell. The boys were a frenzy of flailing elbows and kicking heels. All that could be heard were the sounds of grunts and smacks. More grunts than smacks.

The rest of them stood there, watching. Even the baby, held in Annie's arms, looked stunned. His eyes and mouth were three little round O's. Uncle Hank whistled, long and low, then he and Jimmy Fisher started betting to see who would win until Fern put a stop to that.

M.K. looked worried. "Dad—what's wrong with them?"

Amos stroked his beard, wondering when he should step in. "Those two are butting heads over our Sadie."

"But why?" M.K. couldn't take her eyes off the two, dancing and sparring.

Amos glanced at her. "I believe it's called a love triangle."

"But that would mean . . ." She scrunched up her face. "Could Sadie be in love with two different boys at the same time?" She scratched her head. "Where could you look up a thing like that in the library?"

In the midst of the boys' tussle, Amos turned to M.K. How could he make this clear to her? She was just twelve. She wanted simple definitions of love. Love was many things, but it was never simple. Before he could think of how to answer M.K., Fern interrupted him. "Amos Lapp, would you please stop those two before Gid ends up losing his teaching job!"

"What?" M.K. was horrified. "Does that mean Alice would have to take next year's term?" She covered her face with her hands. "Dad! Please! Stop them!"

"They can't keep this up," Amos said, but they did.

Finally, Sadie had enough. She ran to the hose spigot and filled a bucket with water, then rushed over and tossed it at the two. They stopped fighting, shocked and soaked.

"Gid, stop it!" she yelled. "Go home!"

Gid limped to his feet. "I'm not going anywhere." His shirt front was dripping with water and blood. He held one hand, already swelling, close to his chest. You could tell that he'd broken it. He took a few steps toward Sadie until they were practically nose to nose. She glared at him. Amos had never seen his daughter look so angry.

Gid looked at Sadie through a closing eye and repeated himself. "I'm not going anywhere."

Sadie was furious. Mad at Gid, mad at Will. Will came out of the fight with surprisingly less damage than Gid, but he seemed to sense he should make himself scarce, and after Fern gave him an ice pack for his eye, he quietly slipped off to his cottage. Fern told Gid he needed a splint made for his hand before he headed off to the hospital's emergency room for an X-ray. And Sadie was the only one who knew how.

In the kitchen, Sadie wrapped the gauze around the splint she had made to keep Gid's broken hand immobile. They carefully avoided looking at each other. Amos had gone down to the shanty to call a taxi and offered to go with him to the emergency room, but Gid said no, that he could handle himself just fine.

Mary Kate sidled into the room, watching Sadie clean off Gid's face cuts with cottonballs and alcohol. "It was my fault," she whispered.

"What was?" Sadie said, dabbing Gid's wounds so that he flinched. She could have used something that wouldn't sting quite as badly, but she didn't mind seeing him squirm.

"The cradle. The night Gid brought it over—I was carrying it into the house and I was running . . . and Doozy made me trip. I fell right on top of it, hard, and the whole thing kind of collapsed. Nothing broke—it all fit together like a glove. But I didn't know I should have used glue." She looked down at her bare feet.

Sadie stared at her, dumbfounded. "Why didn't you say so? Mary Kate, why would you let me think Gid did it on purpose?"

M.K. studied a fly buzzing on the windowsill with great interest.

"Mary Kate, look at me. When are you going to ever learn? You create problems for other people—and then you let them pick up the pieces!"

"Geduh is geduh, Sadie," Gid said quietly. *What's done is done.* "Let it go."

Sadie looked at Gid, shocked.

"I don't think you can blame her for the cradle collapse. The fault was mine for bringing the cradle over too soon. I should have waited a few more days until the glue cured." The taxi pulled up outside, so Gid picked up his hat with his unbandaged hand. He walked to the door, turned the knob, and opened the door a crack.

Gid released the doorknob and turned to look at Sadie. An uncomfortable silence settled over them. "You're always preaching about how important forgiveness is. You tell other people they need to forgive. But you . . . you won't forgive me. When God forgives, he does it once and for all. He doesn't keep dragging out reminders the way you do. I've tried every which way I can think of and you still treat me like I'm . . ." His voice trailed off. "Maybe . . . you need to take a dose of your own medicine."

Sadie's jaw dropped. This was by far the longest speech anybody'd ever had out of Gid. His words bit to the quick.

19

Annie stopped by every day to see the baby. She fed him, rocked him, cuddled him, offered him her finger to grasp. She lifted her hand with his fist clamped about her index finger to her mouth and kissed his plump little hand. When she got ready to leave, Annie pressed one last kiss on the baby's cheek. Sadie shifted Joe-Jo to her shoulder and patted him as she watched Annie walk down the hill. Annie was such a lonely little figure, and she was heading home to be with her nutty grandfather. The sight of her tugged at Sadie's heart.

Amos came out of the barn and crossed over to where Sadie stood with the baby. "Annie and I have had a lot of talks these last few weeks—about why she left and why she came back," Sadie said. "Good talks. She seems much stronger now, much better prepared to face her responsibilities."

Amos put his hand on the fence post.

"Dad, I think the time is coming when we need to think about letting Annie have Joe-Jo."

"Fern has mentioned the same thing," Amos said. "But we felt it would be best for you to make that decision."

"Maybe we could start slowly. A day here and there, then maybe an overnight. To help her adjust."

Amos took Joe-Jo out of Sadie's arms. "You know that could very well mean she will move to Ohio to join the colony in the fall."

Sadie gave a slight nod. "I keep trying to think of what Menno might have wanted, if he could understand the situation."

Amos kissed the baby's smooth forehead. "I think he would understand that Annie is the baby's mother. She's trying to do the best she can. And he would be pleased that we are trying to help her."

Sadie couldn't stop thinking about Gid's words: *When God forgives, he does it once and for all. He doesn't keep dragging out reminders the way people do.* The way she did.

She gave her father a sad smile. "Soon, then."

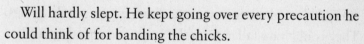

Will hardly slept. He kept going over every precaution he could think of for banding the chicks.

Miner's hard hat with LED lamp. ✓

Red helium balloons to tie on his backpack. ✓

Air horn to scare off Adam and Eve if they flew too close to him. ✓

Protective goggles. ✓

Fingerless leather gloves so he could handle the bands. ✓

Cell phone to call for help if Adam attacked him and left him for dead. ✓

A little before 4:00 a.m., he threw back the covers and got out of bed. Bird-watchers were a little on the obsessive side.

A group of them had figured out he would be banding today and told him they would set up their scopes at dawn. They knew that banding was done when the nestlings were about three weeks old because, at this stage, they didn't run out of the scape or attempt to fly off. What Will doubted that these birders would know was that at three weeks of age, the young birds could be sexed by measuring the width of the legs. He had promised Mr. Petosky a male and a female. Last night, Mr. Petosky said he decided he wanted three, not two, and Will put his foot down. Two was his limit. Two left in the wild, two brought in for captivity. It seemed fair.

His plan was to get out there, get up the ridge, wait for Adam and Eve to leave the scape, band the birds, remove the two bigger ones for Mr. Petosky, and be done with it. He would lie and tell Mahlon that only two were found in the scape. Mahlon would wonder what had happened to them from dusk the night before—the time of Will's last call to him. But Will wasn't too concerned—there were all kinds of reasonable explanations as to the disappearance of fledglings. They could have fallen from the scape and ended up as dinner for another animal. Even Mahlon said he didn't expect that fourth chick to survive. They competed with each other in the scape, and the older chicks had the advantage: bigger, bolder, quicker. Once the deed would be done, Will was sure he wouldn't feel needles of guilt anymore. It was that time of indecision, of anticipation, that made this whole business seem sketchy.

Dressed and prepared, Will climbed the steep, uneven ridge to reach the scape, just like he had practiced. He stopped at a level place, behind the scape, where he would band the chicks.

He planned to band them one at a time. He would pluck one from the scape and band it down below. He would also check it for overall health and condition. If he could get the birds banded quickly and back into the scape without Eve getting too aggressive, he would try to collect eggshell fragments and prey remains for examination. That would make Mahlon happy and hopefully deflect his attention from the two missing chicks. The eggshells could be analyzed for contaminants and the prey remains could provide additional insight into peregrine falcon feeding habits. The use of DDT in the 1950s and 1960s had practically wiped out the peregrine falcons by causing thinning of the eggshells. Even though they were recovering, it was still important to analyze the eggshells for contaminants. With a little bit of luck, he would be done in ten minutes and his pulse could return to normal.

He did have luck—more than a little. Adam was already out hunting. He heard the quacking, duck-like sound he made as he soared over the fields. Hopefully, Will could coax Eve out of the scape with some quail left on a lower rock. Then he could get in, do the deed, get out.

Everything was going according to plan. It was eerie, how easy it was. The bird-watchers wouldn't arrive for another hour, which made Will feel considerably less anxious. He opened his backpack and pulled out a flashlight, turning it on so he could light the area where he would band the chicks. He set out the tools he would need: bands and pliers. A strange thought burst into his mind . . . this must be what it was like as his father prepared for surgery.

Now was *not* the time to think about his father. He quickly dismissed the thought and got back to work.

Will tossed a quail—Eve's favorite morsel—on a rock way out in front of the scape. He held his breath, watching her carefully to see if she noticed it. The scape was so much smaller than he would have expected—only about nine inches in diameter. The depression was only about two inches deep. After a long moment, Eve hopped to the edge of the scape and took a short flight to reach the quail. Will held his breath, watching her for a moment. He thought she might bring it right back to the scape, but she stayed put. Probably hungry.

Okay. *Go!*

Will scaled the rock where the scape sat, grabbed a chick, and jumped back down. He whipped off a glove and picked up the bands Mr. Petosky had given to him. The downy white chick looked at him with those eyes—dark, penetrating eyes, ringed with gray fuzz. It just stared at Will, unblinking. This—this was why falcons have played a prominent role in human history, he suddenly realized. As he gazed back at the chick, he felt the strangest connection. As if the bird knew what he was up to and was disappointed in him. He could almost hear Sadie's voice, poking his faulty conscience: "Is this the kind of man you've become? After all you've learned about yourself this spring, about the God who cares for you . . . this is who you want to be? This is the moment of decision, Will. Yours and yours alone."

Panic crashed through his mind like waves at high tide, his emotions a brackish mixture of embarrassment, confusion, self-reproach, guilt, fear. A cord of guilt wrapped around him and squeezed hard. He'd created this moment, built it one conversation at a time, and now he was terrified of it. His hands were trembling.

Will heard Adam's quacking sounds grow closer. He heard Eve answer back in alarm. They had spotted him. He had to finish this task. He had to.

⸪

Will stared at the cell phone in his hand. He had been hemming and hawing for the last hour. He was about to make the hardest phone call of his life. His heart was pounding, his hands were clammy. Finally, he pressed the button. One ring, two rings, three rings, then a fourth.

"Will?" His father exhaled, impatient. "I've only got a minute. What is it?"

"Dad . . . I'm in some trouble. I need your help."

⸪

A woven-wire fence enclosed the cemetery. Amos, Fern, Sadie, M.K., and Uncle Hank met with their neighbors to help clean up the graveyard after the recent storm. They went in by the gate to join the others. They knew a good many residents of the graveyard, though the oldest part went back to the early 1900s. Uncle Hank stopped to examine a small tombstone. "WHY, LOOKY HERE! If that isn't Lovina Shrock! She was my first customer for my coffin-building business. Howdy, Lovina!" He stopped to pull a few weeds around the stone.

"What ever happened to that particular line of work?" Edith Fisher said, coming up to him with a shovel.

Uncle Hank's face lit up. "My clients never laughed at my jokes!" He took the shovel from her. "But at least I never got any complaints." He roared with laughter and Edith rolled her eyes, until a rusty laugh burst out of her.

So Edith must have finally forgiven Hank for pulling a practical joke over her on a fishing trip. Now that twosome, Amos thought, watching the two of them wander off to weed a row of graves, was one of life's great mysteries. M.K. ran off to join her friends as Sadie set the baby in the shade. Fern started to work with a cluster of women.

Amos wandered down a path to Maggie's grave, under a willow tree, near the fence. Menno's was next to her. A branch had cracked and he pulled out his handsaw to trim it. Then he dropped down on his knees to clear away the brush. He traced his finger over the lettering on the headstone:

Margaret Zook Lapp

Beloved wife and mother

He glanced around, making sure he was alone. Satisfied, he started to talk to Maggie as he knelt down to clear weeds and debris from her stone. He did that, sometimes, when he had important things on his mind. He never told anyone. He knew she wasn't in that grave. He believed she was in Heaven, in the presence of the Almighty. But it made him feel closer to her.

"Maggie, you know how I loved you. No one could ever take your place. Not ever. But I remember a time when you were expecting our second baby, and we wondered how we could ever love a child more than we loved our Julia. Then Menno came, and Sadie, and M.K. And one night you told me that now you understood—love isn't finite. It expands, like the yeast in bread dough, you said. I remember you were punching down bread dough when you told me that very thing." He reached over and pulled the rest of the weeds from the side of the gravestone.

"Maggie, there's room in my heart to love another woman, and I think I've found someone I want to start over with. I want your blessing, dearest." He brushed away the weeds and rose to his feet, standing quietly before the grave for a few minutes. As he turned away, he found Fern, not three feet from him. He looked her straight in her eyes, his heart beat like a drum. "Don't."

"Don't what?" Fern asked.

Amos took a step closer to her. "Don't marry Ira Smucker."

She lifted her chin. "I told him no."

Amos felt a smile start deep down in his heart and rise to his face. He took a step forward, putting only inches between them. He reached for her hands. "Fern Graber, do you think you can stand being part of the Lapp family for the rest of your life?" He felt so raw, so exposed. His inner adolescent had kicked in, because he feared her response but at the same time hungered to know the truth.

Fern pursed her lips for a moment, appearing to be considering this.

Amos held his breath until she lifted her face to his. Her eyes softened as she gazed at him. When she finally spoke, her low, husky voice wavered with emotion. "Well, to tell the truth," she said, "I don't know how I couldn't."

Two hours later, Dr. Charles William Stoltz drove up the driveway to Windmill Farm in his champagne-colored convertible BMW. Will was surprised to see his mother hadn't come too. Then he remembered that his mother had sent him a text message that she was off to New York City this week to see a new Egyptian exhibit at the Metropolitan Museum of Art. He was relieved. This was hard enough.

Will's stomach knotted. He tried to pretend it was from hunger, not regret.

Will waited until his father was out of the car to walk over to him. His mother always said that she was drawn to her father because he reminded her of Gregory Peck—raven hair, now with white wings at the temples, even with that little divot in his chin. He was wearing his customary off-duty uniform: tassled cordovan loafers, light gray slacks, and a powder-blue dress shirt with a pair of Ray-Bans hooked in the breast pocket. He didn't wrinkle. Ever. He looked like he was going to his country club for drinks with his weirdly cerebral doctor friends who made jokes about aneurisms and neuron tangles. It had always amazed Will that his father had friends at all; he thought he had the personality of a prison warden. And he seemed completely out of place on an Amish farm.

Will took a deep breath to galvanize himself as his father took a long look at him. "How in the world does a person stay on an Amish farm and end up with a shiner?"

Unlike Will, Charles Stoltz never got ruffled or confused. He never lost his sense of purpose, which was why he found it so difficult to understand that Will wasn't sure he wanted to go into medicine. Will touched his eye. "Long story."

"Have you packed?"

"Not yet. It won't take long to finish."

"So." Will's father got right down to business, as usual—no *How have you been? We've missed you.* "What have you done now?" he said in his quiet, detached voice.

Will took a deep breath. He might as well tell. Everything.

If anyone were looking at them from a distance, they would have seen a father and son, side by side, leaning their backs against the car, arms folded against their chests, long legs stretched out, one ankle crossing the other. They would have thought the two were very laid-back. Ha! His father was as laid-back as a mountain lion. And they wouldn't have known that Will's heart was beating fast, confessing to his father the many ways he had messed up in the last few months. This confession made getting suspended from school and losing his spot in medical school to be a mere blip on the radar. This was big—it involved the law. The DUI. The shady lawyer. Illegally selling a noncaptive endangered species to a breeder. And now, trying to backpedal and get out of it all.

When he called Mr. Petosky to tell him he couldn't do the switch, that he had banded all four chicks with the game warden's bands, there was dead silence, followed by a stream of cussing like he'd never heard before, even in a fraternity house. Mr. Petosky told him to expect to find out that his DUI blood alcohol limit from the night of his arrest was now at the highest level, thanks to a friend at the police station who didn't mind altering official records. Expect jail time, Mr. Petosky told him. Expect a huge fine. Expect to have your license revoked. Expect to say goodbye to ever getting a decent job. And then he flung a few more swear words at him and hung up.

His father listened carefully, asking a few questions here and there. He was completely unreadable. No fury, or worse, disgust, as Will thought there would be. Nor did he offer any answers or solutions. He simply listened. He could have been taking history on a patient, he was that impassive, that detached. If anything, his father grew more outwardly calm, never a good sign. As Will finished his long tale, he saw the Lapps' buggy pull up the drive. He was grateful they had been away up to this point.

His father noticed the buggy too, and made a dismissive gesture with his hand. "We can . . . finish this later." He glanced at Will with eyes narrowed. "I don't think I've ever been so disappointed in you."

Just like that, Will was eight years old again, and those same cold eyes were judging him for getting a B+ in P.E. on his report card. If only his father could have been like Amos, who only cared about his children's happiness and well-being. Will tried to play it cool, but his guts were in a knot.

M.K. was the first to spill out of the buggy. She hurried over to meet Will's father. Sadie went straight to the house with the baby, which didn't surprise Will. He knew how shy she was around strangers. Amos and Fern walked over to say hello. "You must be Will's father," Amos said, offering his hand to Charles. "You raised a fine young man. We think the world of your boy."

Will winced. How could he face Amos once the truth about him was out? He had been so good to him.

"Oh, I think a lot of my son too," Will's father said dryly, shaking Amos's hand. Zing! Aimed at Will, but one that was lost on the Lapps.

Fern tilted her head in that way she had, sizing up Will's father. Will wondered what she was thinking—did they resemble each other? Did Will fall short? Of course he did.

Then her eyes went wide. "Why, Little Chuckie Stoltzfus. I haven't seen you since you tied an oily rag to my cat's tail and set it on fire."

As Amos heard Fern talk to the fancy doctor like he was a small neighbor boy, he thought that just possibly she had completely lost her mind. Had that intimate moment in the graveyard unhinged her? Fern kept circling back to the cat—how it was her favorite cat in all the world and she still mourned for it. Amos knew, for a fact, that Fern didn't particularly like cats.

The fancy doctor glanced at his watch, tapped his foot, seemed as coiled as a cobra. His face was stone, his eyebrows knitted together. And still, Fern chattered on about that cat. Amos was baffled; Fern wasn't a lengthy talker. Short, pithy remarks that brought a person up short—those were her trademarks. The doctor's cheeks were turning fire red. So rot as en Kasch! *As red as a cherry.*

Amos worried the doctor might explode and how could he blame him? Fern was describing, in infinite detail, how the burnt smell of cat fur lingered on and on. He was just about to step in and muzzle her when the fancy doctor met her gaze, head-on. "Fern Graber, I did not set your cat on fire," he said. His voice was smooth, no friction between the words. "My cousin Marvin did."

You could have heard a pin drop, a heart beat. Will's eyes went wide, his mouth dropped open, noiseless.

So, Fern had been after something! Amos's heart swelled in admiration for her. Somehow, she seemed to know just how to pressure this man into cracking, admitting something he apparently had kept hidden for—well, at least for Will's twenty-one years. It boggled Amos's mind—to think Fern grew up in the same church as Will's father in Millersburg, Ohio! Even more astonishing was the shock registered on Will's face. To think that Charles Stoltz, a.k.a. Little Chuckie Stoltzfus, had never told his son that he had been raised Amish.

Fern insisted he stay for dinner, overruling Charles Stoltz's many objections. Amos suspected there were only a few people who ever told this man what to do—and his Fern was one of them.

Dinner was torture. As they settled in to eat, Will sat there, stunned, wordless. Amos felt sorry for him. Will had shared a few stories about his father with Amos—never in his wildest dreams would he have thought that fancy doctor, with all his degrees, had been raised Plain.

Nothing about Dr. Stoltz seemed Plain now. Certainly not the outside trappings—the clothes, the car. Not a trace of a Deitsch accent. Not a mannerism. Not a single hint of his humble beginnings. Even his surname had been modified. All evidence of his upbringing had been washed away, swept clean.

No one said much at dinner. Except for Fern. She just kept on talking, reminiscing about stories she remembered about Little Chuckie—which seemed to mortify him—updating him about the people in his church as if he had asked. Amos thought she might be trying to squeeze information out of him for Will's sake. "So if I remember right, you were dead set on going to college."

"That's right." It was pretty clear that Charles Stoltz didn't want his past sifted through.

"And your father was dead set against you getting a college education." Fern swallowed a bite of chicken. "He was determined to have you farm alongside of him."

Charles remained unresponsive and helped himself to a spoonful of mashed potatoes. He cut two precise squares of his chicken.

"Broke your parents' hearts when you ran off," Fern said. "I sure do remember that."

Charles cut his meat with such intensity that Amos feared he might go right through the plate.

"That's sort of flip-flopped," M.K. said as she poured a pool of gravy over the potatoes on her plate until Fern stopped her. "Your dad wanted you to be a farmer and you ran off to be a doctor. You want Will to be a doctor and he ran off to be a farmer."

At the exact same moment, as if it had been orchestrated, Charles's and Will's forks clattered against their plates.

No one said much else for the rest of the dinner. Except for Fern.

20

As soon as dinner ended, Will's father leaned over and quietly told him to go get packed up, that they needed to leave as soon as he was ready. Will nodded once and said only, "All right."

As Will crested the small hill that led down to the cottage, he couldn't believe what he had learned about his father tonight. He felt a shock go through him, as real as lightning. Once he had opened a hot oven at eye level to put in a frozen pizza and he was hit by a wave of heat so strong and severe that it temporarily blinded him. The discovery about his father had the same effect.

His father was raised Amish? Dr. Charles William Stoltz had once been Chuckie Stoltzfus, a simple farm boy? Did his mother know? It was too much to take in.

So he wasn't the only one in the family who kept secrets! He grew somber. The revelation about his father—as big as it was—only served as a distraction. The reason his father was here tonight hadn't gone away—Will was facing some serious problems.

Will stopped at the doorway of his cottage. The sun had dropped low on the horizon. He watched, transfixed, as the sky filled with deepening hues of red and orange, then purple. In the morning, the sun would rise; tomorrow evening, about this time, it would set. A regular cycle. He stood there for a long moment, marveling at the earth's precise alignment on its axis when so many other things in life seemed crooked.

Suddenly the fact that he was looking at the last little bit of the sun for this day, knowing that it would rise again in the morning, that it was a solid fact the world could count on—it was a very comforting thought. And the fact that the sun had hung in place since the creation of the world and would be there until the heavens passed away—that God had ordained all of this into being. It struck Will that this same God might have a thought or two for him and his future, as well.

The sun had slipped below the horizon, but the sky was filled with an extraordinary lighting. The world seemed different. The cornfields seemed extra green, the pine trees so vivid they were almost jarring. It was like getting a pair of glasses that were overcorrected. Everything seemed startlingly clear to him.

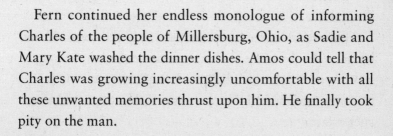

Fern continued her endless monologue of informing Charles of the people of Millersburg, Ohio, as Sadie and Mary Kate washed the dinner dishes. Amos could tell that Charles was growing increasingly uncomfortable with all these unwanted memories thrust upon him. He finally took pity on the man.

"Let's go outside. I'd like to show you the falcon scape before it gets too dark."

Charles bolted from his chair before Amos finished his sentence. They walked to a high spot that held one of Amos's favorite views—you could see rolling fields in every direction. Will had tilled and planted those very fields, Amos told Charles. Since the corn and wheat were knee-high, you couldn't see the wavy furrows and Amos was glad for that. He had a hunch Charles would find fault with Will's plowing.

"I'm glad Will was able to help you," Charles said.

Amos nodded. "We're sorry to think he will be leaving us tonight."

"He's banded the chicks. He's done what he needed to do here for Mahlon. And Will has . . . some things to figure out. I think it's best if we do it together. At home."

It was late and the sun had already slid down the horizon, turning the wispy clouds in the sky to gold, purple, and red. Charles noticed. "I'd forgotten the sheer beauty of nature. Sunsets on a farm are like no other."

Amos nodded. The sunset was particularly spectacular tonight. Maybe it was God's gift to Will, a blessing and a benediction. "I don't know how anyone could possibly visit this part of the world and not believe in the perfect hand of God."

Above their heads Adam floated across the cornfield and let out a shrill whistle. "That's the tiercel."

"The male falcon, right?"

Amos must have looked surprised that he would know such a fact.

"The first car I ever bought was a Toyota Tercel." Charles Stoltz's cheeks pinked a little. "I've always liked birds." He kicked at a dirt clod with his loafer. "I guess there is a small part of me that is still Plain."

"Oh, I have a hunch there's probably a lot of you that is still Plain."

Charles jerked his head around. "I don't think so. I left at nineteen and never looked back. Never wanted to. Nor was I welcomed back."

Adam dove straight down in a stoop, like he was performing for them. They watched his shape shift into an aerodynamic missile. Dozens of small songbirds scattered like buckshot. There was no love lost between the tiercel and the other birds. "Doctoring always seemed like farming to me," Amos said.

Charles raised an eyebrow.

"You learn to fix things, to make things right again. You do your part—do it well, do it thoroughly, and God provides the rain and sun to do the rest. Just like the work of healing."

Charles's eyes were riveted on Adam, who had snatched a barn swallow midair and swooped up to carry it back to the scape. Adam would be back soon. It was taking more and more hunts to keep his family fed. Amos waited a moment, hoping Charles might say something, but he didn't. So Amos did. "Do you know much about falconry?"

"Its history, mostly, as a sport of game hunting, where they wear those little hoods." He looked up, as if gathering details in his mind. "Let's see . . . the first record of falconry was in China in 2200 BC. The tradition made its way around the world—Africa, Egypt, Persia, Europe." He stroked his chin. "Shakespeare was an avid falconer. Then the sport of falconry declined when firearms came on the scene."

Oh. This Dr. Stoltz knew quite a lot about falconry. If Amos ever needed brain surgery, he decided he would definitely want this man to do it. "Falconry is having a revival of sorts. I've read of a blueberry farmer in eastern Washington who uses trained falcons as bird abatement. Not peregrines like our falcons—he uses alpomado falcons. The falcons keep raiding birds out of his crops. He calls them his falcon patrol. Uses about twenty birds. All of the handlers have to get permits to become trainers. It's supposed to be very successful." Amos grinned. "We've been blessed here on Windmill Farm to have Adam and Eve—that's what Will named our falcons. They've helped keep down aviary damage on our crops this spring. Cut way down on those pesky starlings. We're hoping they'll come back to breed here next year."

"Interesting." And Charles Stoltz did seem interested. Amos had finally hit on the right subject to snag this man's attention. Above them, Adam did a looping figure eight. "They are . . . fast."

Amos nodded. "So much of a falcon's life is spent in the air. The scape is only a place to lay and incubate its eggs, to house its fledglings until it can push them out."

The two men were mesmerized by Adam's aerobatics. The falcon was swooping and diving and darting, as if it was having the time of its life.

"Working the falcons is something of an art. The bond between a falconer and its falcon is interesting. It's a relationship of trust. Every time a falconer lets go, the bird has a choice as to whether it will return or not." Amos shrugged.

"It could be in Mexico tomorrow." He looked at Charles. "But it has to choose to come back."

"Why would it? Why doesn't it just fly off?"

"Being a predator—it's a hard life. The falcon has learned that life is easier if it returns to the falconer. It will always get fed, even if it doesn't catch something. Even if it's not successful out there. No matter what." Amos watched Adam circle high above and stoop down to nab a bat, then sail with it back to the scape to feed a chick. "Maybe the falcon just knows a good deal when it sees it." He looked back at the little cottage. "But the falconer gives the falcon the choice to return." He walked a few steps, his hands clasped behind him.

Charles remained behind. Glancing at him out of the corner of his eye, Amos realized Charles knew exactly what he was getting at.

At the bottom of the rise, Amos turned to wait for him and pointed to the cottage. "Will's probably about done packing. I imagine he could use some help carrying things to the car."

Amos jerked his chin toward the farmhouse. "I might head on back. Give you a moment to talk to your son." He strode up the hill.

"Amos Lapp?" Charles called out.

Amos spun around.

The hint of a smile tugged at the corner of his mouth. "Why do I feel as if I've just been counseled by an Amish farmer?"

"No charge!" Amos started up the hill again, grinning.

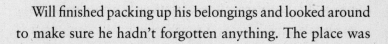

Will finished packing up his belongings and looked around to make sure he hadn't forgotten anything. The place was still a mess. He shouldn't leave the cottage like this for Fern, though he remembered a remark she had made when he had tried to help her with a cleaning project at the farmhouse: "Unexpected things happen around you, Will, and cleaning is not always one of them." *Well, Fern, today I am going to surprise you.* He would leave the cottage as clean as it was when he arrived. He would try to, anyway.

He started a fire in the stove and set a big pail of water on it to boil. Squeezing some dish soap into the sink, he ran cold water and swished his hand in the sink to get the water sudsy. He hadn't heard his father come in, but suddenly, there he was, stacking dirty dishes on the small counter.

"It won't take long to wash these dishes," Will said, glancing at the water that wasn't even close to boiling. "This is the last thing I need to do."

"There's plenty of time," his father said.

Will almost dropped the dish he was holding. He had never remembered a time in his life when his father wasn't tense, eager to move on to the next thing. But here he was, patiently stacking dirty dishes with dried food crusted on them. Will set the dishes in to soak and waited for the water to boil. He and his father stood there, awkwardly, side by side, waiting to see bubbles rise to the surface. Why was it taking so long? In his mind, he heard Fern's voice: A watched pot never boils. Or was it, a boiling pot is never watched? He should have written down her sayings so he would remember them.

Quietly, his father said, "Why didn't you ever tell me you didn't want to be a doctor?"

Time skipped a beat before Will said, "Why didn't you ever tell me you were raised Amish?"

His father wasn't used to someone crossing him. An eyebrow lifted, but he didn't respond. Nor did he meet Will's eyes. He seemed uncomfortable. In a clipped, controlled voice, he said, "I lived under my father's very large and very heavy thumb. I had to break free."

Will snorted. "*That* . . . I can understand."

Then there was silence. It went on that way for a while, the two of them staring at the pot of water, which seemed to refuse to boil, neither one speaking. A perfect example of how things were between Will and his father—neither one would budge.

Sadie had told him that forgiveness was a process, that it didn't happen overnight. She likened the process to filling a bucket of water at a well. God was the well, forgiveness was the water. Sometimes, she said, the bucket would be leaky and it would require numerous trips to the well. But the important thing, Sadie said, was to keep going to the well to fill the bucket.

She also said that someone had to be willing to take the first step. Will blew air out of his cheeks. This was the hardest thing he had ever had to do . . . but it had to start somewhere. Things had to change.

"Dad, I'm sorry." The words erupted from Will in a sob. He pressed his thumb and forefinger into his watering eyes. "I'm so sorry," he repeated, his voice in shreds. "I've made a mess of . . . everything."

Then his father's arms were around him. Will buried his face in his father's neck. He wept, unashamed of his tears.

"I'm sorry too," his father said. "You made some of those choices because you felt trapped." His father released him and stepped back. "Of all people on this earth, I should have known not to assume you were going to do what I wanted you to do with your life." He blew a puff of air. "I'm my father's son. Same song, different verse." He rested his hands on the counter. "Where do we go from here?"

For the first time that Will could ever remember, his father looked unsure of himself. He never second-guessed himself, and here he was, looking baffled, sad, confused. He had Fern to thank for that. She had completely baffled an unbafflable man. Will felt a twinge of pity for his father. "You haven't met Hank—he's Amos's uncle—but he says life is full of turnarounds."

His father looked at him sharply. Another awkward silence fell.

"Maybe . . . we could start again. You know . . . this time as father and son. Instead of . . . brilliant brain surgeon and numbskull protégé."

To his surprise, his father's eyes closed in pain. "I . . . wouldn't know where to begin."

His total helplessness touched Will. This wasn't easy for his father. "Maybe you could just give it a try."

The water started to boil then, rolling, gurgling bubbles. "Let me show you how we used to wash dishes on the farm," his father said, rolling up his sleeves.

As Will and his father scrubbed and rinsed and dried dishes together, they started to talk. It was clumsy, uncomfortable, stilted, painfully awkward. It was wonderful.

After Will said goodbye to Amos and Fern and M.K., he jerked his head to the side in a silent bid for a private conversation with Sadie. He turned to his father. "There are a few things I need to discuss with Sadie. Could you give us a moment of privacy?"

His father told him he would wait in the car for him. Once Sadie followed Will outside, he didn't waste time. He knew M.K. was watching them from the family room window, but he didn't care. He took both her hands in his and said, "Let me get the worst of this over straight off. Gideon Smucker is absolutely correct. I came to Windmill Farm with the intention of doing something illegal. I was going to try and sell a falcon chick to a private breeder. Then he wanted two chicks. Then three. I needed the money and I was going to do it, Sadie."

She gasped. Other than the sharp inhalation of breath, she neither spoke nor moved.

"In the end, I couldn't see it through. That's why I called my father today. That's why I'm leaving tonight." He took a step closer to her. "Sadie, I care for you in a way I've never cared for a girl before. I couldn't leave here without telling you. I came here as one kind of man, but I'm leaving as another. I'm a better man because of you." The words slipped out as though his tongue belonged to someone else. He didn't try to snatch them back or pretend he hadn't confessed something so serious aloud. Will opened his mouth to comment on her lack of reaction, then realized this must be what she was like as she listened to her clients spill forth their problems—she seemed calm and still and ready to hear anything. "Have you nothing to say to me, Sadie? No words of goodbye?"

Finally, she looked up, her eyes filled with tears. She looked at him as if she was memorizing his features. Then she brushed his cheek with her lips. It wasn't the kiss he wanted. It was a kiss for a child, with something final in it, something of a farewell. Yet she moved nearer than she probably meant to. He wasn't just looking for a sign; he knew—deep down, he knew—something in her wanted him to take her in his arms. He knew it, and he knew she wouldn't let it happen. Sadie who never wavered might have come near the brink, but she stepped back again.

"We'll meet again, you know," Will said.

"Will we?" she said, sounding as if she didn't believe him. Her eyes became blurry and she turned away, but he put his hand under her chin and made her look at him.

"I need to get some things sorted out . . . like, my whole life. But I promise you that we will meet again." He cupped her face with his hands. "Sadie, you and me, what we have—it wouldn't have been the end of the world if we'd seen it through."

She lifted her eyes and looked at him as if she couldn't believe she'd heard him right. "But Will, it would have been the end of my world."

———— ❖ ————

Sadie followed Dr. Stoltz's car out of the driveway, waving until her arm ached. She wondered if she'd ever set eyes on Will again, wondered if what he had said might someday come true. Would they ever meet again? She'd had a sense from the beginning to hold onto him lightly.

Pity for Will welled inside her, along with sadness for what he'd missed in his life. He didn't seem to know what he had been lacking until he saw it this spring with the Lapps. Yet she could see something had shifted inside of him today. The time he spent at Windmill Farm was no accident. It was a chapter in Will's book, but the ending wasn't written yet. That would be up to Will. "May God go with you," she said aloud, as the car's brake lights went on, preparing to round the bend in the road.

Just as the car turned toward the bend in the road, a buggy appeared on the opposite side. A long pole stuck out of the buggy window, and on it, a blue bird feeder. The car honked loudly and then swerved dramatically to avoid the bird feeder. In the buggy was Gid, heading up to Windmill Farm. He waved to Sadie from down the road, using his left hand, still in a large white cast. Sadie knew he had built the blue bird feeder to replace the one he had ruined in the ridiculous tussle with Will. It was a silly sight, really, to see a bird feeder sticking out of one side of the buggy and a big white cast waving to her from the other side.

Gid pulled over to the side of the road as he reached the end of the driveway. "I brought you a new bird feeder." He picked up a dinner dish with a hole drilled in the center and held it up to her. "The squirrel thingamajig too."

Sadie looked at the bird feeder. "How did you ever manage to build it with a broken hand?"

He shrugged. "Simple."

"Nothing's simple, Gid," she said. She lifted her eyes to gaze at him. "But you know that."

The tips of his ears began to turn pink. "Well, you can test it out when I finish installing it."

She took her time, paying attention to her words as she always did. Tilting her head. Taking him in. His eyes found hers, and she felt her mouth curve, offering him a shy smile. "That's all right," Sadie said. "I think it's going to work."

Discussion Questions

1. This story begins like the child's game of telephone—Mary Kate tells exciting news about Sadie to her friend, who tells another friend, and another. Soon, the story spreads like wildfire. Have you ever been the victim of a hurtful rumor? Certainly, most of us have participated in them. What is the difference between sharing information and spreading gossip? This Amish proverb might help: "There is a vast difference between putting your nose in other people's business and putting your heart in other people's problems."

2. Will Stoltz could charm even a crying baby with ease, yet he kept himself carefully hidden behind that casual, lighthearted facade. Have you ever met someone like Will—easy to like but hard to know? How did your feelings about Will change after you learn more about his father? How did his autocratic father affect him?

3. Oddly enough, Sadie—from an Amish community—felt free to choose the life she wanted. Will—from a wealthy, professional family—felt no such freedom. What's behind that irony? What does it say to you about choices?

4. As Sadie found her purpose as a healer, she started to bloom—just as Fern had hoped she would. Have you ever found yourself blooming unexpectedly? In what way? Or maybe you have a dream that hasn't yet been realized. Are there people in your life who could help you realize that dream? If not, pray that God will bring an encourager, like Fern, or a mentor, like Old Deborah Yoder, into your life.

5. How did Sadie's friendship with Will help her to become a more confident person? Do you think Sadie's newly acquired boldness might have backfired on Will as he attempted to romance her? In what way?

6. *What a fluke!* Will thinks. "To end up on a quiet Amish farm and find himself reenergized, renewed, inside out. But it didn't feel like a fluke. It seemed that this place, Stoney Ridge and the people here, had been prepared for him, designed ahead of time as a nurturing nest, a soft place from which to grow new wings." Have you had a similar experience of God's provision in an unexpected way?

7. Free will is a theme in *The Haven*—for the falcons; for Will—who is flirting with the wrong side of the law; for Annie—a young mother who abandons her baby. Each

has a choice to make and consequences to bear. In what way does that parallel God's relationship to us?

8. Do you think Annie deserves a second chance? Discuss how you felt about the way the Lapps handled Annie's return.

9. In order for Annie to succeed, the help of the Amish community will clearly be needed. How can strong communities—churches or neighborhoods or circles of friendships—help when a member struggles through difficult situations? When has your community helped you in a time of need?

10. Amos believes that trust is a fundamental part of the relationship between a falconer and his falcon. When the falconer releases the falcon, it has a choice to return. What message is he trying to get through to Will's father? Is there someone in your life whom you have to "let go"? So much of the Christian life is about trusting God. How can you trust that, as you let go, you are really handing that individual into God's care?

11. The story doesn't end with the reader knowing, without any doubt, who Sadie will end up loving—Gideon Smucker or Will Stoltz. How would you finish Sadie's love story? Which young man do you think Sadie will ultimately choose, or which one should she?

Acknowledgments

In the writing of this book, I had the pleasure of learning about the art of falconry through Kit Daine, falconer extraordinaire. Kit provided more than just information—she gave me a sense of the rare and wonderful bond of trust between a falcon and its trainer. Thank you, Kit, for your time and for sharing some valuable resources. A heartfelt high five to Mela Brasset, for linking me to Kit. And a grateful shout-out to Cheryl Harner, president of the Greater Mohican Audubon Society and blogger behind the Weedpicker's Journal (http://cherylharner.blogspot.com).

On the publishing end, my gratitude goes to the incredible group at Revell. To Andrea Doering and Barb Barnes, thank you for being everything a writer could hope for in editors. Thanks for your guidance, astute suggestions, and encouragement, and for helping Stoney Ridge come to life.

To the crew in marketing, publicity, and art (Deonne, Twila, Michele, Janelle, Claudia, Donna, Cheryl)—I so admire the awesome job you do in bringing the books to the shelves. To my agent, Joyce Hart, thanks for taking care of business so I can focus on writing.

Gratitude beyond measure goes out to reader friends, far and near. Thank you for sharing the books with friends, recommending them to book clubs, and taking time to send little notes of encouragement my way via email and Facebook. Thank you, all of you, for being a blessing, a joy, and a treasure. I hope you find a few treasures of your own in Stoney Ridge, and that this story returns the joy and the blessings in some small measure.

Last but never least, an over-the-top, words-can't-express thank-you to God for the opportunity to write stories of faithful people.

Suzanne Woods Fisher is the author of *The Choice*, *The Waiting*, and *The Search*—the bestselling Lancaster County Secrets series. *The Waiting* was a finalist for the 2011 Christy Award. Suzanne's grandfather was raised in the Old Order German Baptist Brethren Church in Franklin County, Pennsylvania. Her interest in living a simple, faith-filled life began with her Dunkard cousins. Suzanne is also the author of the bestselling *Amish Peace: Simple Wisdom for a Complicated World* and *Amish Proverbs: Words of Wisdom from the Simple Life*, both finalists for the ECPA Book of the Year award, and *Amish Values for Your Family*. She is the host of *Amish Wisdom*, a weekly radio program on toginet.com. She lives with her family in the San Francisco Bay Area.

Meet Suzanne
online at

 Suzanne Woods Fisher

suzannewfisher

www.SuzanneWoodsFisher.com

She is the host of *Amish Wisdom,*
a weekly radio program on **toginet.com** and
available to download at iTunes.com

A family. A farm. A heart.
All in need of repair.

"*The Keeper* is a keeper. From a fabric of likable and original characters, Suzanne has crafted a moving story of faith and loyalty, a story of hope shining out of the darkest places. A captivating read."

—**Dale Cramer**, bestselling author, *Levi's Will*

 Revell
a division of Baker Publishing Group
www.RevellBooks.com

Available Wherever Books Are Sold

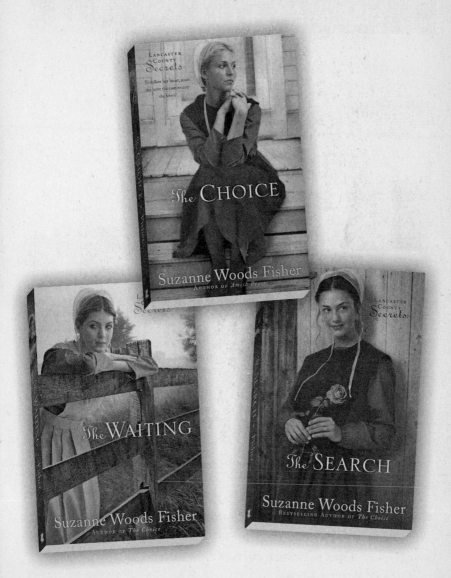

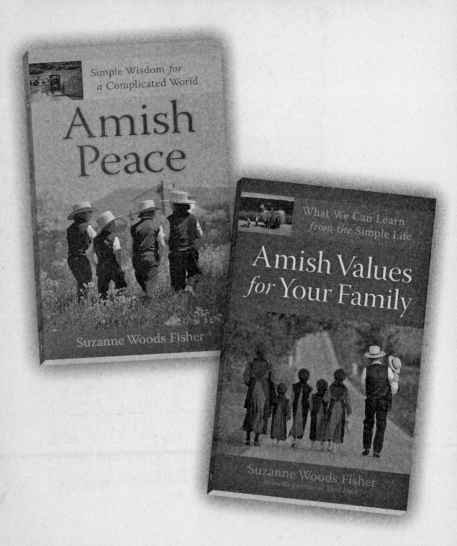